Praise for Vivian Arend's
Rocky Mountain Desire

"The bitter cold of Alberta, Canada, is made toasty warm by the super-sexy Coleman brothers of Six Pack Ranch."

~ *Publishers Weekly*

"I absolutely adore the Coleman family, from Mamma and Daddy Coleman to the little Colemans. The Six Pack Ranch series is one not to miss and has a permanent spot on my favorite series and my will read over and over again shelves."

~ *Guilty Pleasures Book Reviews*

"All in all this was a naughty read that had a lot of momentum and lots of interesting story lines going. The whole Coleman clan was present with updates on previous couples and hints at future ones."

~ *Night Owl Book Reviews*

"This was a terrific story, you feel for both Matt and Hope as the sail into uncharted waters... Another wonderful chapter in the series, can't wait to read the next one."

~ *Sensual Reads*

Look for these titles by
Vivian Arend

Now Available:

Granite Lake Wolves
Wolf Signs
Wolf Flight
Wolf Games
Wolf Tracks
Wolf Line

Forces of Nature
Tidal Wave
Whirlpool

Turner Twins
Turn It On
Turn It Up

Pacific Passion
Stormchild
Stormy Seduction
Silent Storm

Six Pack Ranch
Rocky Mountain Heat
Rocky Mountain Haven
Rocky Mountain Desire
Rocky Mountain Angel

Xtreme Adventures
Falling, Freestyle
Rising, Freestyle

Takhini Wolves
Black Gold
Silver Mine

Bandicoot Cove
Paradise Found
Exotic Indulgence

Print Collections
Under the Northern Lights
Under the Midnight Sun
Breaking Waves
Storm Swept
Freestyle
Tropical Desires

Rocky Mountain Desire

Vivian Arend

SAMHAIN PUBLISHING

Samhain Publishing, Ltd.
11821 Mason Montgomery Road, 4B
Cincinnati, OH 45249
www.samhainpublishing.com

Rocky Mountain Desire
Copyright © 2013 by Vivian Arend
Print ISBN: 978-1-60928-900-3
Digital ISBN: 978-1-60928-633-0

Editing by Anne Scott
Cover by Angela Waters

First Samhain Publishing, Ltd. electronic publication: March 2012
First Samhain Publishing, Ltd. print publication: February 2013

Dedication

Tracey West kick-started the Colemans, and I'm so glad. Thanks, Tracey, for believing in me, and for your words of encouragement to a newbie writer. You made a difference.

Prologue

Whoever invented the debauchery of a traditional bachelor party ought to be slathered with grease and tossed in a sand pit. Matt Coleman worked his way down the length of the bar, tray full of beer jugs balanced precariously as he manoeuvred his burden over the rowdies crowding the floor.

There were too many bodies, too many familiar faces to cut and run like everything screamed for him to do. This wasn't where he wanted to be, not by a long shot. But his personal preferences didn't free him from his responsibilities as the oldest single male in his family.

His brother was tying the knot? Matt would take a trip into hell itself to make sure all the rituals and customs were followed. Even the stupid ones.

A loud roar sounded from ahead of him, and he hurried his step, hoping to control the damage before someone—probably one of his younger brothers—went totally out of control.

"To Daniel, who not only got his balls chained but sleepless nights with kids thrown into the bargain." One of the many cousins in attendance shook a stuffed bear in the air. The attached set of handcuffs rattled, and laughter rang out before he tossed the gag gift onto the table with the others.

Matt lowered his tray in time to see Daniel's response all too clearly. The familiar ear-to-ear grin his brother had worn for most of the past year proved he didn't give a shit his freedom was about to officially disappear into the sunset.

The music picked up, both in volume and tempo, and enthusiastic hoots rose from the males crowding the private room at Traders Pub. The door on the far side of the raised platform opened and a pair of long, slim legs appeared.

Someone yanked on his shirtsleeve. Matt leaned in close enough to hear Daniel above the rest of the boys' caterwauling.

"Strippers? You trying to get me killed?"

"I stopped at dirty dancers. Beth won't kill you unless you touch 'em." Matt lifted his shoulders briefly. "Face it, bro, this part of the party ain't for your sake anyway. You tell me the entire clan would accept your idea of a steak dinner and a brew down at the ranch, and I'll suspect you've found a bottle of Unca's moonshine and been sampling it on the sly a little too hard."

Daniel shook his head, raising his drink in salute. "I'm telling her this was your idea."

"Damn right, you give me credit. Had to book the entertainment in all the way from Red Deer." Matt forced a smile, clicking mugs with his brother as he searched the room for the three youngest boys in the immediate family.

Colemans filled the space. With all the cousins and second cousins living in the area, there was no shortage of similar-looking male relatives leering and waving at the pretty blonde strutting her way across the stage. She wore a milkmaid costume that didn't do much to cover her ample breasts. Matt took in the view for a moment before turning away with a sigh. Pretty girls all around him and he would still be partying with his hand once the evening was over. The notable gap in his love life, no, his *sex* life, was getting old.

Screw love, he wanted some out-and-out hard fucking. And soon.

The cheering got louder, and Matt rolled his eyes when he spotted the cause. Figured. Jesse and Joel, the babies of the family—although finally legal in all states and provinces—were front and center making suggestive gestures at the dancer. She squatted in front of them and preened while continuing to display her assets, and once more Matt wondered just what the hell those boys ate for breakfast that the rest of the clan missed.

Women lined up to lie down for the twins.

A hand landed on his shoulder, solid. "Well done, Matt. Where were you when I was having my bachelor party?"

Matt laughed at his brother Blake, the oldest in the Coleman "six pack". "You didn't trust me to organize things. That's why you had Leo set up your party. And if I remember correctly, the police got called well before midnight—what more did you want?"

Blake grinned as he eyed the second woman crossing the stage, this one a brunette wearing a schoolgirl costume. "I'm not complaining. Still, I think Jaxi would have gotten a kick out of this kinda thing."

Matt slapped him on the arm. "Guys only. Just because your woman is atypical and doesn't mind seeing other girls kick it up..."

"Hell, she can dance better than most of these ladies," Blake teased, pulling away in time to avoid Matt's swinging fist.

Bastard was telling the truth. Although, Jaxi's mixed bag of talents and otherwise scheming skills were on hold for a bit. "She's doing most of her dancing with the babies these days, I bet."

The proud expression on his big brother's face had rarely left since May. "The girls are the cutest damn things. Swear they're gonna be as pretty as their mama. I'm polishing my shotgun already."

Matt gave him a pat on the back then headed toward the side of the room where a few of the cousins were swinging their mugs a little too hard. Blake and Daniel both wore the blissful expressions of men in love—and Matt was ready to beat

11

someone to a pulp. He'd worn that expression himself. Fully intended to marry his high school sweetheart, until she'd proved the big city was more important than he was.

The party swirled around him, and he smiled and nodded at all the appropriate times. But when it came down to it, there wasn't a lot to smile about.

He'd satisfy the ache in his groin with women who were willing but not looking for more than a casual fling. Hearts couldn't get broken if they weren't involved.

Hope shivered. The skimpy outfit covered her breasts but not much more, and she prayed the two-sided tape currently tugging at her skin would keep the fabric in place. She'd put on a few pounds since the last time she'd worked a stage, and this costume would have been revealing on her former, less-ample figure.

A rush of adrenaline and fear pumped through her veins. Going down to not much more than skin and a blush had been fine during her college days to pay the bills, but she was supposed to be a mature businesswoman now. This wasn't the way to maintain a respectable image in most small-town eyes. Why had she agreed to this craziness?

Cash. Right. The cash she desperately needed.

The quilting shop had been open for only a few months and due to circumstances beyond her control, i.e. the sister from hell, her savings were nearly exhausted trying to make what should have been payments from two pockets.

Just get it done.

"I hope you remember I'm rusty. It's over six months since I did this on a regular basis," Hope warned the head dancer.

"Honey, you'll do fine. You always were one of my best. I'm so glad you agreed to help last minute." Trish pushed in one final hairpin and stepped back, draping the long wig extensions over Hope's shoulders. "Don't be worried. It's not like anyone can tell it's you, not with this costume. Plus, I've got you on stage second last—by that time all the guys want is to see you wiggle."

Hope laughed. "Wiggling I can do no problem."

"Oh, hush. You've got curves I'd kill for. You ever move to full stripping, you'd make a mint."

As if. "Thanks, no. Dirty dancing is as far as I go."

"No worries. The guy who booked the party specifically said no full nudity." Trish shrugged. "I'm good either way, but the one thing I know is the guys enjoy variety."

Hope pointed at the wig on her head. "Which works well for me trying to stay undercover. Only, a mermaid? Really, Trish? When did you expand the costume selection from hard-working women into the fantasy realm?"

Trish patted her cheek teasingly then handed over a sparkling, sequined half mask. "Be thankful I didn't turn you into an elven princess for the night, pointed ears and all. No one will be staring at your face, anyway."

True. Hope arranged the mask over her eyes before sneaking another peek downward. Right about then, her sense of the ridiculous got the better of her. She had more than enough hips and ass for the guys to stare at. More than she wanted there to be, but the soft curves refused to diminish no matter how many workouts she put in. Not that she had much time for an exercise routine these days with everything she had to accomplish around the shop.

Trish kept babbling, but Hope had lost interest in listening. Just one step at a time. She was going to go out on that stage, shake her boobs at the gathered men. With the extra cash from tonight added to what she had scrimped together, she'd hit the bank on Monday and make her shop mortgage payment by the deadline. Done.

Of course, that to-do list didn't mention the paperwork she still had to complete when she got home tonight. Or the new stock she had to put out in the morning. But if she started thinking about her workload, she'd have no energy to dance, and after all Trish's hard work to glue this costume on her that would be *such* a pity.

She snorted at her own twisted joke. Hope glanced at the mirror again and fought back giggles. At least her concern that she'd be recognized had lessened now that her costume and mask were in place. Maybe that's why Trish had scheduled her to dance near the end—give the boys enough time to drink and the alcohol blur would help cover her features.

Money, that's all this was about.

The most intriguing part of this gig was the shimmering silver wig. She'd worn her hair short during high school, but over the past couple years she'd grown it out so she could wear it back in a ponytail. Dealing with a fancy do while working with customers or bending over a sewing machine was impractical. Still, silver instead of red? Her real colour was probably her favourite feature, but the instant change was amusing. She pulled on the kimono-style cover-up Trish had provided, then made a slow rotation to watch the artificial hip-length hair swirl around her.

Hmm, this could be enjoyable after all.

Another of the girls left the back room, the third to go. Schoolgirl Shelly was back, and she wiggled past Hope, laughing under her breath. "Hot damn—I wish I'd known who'd made the booking before I picked my costume for the night. That was fun, but more embarrassing than usual."

If Shelly thought taking off most of her clothes and swinging her hips for money was embarrassing, she was in the wrong line of work. Hope had never regretted her dancing days, even if it wasn't what she intended for her future. "Why more embarrassing?"

Shelly winked. "Because the bachelor's hooking up with a teacher."

Okay, that made sense. "You're kidding. Too funny."

"Hilarious, but you know what? There's enough Colemans out there you're bound to find a profession—"

"Colemans?" *Oh shoot.* She'd been so focused on the offer of the instant cash she desperately needed, the one question Hope hadn't thought to ask Trish was the name of tonight's client.

She snuck a glance through the doorframe. Familiar faces greeted her. Guys she'd gone to school with, guys she saw on a daily basis all over town. That part wasn't a surprise—she'd figured the crowd would be locals, but damn... Why had she thought this was a good idea?

The money. Every bit helped.

Staring into a sea of Colemans wasn't what she needed. And when she instinctively managed to find Matt in the crowd, life got just that much stinkier.

"You're up, Hope. Go give them what for." Trish's firm push between the shoulders was the only thing that stopped her from turning tail and racing from the bar without a backward glance.

Matt sat to the side of the room, laughing with his brothers as they joined together in that wall of impenetrable camaraderie she'd always admired. That's what family was supposed to be like, not cutthroat and undermining.

She only had a second to take him in. His dark hair was longer now, and a neatly trimmed beard and mustache covered his chin and upper lip. Oh God, he'd grown a mustache.

She loved what he looked like with facial hair.

Hope snapped her gaze to the ground and stepped forward in time to the music, resisting the urge to glance up and discover Matt's response. Of anyone in the crowd, he'd be the most likely to recognize her.

Ignoring the fluttering sensation in her belly, she lifted her arms to start her portion of the show. She had to concentrate on what she was doing or, substitute dancer or not, the guys would only be so forgiving. She shimmied her hips, forcing the front of her robe to gap, and the whistling began.

It wasn't difficult to get back into the swing of things. She still sang and sashayed around the shop when there were no customers—moving to a beat made her happy even though her days of dirty dancing were supposedly behind her.

She turned her back to the group before allowing another tease of skin to show, baring one shoulder. The robe clung intimately as the heat of the lights brought a slick to her skin. There had always been something ego-stroking about watching men respond. Even if the one guy she truly wanted was stamped off-limits.

"Oh, darling, shake them hips over this way."

"Strip, baby."

The suggestions got raunchier, and the pulse in her veins increased in tempo. When she let the robe slip to her waist, revealing the tiny fabric seashells barely covering her breasts, the roof shook with their shouts.

The heavy weight of the silvery wig's long strands caressed her as she twirled and allowed the silk to puddle to the floor.

"Sweet Jesus."

Matt's voice. Even in the crowd she recognized it. Hope lowered her eyelids to nearly closed, forcing the room to fade until individual faces blurred into nondescript, unidentifiable ovals.

If she didn't know where he was, she wasn't dancing her heart out for him, right?

Daniel passed him another beer, but Matt didn't think he

could swallow. *Holy shit* was the only thing currently filling his brain. The mug bumped his fingers, and he curled his fingers around the glass to stop it from tipping.

"You never seen a woman before, Matt? Because I think you're drooling."

"For a minute I thought..." He was seeing things. It had been six months since Helen had hightailed it out of Rocky Mountain House, swearing she never wanted to see a country road or smell a hay bale again for the rest of her life. But for a moment, just a moment, when the dancer had turned on the stage? He'd seen his ex-lover, her familiar body displayed to the noisy crowd of his kin.

Daniel leaned in front of him, forehead furrowed. "You okay? You look flushed."

"Tell me I'm imaging things—that's not Helen up there, is it?"

Daniel snorted in disbelief before he turned to examine the dancer. He shook his head. "It's not Helen. Trust me, the woman said she wasn't going to set foot in Rocky ever again. Why the hell would she turn up now on the stage shaking her tits for us?"

Matt chugged half the mug of beer to resist responding. Daniel didn't need to know that last part wouldn't surprise him. Helen had no issues putting her wares on display for more than one guy at a time. Even if her lover wasn't around, which had made their breakup easier in a way.

Instead, Matt ignored everything but the woman on the stage. The teeny bits of fabric clinging to her were as close to being naked as a person could get. Plump, round breasts— heavier than his ex's. In fact, the overall curves on the woman on the stage were more pronounced. Matt didn't mind, not one bit.

Long hair pooled around the dancer's shoulders, the

strands covering her breasts for a moment, then flowing out of the way like a peek-a-boo screen. He wanted to run a hand over the swell of her hip to see if the glow was from the heat of her skin or if it was a trick of the light.

He rocked in his chair, willing his dick to settle down. There was still a lot left to the evening, and hell if he'd sit there with aching balls the entire time.

He dragged his gaze back up to the dancer's face, confusion dogging him. She wore a small half mask over her eyes. Part of her costume, he guessed, but the silver material hid enough it was impossible to get a clear focus on her features. He swore there was something familiar about her, but just couldn't nail down what.

Then she made eye contact. Even through the mask he could tell—she was staring directly at him. His breath caught, his cock jerked. Anticipation rose. She shimmied in his direction. Daniel nudged his arm, and when one of the cousins stepped between them, blocking his view, Matt rose to his feet without thinking.

She was still looking his way—as if seeking him out. The slow curl of her lips turned them to a sinful smile that made his body ache.

"I think someone likes you," Blake teased.

"Fuck you."

"Think you're the one who needs a fucking. You've been a bloody asshole lately. Why don't you go say hi? Get her name and you can call her later and ask her out."

"She's a dancer at your party—"

"Who is staring at you as she's leaving the stage." Daniel pushed Matt. "I'm not telling you to jump her or anything, but dancers are allowed to have a private life. You saying you wouldn't date a dancer?"

"Hell, that's not it at all." Matt didn't give a damn as long as she was doing it of her own free will, and the group he'd contracted had a sterling reputation. "Forget it, okay? We're here for you. All discussion of my sex life is over."

Daniel waved a hand. "Fine. Do whatever you want. Just pointing out you're a gloomy ass and we know how to drink without supervision."

Blake nodded toward the far door. "And there will be some serious drinking and cards happening now, since I see Jon and Leo have finally arrived. Bastards cheated the last we got together, I swear they did."

Blake rearranged the chairs at their table, totally ignoring the noise that rose as the last dancer hit the stage. All the earlier girls strutted onto the bar room floor to mingle, but Blake and Daniel seemed oblivious to the revealing costumes and flirty glances, instead breaking out a deck of cards and greeting their friends.

Matt wished he were so happily content with a steady female that he'd be blissfully unaware of the half-naked women, especially the one in the silvery wig. He glanced around the room, pulling on his party-organizer hat, but all the cousins were suitably distracted.

The pile of gifts on the table caught his eye. Most of it was strictly for fun, but there were a few things he figured Beth would want to see. Matt grabbed the bags he'd brought with him and stuffed the gifts away for safekeeping.

It only took a moment before he stood beside the card table, staring down at his brothers and their friends. "I need your keys. I'll stick these in your truck."

Daniel winked as he tossed them over then turned his attention back to the game.

Matt swung across the room as quickly as he could with full hands, dodging the chaos. The party seemed to be a success, although there'd been no fistfights yet and no one was out cold on the floor.

Of course, it was still early.

He wasn't about to haul ass all the way to the front doors and back around to the parking lot—not when he knew the short cut. Matt ducked through the side door and waited impatiently for his eyes to adjust—the long back-hall lighting just bright enough to reveal the flash of a leg disappearing into a side room.

Oh hell, this route took him past the stage backroom. An instant shot of lust smacked him upside the head as he pictured in far-too-intimate detail the dancer in the silver wig. Imagined her hair swaying as she rode him like some wild bandito, her eyes staring through that mask—he could totally go for a few games in the bedroom if he got to play them with her.

He fumbled with the bags for a moment, hesitant to go forward. Feeling stupid, he was even considering going back and all the way around, like a child scared to brave the unknown ahead of him.

Being attracted to the woman wasn't wrong. It *wasn't*. If he happened to meet her, like Blake had said, he could at least talk to her politely.

Or was he so backward around women he'd forgotten how to do that?

The energy in his limbs from the internal pep talk lasted all of ten seconds. Long enough for him to square his shoulders and stride firmly down the hall. Long enough for him to step in line with the open door of a room where a quick, almost involuntary glance revealed a mess of makeup on the counter, clothing tossed over chairs.

And the flash of nearly naked skin as the woman he'd been salivating over earlier peeled the robe off her shoulders to be his own personal temptation. He couldn't stand there and ogle her, but he couldn't seem to walk away either.

Matt gritted his teeth, bracing himself to take the final steps to the exit door. A feminine gasp dragged his gaze off where he'd gotten trapped—her nearly naked breasts, *dammit.* He retreated in a hurry, smashing into the wall behind him as he forced himself to look at the floor.

"I'm sorry. I didn't mean to frighten you. I'm going."

He rushed away, slammed a shoulder against the door and escaped through the exit into the warmth of the July evening air. His heart was still pounding like a freight train after he'd put his load away.

Shit. He was beyond pathetic. Now he was freaking out innocent women. He leaned on the door to Daniel's truck, closed his eyes and took a long slow breath through his nose, attempting to calm his body and his mind.

All he could see was the dancer's body, and his dick got hard.

This was bullshit. So he was attracted to her. Fine. He was an adult, she was an adult. He'd probably never see her again. High on the agenda was to find some way to burn off this fever she'd begun, but it was hardly her fault and not his either. He just had to move on.

Which meant for now, making his feet take him back into the pub and the party, which was so much not what he wanted to be doing. Frustrated, he yanked the exit door open far harder than he had to and someone fell toward him. The woman's long red hair swung in a circle as she poured out the door—she must have been about to lean on the surface to open it when he'd pulled, and now she tumbled into his arms.

He caught her before she could be hurt. The light curses rising from her lips made him smile even as the warm skin under his fingers caused other reactions. Silky heat pressed against his body. She clung to his shoulders, fingers pressed into his muscles.

"Hang on, I've got you." He placed her on her feet and she shuffled away, head down as she muttered *thanks* in a low tone.

God, it was her. His dancer, who he was already guilty of obsessing over. She was walking away and he couldn't stand it. "Wait."

She stopped, face still in the shadows, almost as if she were hiding. Fuck, he was doing it again. As good as stalking a stranger.

"I'm sorry—I keep apologizing to you, but it's just...I wanted to say..." The range of suitable words in his vocabulary seemed sorely lacking so he just went for it. "I know it's wildly inappropriate, but I have to tell you. You're a very beautiful woman. That's all. I wanted you to know that."

It was cathartic to let the words escape. He had no idea what would happen next, but at least he'd been honest.

She swayed on her feet, then her head lifted, light shining off her cheek as she twisted toward him. "Thank you, Matt."

He froze, every muscle gone taut.

That voice—familiar. Too familiar. He'd heard it a hundred times over the years at family dinners with his high school sweetheart. Listened to it on the phone when he'd called to speak to Helen. Oh shit. Oh shit, *no*.

Her name jolted out. "Hope?"

She finished turning and the beam of light from the overhead bulbs hit her face full on. No wonder he'd thought he'd recognized her. Her eyes were lighter than her sister's, a pale blue like a summer's morning sky. Right now they were open so wide he could have driven his truck through them.

"Of course. You mean...? But..." Her smile faded, her hands rising up to cross in front of her body as if she still wore that revealing costume. "I thought you recognized me. Isn't that why you were staring, why you came to the change room? And now, you said that I'm attractive, and I thought maybe you weren't coming to give me hell, but..."

She had thought he was hot for her because it was true, and didn't that make him an asshole, lusting after his ex's little sister.

All of a sudden he felt every inch the bastard he was. "I didn't know."

There was nothing he could say to make this better, but he had to try.

Confess you were a jerk.

"I'm sorry, Hope. I didn't know it was you. I..." She shifted her feet uneasily, focusing on something to the side of him, her bottom lip caught between her teeth. *Say it, fuckhead. Admit you're a shit.* "...I thought you were a stranger who liked me. I don't usually go around pestering dancers, honest."

Her chin rose and she looked him in the eye. "Please don't tell anyone I was here."

Then she spun and raced away into the parking lot before he could apologize anymore. Equal parts relief and guilt poured over him, and he really didn't know what the hell to do.

Chapter One

Five months later

The giggles emitting from the living room were far too mature and feminine to belong to his nephews. Matt paused on his way up the stairs to figure out if he was about to walk into something he'd rather avoid.

"You going to have that done in time for Christmas?"

"I have to have it ready. The only way Gramma is allowed to give a homemade Christmas present to one child is to have something for all of them."

Matt leaned on the railing and grinned. His ma and her brood of friends doing the doting thing again. He'd forgotten about the monthly hen party. Guess he could put in an appearance before disappearing to safer and more masculine pastures.

If his trailer weren't so damn cold, he'd still be out there. But with the temperature dipping toward minus forty, sheet metal and forced air heaters simply didn't cut it.

"Evening ladies."

He rounded the corner, spotting, as he expected, piles of...stuff...everywhere. This time it looked as if a fabric shop had exploded in the living room, and not only his mother, but a half-dozen older women from the community beamed at him.

"Matt. Come and see what I've made." His ma held up a small quilt with a horse print on it, waving it madly for his approval.

"Very nice. Who's that for?"

"Robbie. And this one—" another quilt was raised for inspection, "...is for Nathan, and this one is Lance's."

He could be there for hours if he didn't manage to excuse himself after the first couple minutes.

"Love them all. You've done a fine job, Ma. Hey, I just wanted to say hello." Matt glanced around the room. "It's bitter cold outside—you ladies all have rides home tonight?"

"You want to escort me, you can, young man." Mrs. Katen winked and the room resounded again with laughter. The woman was one of his ma's best friends, and she and her husband had been married close to forty years.

Matt tipped his head. "Your husband might not ride rodeo anymore, ma'am, but I'm still plenty scared of him. I think I'll let him be your backup, if you don't mind."

He gave his ma a kiss on the cheek before turning to leave.

The breath whooshed right out of him as he came face to face with Hope. Long red hair framed her shining face, and her mouth opened and closed a few times as they stared at each other. Then she smiled and tucked her fingers together, standing like a prim and proper maiden in the midst of a singing recital.

All he could picture was her with nothing but tiny seashells covering her breasts.

"Matt. Good to see you. You're a little late to join the quilting bee, but if you want, I've got a lovely printed panel you could start on."

He hoped the heat flushing his face could be excused by the laughter in the room. "I think the family woodworking business is enough of a crafty task for me. Last thing I sewed on was a button, and I was bleeding like crazy by the time I was done."

Hope stepped to the side at the same moment he did, and they bumped. He caught her before either of them fell, the heat

25

of her body drawing him like some strange magnet. The sensation was far too familiar and far too tempting.

He didn't want this.

He was surprised she didn't knee him in the groin.

Hope wiggled from his grasp and stepped back, teetering until she found her balance. "Sorry, I'm very clumsy at times. Two left feet."

Not clumsy when she was shaking her ass on the dance stage.

Matt pulled himself together. "No, totally my fault."

She wore a sweet scent. Something mild and flowery, nothing at all like the stronger spicy perfumes Helen had always worn. He took a deeper sniff before he was even aware he was doing it. Hope's eyes widened, and she paced back farther, opening the space between them. A momentary rush of disappointment hit that he wasn't willing to admit to anyone, least of all to himself.

Not that he deserved any better after their surprise meeting last summer. She'd never returned his calls, never let him apologize properly, and he didn't blame her one bit.

"I'd better head home." Hope's gaze skimmed past his, then she busied herself grabbing bags and piling material into heaps. "If you ladies need anything this coming week you be sure to call. I can coach you over the phone if you want, if you can't wait until you make it into the shop. I know you're eager to finish these projects in time for the holidays."

Marion Coleman spoke up. "Matt, help carry her things. It took three trips for her to bring it all in."

"Oh no, Mrs. Coleman, that's fine—"

"Of course, I'll help." Matt tugged the bags from her grasp. "I'll nab my boots and coat, and meet you at the front door."

The panic on her face vanished almost as quickly as it

arrived, and she smiled. "Thank you. I appreciate it."

Matt dropped his handfuls by the front door then pivoted to fetch his shoes from the downstairs entrance that all the Coleman males still used out of habit. Only as soon as he turned, he smacked right into Hope, and once again, ended up catching hold to prevent her from falling.

The soft material of her T-shirt under his fingers felt way better than it should. And the thoughts that raced through his mind were of dragging his hands off her arms and around her waist to tuck her tight against him to see if she was as good a fit as he remembered from their brief tangle outside the door—

A tiny gasp escaped her. That only brought his attention toward her mouth, shiny from some type of lip-gloss. She smelt so damn good, and if the noise from the living room hadn't reminded him where they were—standing in the front hall one corner away from the sight of the most vocal gossip line in the area—he'd have been tempted to further his mistake from the summer to discover what flavour she wore.

Instead he decided to bluff. Had to, or this situation would drive him mad.

He winked. "I think we're both having troubles keeping our balance today. Not enough caffeine?"

Hope nodded. She seemed as eager as he was to change the topic. "Or too much. I drank a lot in the shop today to stay warm, and your mother served tea and coffee all night. I might need to switch to decaf the next time."

It was as good an excuse as any. Matt hurried down the stairs, donned his winter gear and used the side path to get around and meet her at the wide front entrance to the family ranch house.

The long, low building was set into the hillside, with the walkout on the back giving the illusion from the front of a single-level home stretching across the land. With the

Christmas lights strung along the eaves, twinkling white lights that his mother insisted go up the first of November, the darkness was warmed with a cheery brightness.

Nothing could change the fact it was as cold as a witch's tit. His breath didn't just fog in front of him, it clouded in heavy dregs, or would have if the wind didn't whip it away in a rush. Hope was already on her way back from her first trip, the cleared path of the sidewalk showing a good three feet of snow piled high on either side. She'd started her car, puffs of exhaust streaking behind it like dragon smoke.

"You were supposed to let me help you." Matt opened the front door for her and she stepped in, smiling cheerily.

"As your mom said, it's a three-trip job." She pointed to a pile. "If you get that, I'll take my sewing machine and purse."

Matt scooped up his load with ease. He listened for a moment. The chatting in the living room had resumed. "You need to say goodbye to anyone?"

She shook her head. "I did while you were gone."

He followed her out the door. Why did this feel so prickly? She was a friend. Other than that one weird incident from last summer hovering over them, there was no need for this awkwardness. Hell, for years he'd thought she'd end up his sister-in-law. There was no reason for the strange twisting sensation in his gut.

Maybe it was the memory of just how turned-on he'd gotten before he knew who she was. Plus the realization she wasn't his sister, not by any stretch of the imagination, and wasn't ever going to be, changed everything.

Hope turned from packing her load into her crowded backseat and reached to accept her supplies from him. As she tucked them into the vehicle, he couldn't help but notice it looked a little worse for wear. Even as he passed over the final armful, he took a closer glance at the tiny car. It was filled to the brim with bags and boxes. There was no way she could see out her back window.

"You use a shoehorn to get yourself in there?"

Hope straightened from where she'd been rearranging things to make them fit. She smacked into the doorframe and cursed before snapping her mouth shut and rubbing the back of her head.

"It's big enough for me. And I don't usually haul this much stuff, but with the holiday season being the best time for sales, I didn't want..." She grinned sheepishly. "I guess that's as close to a confession as you'll hear. I didn't want to lose a sale just because I'd left something behind. With this weather, the ladies aren't coming to the shop as often as they used to."

The sharp wind slapped him in the neck and Matt flipped up his collar. "I don't blame them for not going out. I wouldn't if I didn't have to."

"I know. Me neither." Hope forced the passenger door shut before turning and rubbing her gloves together briskly. "Thanks for the help. See you around."

Matt eyed her tires with continued suspicion as she manoeuvred her way back to the driver's side, slipping on the hard-packed snow underfoot and barely catching herself in time. She got behind the wheel, adjusted a few of the bags beside her, did up her seatbelt.

He couldn't stand it any longer. He knocked on the passenger window.

She paused then opened her driver door a crack. "I don't have power windows and I can't reach the crank."

He should have thought of that. He hurried around, worried all the heat she'd built up inside was escaping. When he made it to her door and leaned in close, only a faint bit of warmth greeted him.

"You sure you're okay heading back to town? Why didn't

you turn on the heater?"

"Herbie takes a while to warm up. I'll be fine. Really."

She wiggled the door and he reluctantly moved away. The brittle *clink* of the locks connecting made him cringe. Why was she driving a clunker like this anyway? And she'd named it?

At least she was a competent driver. She backed past him smoothly, waving a gloved hand. Her headlights clicked on, and the tiny vehicle slipped along the long gravel drive to the highway.

Matt watched until the red of her taillights disappeared when she turned, only she didn't head right, down the road that led toward town, but left, and his remaining limited patience vanished.

He spun and headed for his truck. She didn't have to know he was following her, but until she was home, he couldn't relax.

And while he would have done the same for any woman under these circumstances, for some reason knowing it was Hope ahead of him turned the Good Samaritan act into something infinitely more complicated.

Hope twisted the air-selection button. Car manufacturers needed to realize when it was this cold, a setting to blast heat at feet, body and windshield simultaneously was more than a whim, it was a necessity. Either she had a trickle of heat on her rapidly numbing torso and toes, or she had enough air pressure to keep the front window from fogging over and blocking her view. There was no selection in her ancient beater for all three to run at once.

She gripped the wheel tighter, staring into the darkness, and counted gate entrances. She never would have made the trip in the dark, on a night this cold, if she hadn't already been three quarters of the way there. It made no sense to go home and have to drive all the way out in the morning to deliver the package Mrs. Bailey had ordered. The gas savings alone was worth the inconvenience of adding to her already long day.

She just wished it wasn't so dark, so cold, and that the secondary roads were plowed a little better. The locals with four-by-four trucks would have no troubles, but her wheel clearance wasn't nearly as high. She hit another rut and her car shimmied from side to side.

Ignoring her rising sense of foreboding, she turned on the side road leading toward the Baileys' and a half dozen other homes. The plows hadn't touched the fresh snowfall from the morning yet—there must be no school buses on this route— which meant the remote country lane would be one of the last to get cleared.

She pulled to a stop in dismay. The only people moving that day *had* been driving four-by-fours, leaving two narrow wheel tracks the length of the gravel highway. There was no way she could get Herbie down that road, not even for the two miles it would take. The lights of her farmhouse destination twinkled in the distance, and for one crazy second she debated walking. Reason beat away that idea quick. It was cold enough she'd have frostbite if she was lucky and made the trip without any problems. If she did get into trouble? No way. She wasn't stupid.

So much for her time-saving, money-saving plan. Hope sighed in frustration and turned her car toward the main highway. No use backtracking past the Coleman's. She was now far enough out that taking the secondary route into town would be quicker than looping back.

The vehicle was still cold, but as she drove, the memory of bumping into Matt warmed her from the inside out. Good Lord, he must believe her to be a total klutz, along with being a fool.

Her embarrassing blunder last summer had faded enough she now found the situation amusing. His shocked response to her mistaken impression that he was coming on to *her* had made one thing crystal clear. He was not on the menu. Not now, not ever.

It didn't stop her from getting tingles in inappropriate places, daydreaming about his hands moving from her arms to other locations. He was hard, solid and muscular everywhere, and she'd wanted so much to just wrap herself around him and satisfy her curiosity.

Wrong word. Totally wrong word for what she felt. Fascination? Obsession?

She snorted and gave herself a mental kick. He was the last person in Rocky who would ever consider dating her, not after the shitty way her sister had treated him. Not after Helen and him had been together for years. Dating someone in the same family wasn't unusual, not in a town as small as theirs where there just weren't enough people in the dating pool, but he was off-limits for more than one reason. She had to get that through her head.

But the daydreaming remained kinda fun.

The curve of the road slipped under her tires, and Hope tightened her grip in panic as she fought to control the car. There was no warning, no indication she'd done anything wrong, but instead of being in the proper lane on the road she was on the side, headed for the ditch.

She turned the wheel. No response. Her front bumper hit the leading edge of the snowbank and the car bucked. Her seatbelt tightened around her chest, yanking hard as the incline increased. She slid down the embankment and everything went dark as her car was buried under a pile of collapsing snow.

Chapter Two

Matt cursed solidly. He was no more than half a kilometre behind, still wondering what the hell Hope was doing driving the long way home, when her car disappeared. He hit his brakes cautiously, skittering on the icy road and slowing to a stop as close to the shoulder as possible. His headlights shone over the embankment, casting a faint illumination over a broken path through the deep snow. It was a shitty place to pull over, but there was so little traffic he wasn't going to take the time to get farther around the corner, plus they needed all the light they could get. He flicked his fog lights on high and hit the hazard signal, turning the entire truck into a blinking lighthouse. He scrambled out the door, grabbed his shovel from the truck bed, and headed down the tracks left by her wheels, the faint red of her taillights shining like ghostly eyes.

There was no smell of exhaust—either she'd turned off the car or it had stalled, so at least he didn't have to worry about carbon monoxide. Layers of crust broke underfoot, sending shocks through him. Snow crept over the top of his boots, his jeans coated with the heavier, wetter underlayers. He reached her back bumper and slammed a hand on the metal.

"Hope, you hear me?"

"Matt? How did you...never mind. I can't get the door open." The answer was muffled but there.

Relief she wasn't unconscious loosened the knot of panic in his gut. He dragged the shovel forward and attacked the snow blocking her way. "I'll get you out as quick as I can. You okay otherwise?"

"I'm fine. Shook up a little. I don't know why that happened. Damn car. Damn snow."

Then he couldn't hear her as he struggled to clear a path toward the front of the vehicle. Friction had frozen the closest layers, even in the short time she'd been stuck. He eyeballed the opening he'd made. Good thing she wasn't that big. He yanked on the nearest door and it opened all of an inch.

"Hang on, I need more clearance. You're gonna have to climb out through the back."

He peered in the crack he'd achieved. She stared in dismay over fabric and boxes piled to the ceiling, the faint interior light a halo around her toque. "You don't ask much, do you?"

The filled-to-the-brim backseat was her only route out, and in spite of her protests, she was already pulling items into the front beside her. Matt worked for another couple minutes before stepping away and opening the door a grand total of ten inches. Bags and boxes toppled into the snow, blocking her escape.

Hope crawled over the seat, and he reached in and tugged her free from the mess.

"Come on, we'll have to get your car in the morning. I don't have a winch on this truck, and it's dangerous to be messing around in these temperatures."

"Wait." She started tucking items into the car, attempting to close the door.

"Forget it, it's too cold. We'll come back in the morning."

"I can't leave my supplies like this," Hope growled at him. "There's stuff here that's worth a lot of money."

"Worth shit if you die of exposure. Leave it."

Hope ignored him as she attempted to fit some of the jigsaw together.

Wanted to be stubborn? She picked the wrong guy to try it on. He nabbed her around the waist and slung her over his shoulder.

She screamed and clutched his jacket. "Matt Coleman. You put me down right now."

He struggled toward the truck, knee-deep in the snow and floundering with her squirming body weighing him down. "You keep that up and I'll spank your ass, young lady. They're only things. We'll get them in the morning."

Hope went still before relaxing on him. He managed a couple more steps before she spoke. "Fine. Just...let me walk. This is ridiculous."

He lowered her but kept her close, checking her carefully. "Where's your other glove?"

"Lost it when I was moving supplies."

He pulled off his right glove and held it out.

"You need to wear it," she protested.

His patience snapped. "Hope Meridan, you put that damn glove on. Then you march your ass up to my truck and you fucking sit where I tell you and do what I tell you until we get somewhere safe. You understand?"

She sniffed and took the glove from his fingers, slipping it on before twirling her back on him.

He grinned. It was bloody cold out, they were buried to their knees in snow, some of which had already melted into his boots and soaked his socks. The wind whistled past hard enough to snap branches in two, and he was the happiest he'd been in the past six months.

A pissed-off Hope was a pleasure to see.

They both struggled their way up the embankment, slipping and falling as they snagged dead grasses under the frozen layers. Hope got stuck making it over the final lip. Matt braced a hand on her ass and shoved, and she slid onto the road. He scrambled next to her and hauled her to her feet.

"This is right where we don't want to be if another vehicle comes along."

She nodded and they raced for the truck. He kept hold of her—the passenger door was too far to the side and surrounded by more deep snow. He opened his own door and pressed her in ahead of him.

The howl of the wind cut off as he slammed the door shut, leaving a ringing in his ears. He cranked up the heat.

Hope let out a groan of satisfaction. "That's what a heater is supposed to work like." She pulled off her mismatched gloves and held her hands to the air vents.

Matt shivered involuntarily. It was damn cold, and every inch of him felt as if it had been soaked in ice water. He buckled himself in. "Come here. Sit beside me."

Hope snapped her head up. "I'm okay over here."

"Don't be stupid. You remember my do-what-I-tell-you lecture? That seatbelt doesn't work. Get your ass over here, I want to get you home as quick as possible."

Hope lowered her gaze and slid into the center of the bench seat. She settled against him and buckled up before holding her red hands toward the heater again. "Wait—take your glove back. You'll need it on the steering wheel."

He accepted it gratefully before putting the truck in drive and heading to Rocky.

Neither of them said a word for a minute. She was probably worried about her shop shit getting wet and frozen, half-buried in the ditch, not to mention her car door left ajar. "Sorry for yelling at you."

"No, you were right, it's just things. I hope..." She sighed. "No. It's just things."

Music filled the cab. The wind now carried loose snow, reducing visibility, and Matt had to concentrate on the highway.

Only his focus got increasingly scattered as the scent of her perfume mingled with the hot air attempting to force its way past the icy fingers clinging to everything around them.

"I think we hit that cold snap they warned about." Hope wiggled closer, and a small batch of the wetness at his hip was no longer freezing but warm.

"I'm not looking forward to checking the animals, I can tell you that."

"You need to go out tonight?"

He shook his head before he realized she couldn't see the motion in the dark. "Nah. Dad and Travis are on, and we had the main herd back where there're enough shelters and trees the animals will be fine. But Blake and I are on tomorrow working the far fields. In these conditions we'll use the snowmobiles, and the cold is gonna suck."

She shivered. He felt it to his bones. "Not my idea of a good time."

The memory of his ex-girlfriend using that exact phrase cut into his belly like a knife. Helen had wanted him to give it all up. Wanted him to move into the city with her and become something other than a rancher. The pain made his response come out sharper than he'd intended. "It's part of the job, and you take the good with the bad. That's life."

Hope fell silent again. He drove as fast as he safely could. That's all they needed, for him to hit the ditch as well.

By the time they'd reached the outskirts of Rocky Mountain House, it was borderline warm in the cab, which meant he was borderline freezing his balls off in his wet things. Hope had to be just as cold, but she hadn't uttered a word of complaint.

"You still live above the quilt shop?"

No answer.

He stopped for a red light and looked down. Her eyes were

closed, and she swayed slightly from side to side.

Shit. Hopefully she was just plain tired, and not going into shock. He dropped an arm around her shoulders and squeezed. "Wake up. I need to know where to take you."

She shook her head, looking up with glazed eyes. "What?"

"You still live above the shop?"

"Yeah."

"Stay awake, okay?"

"Sure." She shivered, and he held on tight as he drove one-handed through the side streets to reach the back-alley entrance behind Main Street.

He parked in what he hoped was her stall. There weren't a lot of people moving, or lights on anywhere. Seemed most people knew enough to stay home when it was this damn cold.

He got out and pulled her after him. Hope draped her arms around his neck without him saying a word. The outside staircase up to her apartment was buried under an unmanageable amount of snow, so he carried her to her shop back door.

"Keys?"

Hope paused. "Shit."

"In your car?"

She nodded, then her eyes lit up. "There's a spare. I hid one."

She looked so pleased with herself, Matt had to laugh. Freezing his ass off and laughing in a back alley with his hands going numb and his feet and butt turning into blocks of ice.

"You gonna tell me where it is?"

"Oops."

She wiggled free and stepped on a box, reaching overhead behind a light. Then she turned and fell, exactly what he'd expected to happen, so he was ready. He caught her in midair, swung her to her feet and pulled the key from her fingers. "Either you're way colder than you're letting on or you've got a bad case of the clumsies."

"Co...co...old."

He opened the door and pressed her in ahead of him. Faint security lights glowed in parts of the shop, fabric bolts and whatnot on the shelves, and quilt samples displayed on the walls. It was warmer out of the wind, but it still wasn't warm.

"You turned the heat off?"

"Down. Saving money."

She stumbled and Matt read the signs all too clearly. Screw it. Physically she'd lost it. He guided her up the private stairs to her apartment. Every step he took, his socks squelched. Every pace he was more aware of the icicles clinging to his backside.

Hope turned on the landing. "I have a key here too. Wait."

By the time they were through the door, Matt's teeth were chattering like the gears on the old Ford. "Strip."

He had already gotten off his winter coat and was working on his boots before he noticed Hope stood motionless in front of him.

"Hope, you listening?"

She lifted her hands to paw at her zipper before letting her arms fall. "I'm here. The brain is working, honest, but not the fingers. Can't. Too cold."

He dragged off his final boot and wondered what he'd done to deserve this kind of punishment. "Okay, I'll help you. Just...relax."

She nodded, eyes closed. That made it easier—not having to watch those expressive orbs as he peeled off her outer layers and got her down to her T-shirt and slacks. Goose bumps rose on her arms, and he was a bastard for noticing her nipples were rigid under the thin layers of her top. When he led her into the bathroom, she went without a complaint.

He turned on the taps for the tub and she nodded. "Oh yeah, that's what I need. Perfect."

That's when the lights went out.

A million scenarios flashed through Matt's brain where this would be a good thing. If he'd rescued some random damsel in distress from the side of the road who he'd taken back to a hotel and the power had gone off, they'd have to share body heat to survive. One thing would lead to another, and the heat they generated would be most enjoyable.

Hope. This is Hope.

"Matt? I've got candles."

She bumped into him. He'd half-expected it though and managed to keep his balance. Logic and self-control were going to be the only way out of this mess with his sanity intact. "You need a hand?"

"Yeah, but just wait." She snuck past him, clinging to his waist for a second. Something clattered to the floor then a drawer opened. She groped her way down his arm just before icy cold fingers pressed the hard surface of a lighter into his palm. A rosy glow filled the room as he followed her directions and lit the couple dozen tea lights arranged around the room.

"Convenient."

"Pretty," she corrected. "It's a part of my relaxation therapy. Never thought I'd need them for this."

Steam rose from the tub. "Thank God for gas hot-water heaters. I didn't make it too hot though—you're too cold. We can add hotter water once you've warmed up."

Hope nodded. "Matt? You're not thinking of leaving, are you?"

He was thinking things that were going to send him to hell.

He undid the button on her jeans as quickly as possible, opening the zipper. Ignored her soft gasp as his cold knuckles bumped the heated skin of her bare belly. "I'm not leaving until I know you're okay. Take off your pants and get in the tub."

She obeyed clumsily. "You too, right?"

Bloody hell. "Yes, me too. I'm fucking freezing and I'm soaking wet. Don't worry, it'll be crowded, but your virtue is safe."

Hope laughed as she lifted one long leg over the edge of the tub, the sound turning to a moan of pleasure as the water surrounded her.

Matt was a dead man walking. He couldn't get in the tub now, not without her knowing he had a woody the size of a bull's. How he had gotten a hard-on when he was this bloody cold, he had no idea, but the damn thing was there. Insistently there.

She was all the way in, liquid soaking her T-shirt and making it cling to her body. He stared and reconsidered. He could strip and wrap himself in blankets in the living room. He'd already taken a step toward the door when she spoke.

"Matt? I know this is awkward, but if you don't get your ass in the tub right now I'll track you down and make you regret it. I don't care if you've got a hard-on, I've seen one before. I know it's a natural reaction, and it doesn't mean anything."

Shit. "What the—"

"I danced for years, Matt. Put myself through school showing skin, and I know the female body turns guys on even if their brain isn't engaged. I understand what happened this summer. Enough. It's forgotten. Just get in the tub."

Matt figured he was about fifty shades of red, but obeyed. Dragged his jeans down his thighs, deliberately not looking to see if she was watching. Because if she had her gaze on him and there was even a hint of attraction, he wouldn't know what to do.

And if she was watching with total disinterest that might be worse.

He stripped to his T-shirt and boxers before glancing her way. She sat in the middle of the tub, leaning against the side. Her body was curled into a ball, head back on the tiles, eyes closed. There was enough room for him at the top of the tub to step into the heated water—he groaned as loudly as she had, it felt so damn wonderful—before he sat and tugged her into his lap.

"I'm glad you have such an open mind about things, darling, but if it weren't for the fact I'm afraid you'd fall asleep and drown, I'd keep my carcass out of your way right now."

Hope twisted until she lay flat out on top of him, hip tight to his groin, head turned so her cheek rested on his chest. "Fine by me, any excuse you want to use. Just get your hands back in the water before your fingers fall off and my guilty conscience forces me to sew you special gloves for the rest of your life."

Matt snorted, but obeyed, slipping his hands around her and resting them on her belly. He linked his fingers together to be sure he didn't accidentally touch anything he shouldn't.

No matter how much he wanted to.

"By the way, thank you for rescuing me." Her voice, soft and low, tickled his ears.

"No troubles."

She shivered once more before relaxing with a deep sigh. "So, Matt Coleman. Can we start again?"

What was she up to? "Start again?"

Her body shook with soft laughter. "We're sitting in a tub of water in our undies. This situation calls for some explaining. Since we're not going to be lovers, I'd like us to go back to being friends. I've missed having you around since Helen deserted us.

I'm sorry she was a shit to you, but I hope you won't hold her actions against me."

The matter-of-fact way she said it, with a cute, slightly sleepy after-yawn, wiped away the sexual stress and chaos of the past hours. He hadn't realized that Helen had abandoned others as well.

Hope was smart, quick-witted...and a desirable woman, but the sexual part would just have to wait for someone other than him. "I would be honoured to be your friend, Ms. Meridan."

She lifted one hand out of the water, palm toward him, and this time he laughed as he gave her a high-five, like he'd done off and on over the years since they'd been teenagers.

Friends. Yeah. He could do that.

Chapter Three

The nonchalance she'd donned like a cloak was harder to maintain once she was warm enough to concentrate on something other than the ice in her limbs. Things like his firm body under hers.

The tingling in her extremities slowly faded. The tingling in her core refused to go away.

"How do you like running the shop?" His deep growly voice tickled her ears at the same time he wiggled just enough to scrape his whiskered chin over her shoulder. She hoped the lingering chill in the air would stand as a good enough excuse for the goose bumps that rose in response.

"Stitching Post?" Hope shrugged, then froze as that motion slid their skin together too intimately. "It's amazing. Although, there are moments, like when I've got more work to do than seems humanly possible, I wonder why in the world I thought being a business owner was a good idea."

Matt chuckled. "The chores can seem unending, can't they?"

"Like ninety five percent of the time?"

"At least you don't have to muck shit."

A laugh escaped her and she manoeuvred carefully to the bottom of the giant tub, slipping between his knees as she dipped her hands in the water one last time. "There is that. You're right. If we want to play 'who has the dirtiest tasks', I'm pretty sure the ranch wins. But mindless? Matt, you need to try restocking the thread bins sometime."

He sat straighter, his wet shirt clinging to the ridges of the six-pack muscles covering his abdomen. Oh dear. Hope dragged her gaze away.

"Those little white spool things? They got numbers on them, right?"

"Yeah, only they slip out of the rack on a spring-loaded system, which makes it oh-so-fun for the kids who get away from their moms to stand and one after another make them go *ping ping ping* across the room. One day I swear I reloaded that thing four times before I caught the little vermin and tied them down."

Matt was laughing as she stood and reached for the towel. The timbre of the sound changed then cut off. She steadily ignored him, stepping onto the bathmat to catch the drips.

Yeah, she had enough body to catch anyone's attention. She wasn't unaware of it. Only she wasn't trying to make this any harder for him than it already was.

The sheer dirtiness of her thought patterns made her want to snort. Poor baby. Hard?

"You warm already?" Matt crossed his hands over his lap casually, pulling his knees up to hide what must be another erection. Although she didn't think he'd really lost the first one.

"Warm enough to go..."

The power was still out. What in the world was she leaving to go do?

Matt smirked. "I think you need to reconsider your options, friend. You were pretty chilled. The apartment isn't getting any warmer."

"So we're going to sit in the tub all night?"

"Until we're wrinkled like prunes."

She shivered, and his expression changed, this time from lighthearted to deep concern.

Not even that was enough to stop her from getting out of temptation's reach. "Now don't look like that. I'm okay. Let me get a bunch of layers on, and I'll be fine. You stay in the tub for a bit then we can talk about what happens next."

It was the best idea—he couldn't argue with her logic. When he nodded, she picked up one of the candles and used it to reach her bedroom.

Fifteen minutes later she had a flashlight to illuminate her way. Long johns, two layers of socks, a thick long-sleeve sweater and a quilted hoodie she'd made completed the outfit. She'd also dug up a few things for Matt, although she wasn't sure how happy he'd be to receive them.

She tapped on the bathroom door. "Knock, knock. Is it safe to enter, your majesty?"

"My kingdom consists of six feet of water, two feet deep. One knock will suffice."

Hope laughed and opened the door, her amusement dying away as she took him in. Candlelight glowed over Matt's naked skin—he'd taken off his wet T-shirt, and all those ridges she'd felt under her before were now out in public. It wasn't clear right off if he'd also removed the boxers. She wasn't sure she could handle knowing.

Sweet mercy, what evil thing had she done to be tormented like this?

Ignoring him completely—*ha!*—Hope strode to the sink and plopped down the pile of clothing. She clicked on the spare flashlight and set it on the counter as well.

"I found some things that should fit you. If you're warm enough, I thought you could get dressed. You could be home pretty quick." She turned and looked him in the eye. "I have tons of quilts. I won't freeze. And if you're worried about the roads, you're welcome to stay as well."

Matt returned her gaze steadily. "I'm not worried about the

roads, but if we went to my folks' place, there's a fireplace..."

"I'm sure the power will be back on soon. You hungry?"

He had to realize she was deliberately changing the topic. She was damn stubborn when she needed to be. She was not leaving her place and that was final.

Matt nodded. "A sandwich would be good."

Then he moved to stand and she fled the room as casually as she could. Because there was no way, even with talk of being friends and all that nonsense, that she could watch his beautiful body any longer without giving in to the desire to drag her fingers over him. To follow her fingers with her tongue.

Yeah, friends. What had seemed like a simply marvelous idea at the time simply sucked.

She'd brought him his own clothes. A pair of sweats. A T-shirt. Thick sweatshirt. The only thing that didn't belong to him were the socks, and those looked hand-knit.

Matt dragged the towel over his skin harder than needed to dry himself. It was useless though. Scrubbing away the pain of the past was impossible.

Another sign of his fucked-up relationship—he tugged on the sweats. A pair that he'd left at Helen's one day. The T-shirt? One she'd said was her favourite. He could picture her pulling it on her naked body after they'd made love. Could imagine he still smelt her scent on the fabric, and a knife drove through him hard enough to kill the lingering sexual frustration that had built over the past hour.

Matt sat on the edge of the tub and wrestled with the demons in his soul. Helen hadn't only left him, she'd cheated on him first. Called him and his choices stupid and shitty. Blaming her words on the alcohol she'd consumed over New Year's Eve could only excuse so much. Drunk as a skunk, what she'd really been thinking and feeling had exploded out. Even her

47

apology later that week before she left town for good had been no kind of an apology. More of a rationalization on her part, as if he had to agree that the big city had more to offer.

The fact Helen had the guts to beg him to join her—to abandon his family and simply up and leave—the memory of that scene cut off any sympathy he might have had for her.

He pulled on the T-shirt. It was just a chunk of material. The sweatshirt would keep him warm. They had nothing to do with any past memories.

If he kept pretending, maybe that would make it true.

He didn't bother to look in the mirror, because he knew his expression was dark and angry. Matt blew out the candles one after another, trying to blow away his frustrations at the same time. Because out in the living area was a different woman than the one who had hurt him so badly. Hope wasn't responsible for her sister's offenses.

The knit socks cradled his feet on the hardwood floor, like furry caterpillars cocooned around him. He found Hope in the kitchen, the diffuse flashlights making her eyes darker as she handed over a plate and nodded toward the living room. "I'm having a bite then heading to bed. If you want to stay, you're welcome to."

Matt accepted the food and followed her into the living room. She plopped on the floor in front of him, dragged a quilt around her shoulders and basically all but vanished from sight. The only things still visible were her hands as she took up her sandwich and brought it under the hanging edge of the quilt draped over her head.

He sat on the couch and tossed the jean quilt behind him over his lap. It was cold in the room, but not cold enough he needed to hide. "You do have enough quilts to outfit all of Rocky."

Her smile peeked out from under the covering. "I will never

freeze. The apartment pipes may burst, but a woman who can sew will never go cold."

The sandwiches slid down easily. Hope had turned on her iPod, plugging it into a speaker system. Music filled the quiet around them.

"Batteries?"

The pile of fabric nodded. "Lasts a few hours at least. I like being able to take my own music with me wherever I go. I've got another speaker set up in the shop, although the play list is more applicable to the average customer's tastes. This..." she nodded at the player, "...this is my shit."

It was louder and raunchier than what Matt usually listened to. "That's not country."

A laugh burst out. "Damn right it's not."

"That's almost sacrilegious, isn't it?" Matt finished the final bite of his sandwich and followed it down with the pickle she'd popped on the plate.

"I enjoy country in moderation. Get to listen to it in all the grocery stores and everywhere else in town. So when I'm on my own, I balance it with other flavours."

She leaned over to hit the forward button, and the quilts fell away, the combination of the long line of her neck and her bright smile warming him inside more than it should.

The music changed, and this time it was his turn to laugh. "Is that an accordion?"

"Yeah, I've got eclectic tastes. Keeps things interesting."

She yawned then rubbed her hands together briskly. "Sorry for abandoning you after you saved my butt and all, but I'm exhausted. You planning on staying or heading home?"

Matt checked his watch. *Shit.* "I have to get up in four hours. If you don't mind me staying..."

Hope rose, still clutching the bundle around her.

"There's—" Her eyes went wide and she stared in consternation. "Oh, fuck it. It seems I'm going to keep kicking you in the balls, Matt Coleman, even though that's not my intention. You can sleep out here on the couch that's way too small for you, or you can have my bed. Or you can have the spare bedroom, but that was..."

Fuck it was right. "Helen's room."

Hope nodded slowly.

It wasn't the end of the world. "It's just a bed. I'd head home now, but it makes no sense to start the truck, scrape the windows clear, fight my way through the fresh snow to my trailer and then have to do it all over in three hours' time."

Hope nodded, more briskly this time. "This way. There's a wind-up old alarm that used to belong to my grandpa if you want it."

She grabbed for the quilts on the couch. All the way down the hall, Matt wondered what evil karma he'd earned to deserve getting the hell beat out of him this way. When she hustled him into the room and piled the bed high with quilts, there was nothing left but to deal with his torment.

Hope stood in the doorway, hands clutched together. "You got what you need?"

Matt nodded. "I'll leave as quietly as I can in the morning. Okay if I just pull the door locked after me?"

"Perfect, because honestly, I'm not getting up with you. Help yourself to whatever you want out of the fridge." Those blue eyes of hers caught him again, her expression serious. "Again, thank you. This evening could have ended way differently if you hadn't come along."

Then she was gone, the wink of her flashlight disappearing behind her door.

He turned to face his fate.

It was just a bloody bed. He crawled in with his clothes still on, tugging the quilts right up to his chin. Lying in the dark, slowing his breathing, trying to calm the wild activity in his brain.

It was no use. It might be self-torture, but he had to do it. He sat up and shined the light around the place, looking for signs of Helen, looking for anything that would poke him and make him bleed.

Nothing. It was just a bedroom.

The ghosts wavered and faded to mist. There was enough heat generated from his body and the food in his belly to allow him to relax. He turned off the light and covered his ears. Yeah, the only thing haunting him right now had nothing to do with the knowledge that his ex-lover had slept in this room.

It was the bright-eyed woman on the other side of the wall, her enthusiastic laugh and her kindhearted actions that dogged his thoughts as he fell asleep.

Chapter Four

The welcoming tinkle from the bells attached to the shop's front door brought Hope from her inventory to greet a massive armload of familiar-looking supplies moving toward her.

"How...?"

The boxes lowered to reveal another familiar sight. Clay Thompson, old classmate and sometime dance partner, flashed her a smile. "Got a few things for you. Must have fallen out of Santa's sled or something."

"That's the stuff from my car." She came forward to pull the topmost of the pile off and lay it on a table. "Oh man, thank you for grabbing it for me. When I called this morning your dad said the tow truck was already gone."

"Yeah, Matt Coleman phoned first thing. We had to rescue a couple others before your car, but she's at the shop now."

Hope wished she could stop the heat that rushed to her cheeks. She wondered if Clay would ask what Matt was doing phoning for her. He'd been gone when she got up, but obviously had taken time from his chores to put in the rescue call.

Clay lowered the rest to the floor. "We'll look the car over and let you know what needs to be done to make her roadworthy."

"You do miracles?"

"Ha. Yeah, she's in rough shape, but until they're completely dead, there's always hope."

His joke fizzled as she thought about how much harder having no vehicle was going to make life.

He motioned to the pile. "I think we found everything before we messed up the snow hauling your car from the ditch. Len's got another load coming in a minute."

"Len has the load right here."

Hope turned as a second massive male stepped through her doorframe. The past twenty-four hours had brought far more testosterone into her shop than she'd had around for ages.

"Thanks for bringing it all over, guys. You didn't need to do that."

Clay grinned. "What? Not take the chance to skip out of work? You've got to be kidding."

"Your dad will know something is up if you're more than five minutes behind schedule." Hope helped settle the supplies in one spot, embarrassed by how much she'd actually had crammed into her vehicle.

"This is a business meeting." Len retreated to the front counter, his broad shoulders stretching the fabric of his work coverall. "Why didn't you ask our garage to be a part of your spring fundraiser?"

Hope stared in confusion, distracted as Clay worked his way to her side, watching his six-foot-three frame pass between the rows of quilting supplies a little like seeing a bull manoeuvre through a china shop. "Fundraiser? Oh, the quilt raffle? I just got started on setting up the challenge. It doesn't officially begin until after the New Year. How did you hear about it?"

"Mason from the fire hall was bragging the other night that he and the volunteer firefighters are going to win."

Hope laughed. "Good for him. I'm looking forward to seeing what quilt design they finish."

Len jerked upright. "They have to sew a quilt?"

"Still want me to ask you to join in?" She laughed out loud at the chagrin on his face. "Come on now, it's for a good cause. Only rule is the quilt you put up for auction has to be made by all the members of the sponsoring group, *not* their girlfriends or mothers."

Clay swore. "You're serious?"

"Dead serious. Proceeds go to the Big Brothers and Big Sisters Club. The shop teacher at the school is training the Big Sisters' participants so they can offer car tune-ups during the fair."

"We can't sew."

Hope took her time looking them up and down. "Then I guess the firefighters will get bragging rights for the year. Because if they make the only quilt to be raffled off at the spring fair..."

Len and Clay were making the most hilarious faces at each other. Her smile was real as she turned to examine the pile of supplies and start sorting them. A few things were completely fine—she put them to the side for reshelving as soon as the guys went back to the garage.

Her happiness faded as she picked up a plastic bag filled with wet yarn and grimaced. Here started the troubles. Maybe she could recover it enough to put the yarn up for a discount. Or use it herself for a sample item.

Clay dragged her back from her labours with a tug on her sleeve. "You plan on giving lessons? If we sign up for the challenge?"

"Sewing lessons? Of course, that's part of the fun. And I've arranged for loaner sewing machines from the high school for anyone who needs one. I can come to your place or you can come here." She eyeballed the tiny workspace at the back and pictured the five oversized guys from the car shop all fitting in there. "Maybe I'll make it a rule I come out to the challenger's place. That will help keep the designs a secret as well."

"Secret designs. Now it sounds like a spy show and not sewing. This could be fun."

Hope glanced at Len. "He's getting you into trouble."

Len grinned back. "Does it all the time. I'm used to it."

"Go on, blame me. But hell, if the fire crew can do it, so can we." Clay nodded. "I have to double-check with the rest of the guys, but I'm pretty sure they'll agree."

"Really?" She'd only begun setting up the challenge, but having two solidly male teams involved was exactly what she needed to get interest going. "Sponsoring teams pay for materials at cost, we'll have the quilts displayed during the fair, then all the proceeds from the raffle go to the club."

Clay glanced around the shop. "I figure you can find us a manly enough design, right?"

"Sure. Moose and rifles? Beer cans and barbecues?"

Len laughed. "We'll talk about it more after New Year's. I'm heading back to the shop. You coming, Clay?"

"In a minute."

Hope waved Len off and stared at Clay as he shifted to the side of the display unit, grinning down at her. There was a flicker of interest—he was a handsome fellow. Having Matt Coleman under her roof might have revved her up, but Clay was sexy enough on his own to get a rise out of her without even trying. "You need something?"

"Yeah, an answer to when I get to see you again. When I asked you out in August, you said you were swamped with fall preparations, what with getting classes going. And then you were hard at it in October getting ready for the holiday rush. Now you're going to tell me that after Christmas you'll be busy with something else like this fundraiser?"

Hope took a deep breath and pulled a fabric bolt from the

pile on the floor, refolding it to give her something to do with her hands. "Well, it is hectic running the shop."

"It's demanding working on cars and pulling people out of trouble. I still make time for fun. "

Oh boy. Fun. She could go for some of that. Hope stopped her fidgeting and leaned forward on the table, glancing over his tall frame. Good looking, a decent dancer—she'd enjoyed his company in the past. "I have been busy."

Clay shrugged. "That's why I haven't been bothering you more. You ended up with a shop to run on your own. Just figured that you could use a little time away from being completely grown-up. Come and play for a while."

She was tempted. Not only would she enjoy some adult company, it might be what she needed to knock Matt Coleman permanently out of her system.

Guilt at making Clay almost a rebound date, when he didn't deserve that, held her back. But only a little.

"Okay." His face brightened and she held up a hand. "But not right away."

"Hope..."

"I'm not putting you off, really. Just give me a few days to finish dealing with the extra orders from the ladies who need help finishing projects in a rush for Christmas. I could end up with—" Clay crossed his arms and she stopped, partly because of his expression, partly because she was distracted by the sheer size of his biceps in that position. "Maybe instead of the quilts I should organize a beefcake calendar or something. Good God, you're making me drool."

He rolled his eyes. "Way to change the topic. I'm holding you to calling me when you have time."

"I will." Hope let her appreciation show. "Honest, I will."

Clay stepped into her personal space. Close enough she

had to look up at him. Close enough she wasn't sure if the heat she felt was from his body or hers.

He tilted her chin with a finger. "And Hope? If you don't call before we start working on the quilts, I'm going to think you're just after me for my sewing skills."

Hope laughed. "I'll call."

Someone entered the shop and Clay made a quick getaway. Hope switched her focus, but there was a different feel to her day. A pile of questionable supplies she needed to deal with, a car she needed to arrange repairs for.

But...more happiness coming her way in the future? Maybe it was time to work harder for the things she could have.

Time to put aside the things she couldn't have.

Things like Matt.

Matt flew around the corner and pulled up sharp to avoid crashing into his sister-in-law.

"Damn it, Jaxi. What the hell are you doing?"

The tall blonde gave him a dirty look. "What? I'm not allowed in the barns anymore?"

He snorted. "As if I'd try to boss you around like that. No, I meant right now. It's damn cold outside."

"Oh, you noticed?"

Her sarcasm was so blatant warning bells went off. Jaxi had been a part of the Coleman family officially for just over a year, but she'd been around forever. He grinned and mock bowed. "Did I screw up? Because life is much more manageable if you simply tell me what I've done wrong."

Jaxi grinned. "Sorry, although, you're right, if everyone would do what I want all the time, the world *would* be far more fabulous."

She skipped past him and grabbed a rake. Figured. She couldn't just talk. Had to work at the same time. Matt followed her example and headed into the next stall with his own rake.

"Heard you had a little run-in with Hope the other day."

Gossip around small towns never slowed down. "Rescued her, more like it. The woman shouldn't be allowed on the road with that death trap of a vehicle. Herbie should be crushed and buried."

Jaxi's snort of amusement carried over the top of the stall. "Herbie?"

"Her car."

"Is it even running anymore?"

"Doubt it. I got the shop to haul it out of the ditch for her, but I haven't heard anything after that."

A solid thump hit the wall between them. Matt paused then peeked cautiously around the corner. "Jaxi? You having problems controlling that rake?"

She slammed the head to the ground hard enough for puffs of dust to rise up. Then she leaned forward and glared at him. "The rake ain't hitting anything I don't intend it to."

Not an auspicious announcement. Not with her glaring as if he'd just tracked mud through her entire house. "You're pissed at me, that's clear, but hell if I know what I've done."

"Okay. So, you rescue a woman from a storm, then get her car hauled home."

Matt waited. She wasn't making this easy. "And...yeah. That's about it."

"Shit, Matt. What is wrong with you?"

"Not sure, obviously. I'll wait for you to tell me."

Her face lit with laughter for a second before she must have remembered she was upset with him and planted her hands on her hips.

"No, you tell me. If I'd gone off the road, is that all you'd have done? Hauled my ass home then got my car dragged to the shop the next day? Bull. You would have at least called later to find out if I was okay. Heck, you probably would have gotten the car out for me yourself, maybe helped gather some of the stuff that might have gotten ruined from being dumped in the snow."

Hope's stuff. He'd forgotten about that. He'd been working so hard at forgetting all the other things about her, like how soft her skin felt against him, that he'd forced her out of his thoughts every time she'd popped up.

Which was disturbingly often.

Guilt hit for a moment before he jerked to a stop. "Wait—but that's you. You're family."

"Matt Coleman, you're not actually going to tell me your mama would be happy to know that you left someone like Hope to fend for herself, power still off when you left her apartment—"

"Whoa, right there. How the hell you know all this? Did Hope complain to you?"

"Course not. That girl complain? She's got bigger balls than any of you Coleman boys, and she'd never think of bitching about losing money or being ignored by someone who said they were going to be her friend."

"Okay, now I know you talked to her."

He hadn't said a word about staying the night at Hope's because it was nobody's damn business. Nor had he shared their talk about being friends.

And he certainly hadn't mentioned crawling into the tub with her, and if Jaxi knew about that part, he wasn't sure what he was going to do.

Jaxi marched in closer. "I heard the first bit from the repair shop—Mr. Thompson called the house looking for you since you'd put in the order for the tow. He was mixed up. Thought it was your car and wanted to know what to do with *Herbie* since, as you said, they think it's a sorry hunk of junk worthy of not much more than hauling to the dump. So I took a trip to town to talk to Hope, and found her using a hairdryer to try and salvage the stuff that had gotten wet. She's not mad at you, by the way. Said you were right to leave it."

"But you're mad at me."

"Damn right, I am. She's got no one, Matt. She's not going to complain, so I'm going to do it for her. That night going off the road probably shut down most of her profits for the holiday season."

And she'd already said she'd been trying to get a few extra sales because of the bad weather. Matt dragged a hand through his hair.

"Well, I'm sorry, but I'm still not sure what else I can do. Yeah, I should have followed up faster afterward, but—"

"You were too busy being a chickenshit." Jaxi gave him a *fuck you* look, then went back to raking. Her shoulders moved easily under her coat as he watched her work for a minute.

"You know, you might be married to my brother and all, but I can still turn you over my knee and spank some sense into you."

Just like he'd anticipated, that got a rise out of her. Jaxi carefully leaned her rake against the wall then turned to smile sweetly at him. "You and what army?"

Matt held up his hands pleadingly. "Come on, give me a break. Explain."

Jaxi rolled her eyes. "Fine. Hope scares you to death, doesn't she?"

"Bullshit."

"Not bullshit. I've seen you, Matt. You go five miles out of your way to avoid the girl. Either you're trying to avoid her to stop from jumping her bones, or she's like the devil incarnate and you think associating with her will make her sister pop out of the woodwork to kick you to hell and back."

Fuck. That one hurt. He might have even bent over a little to protect his gut from the impact. "Is there nothing sacred with you, Jaxi?"

"What? That I care enough about you to not let you hide? Helen hurt you badly. If I could have I would have scalped her, but she's gone. You need to stop seeing her everywhere. Including associating Helen with her sister."

"I'm not."

Jaxi raised a brow. Deliberate-like, almost taunting him to protest again.

Was he? Was he really running that hard?

Jaxi went back to work, as if to let him think it through. Yeah, Helen had kicked him brutally. And he didn't know what he'd do if he ever saw her again.

But Hope—between the scorching-hot attraction he'd felt last summer and his current strange stirrings inside every time she was around—was he avoiding her for the right reasons? And what were the right reasons?

He didn't want to be involved with her. Didn't want to be involved with anyone other than for no-strings sex. And that sure wasn't something he wanted with Hope.

Liar.

Okay, he'd totally go for some no-strings sex with the woman. Touching her skin, grabbing her hips and riding her into oblivion would be fucking great. But that's all it would be— fucking—because there was no way in hell he was letting anyone near his heart.

Physical attraction was uncontrollable. Instinctive. But so was self-preservation, and he wasn't going to willingly edge into pain ever again.

Jaxi switched to the next stall over, still not saying anything. Matt methodically worked to finish his first. What had she accused him of? Running from Hope? Associating her with her sister?

Wasn't unreasonable, but then... He wouldn't want to be judged by his brothers' behavior all the time either.

He slipped out and stepped behind Jaxi, tapping her on the shoulder.

"Okay, since it seems you think you run my life as well as Blake's, tell me. If I agree that Hope is not her sister, and that I can be friends with her, then what does my friend need right now?"

Jaxi poked him in the chest. "Well, you might try asking her that question yourself, but since I know she's as stubborn as you, I suggest you go over and tell her you'd like to do some repairs around the shop."

He bit back a groan. "Like building shit?" She narrowed her eyes and he backpedaled. "Fine, makes sense. She won't take money for the stuff that got lost, right?"

Jaxi shook her head.

"But I can go over and fix things."

"Because that's what friends do. They help each other."

"Still want to know why you think we're friends."

Jaxi grinned, all her disapproval wiped clean now that he'd agreed to do her bidding. "Because either you're friends or you've got the hots for her, and I figured you'd be more comfortable with *friends* for a while."

She was far too intuitive. "That offer of tanning your hide still stands, girl."

She stuck out her tongue cheekily. "All my spankings are saved for Blake."

"Oh God, thanks for that image." Matt hugged her tight for a minute then shoved her toward the door. "Go bother someone else for a change. Squeeze the babies for me or something."

She waved then left him.

Left him alone with thoughts that were on a whole lot different path than they'd been when she walked in thirty minutes earlier. Family. Wrapped themselves into your lives and refused to let go.

And that was both a bit of heaven and a slice of hell.

Chapter Five

The bell over the shop door rang, and Hope looked up from her organizing, optimism rising. A couple more sales would go a long way to making her quota for the day.

When she spotted Matt, she wasn't sure if it was exactly disappointment that rolled through her. He wouldn't be buying any supplies, she was fairly certain of that.

The flutter of constant sexual interest she fought whenever he was around made it easy to smile at him. The tough part was making sure she didn't look hungry at the same time.

"Mr. Coleman."

Matt glanced over his shoulder. Hope laughed before she realized he hadn't done it to fool around. He was actually blushing when he turned back, his cheeks flushed from more than coming in out of the cold.

"Sorry, but that's my father's name, and I couldn't figure out how the hell he got into town faster than me when last I saw him..." He faded off then simply grinned. "Hi, how you doing?"

"Good. You doing your Christmas shopping?" There was a possibility, although she'd probably discount the sale too far to actually make any money if he was buying something for Marion. Guilt and desire were bad companions to private enterprise.

"Actually, I'm here to apologize. I was thinking about when I rescued you, and I messed up badly. I've been feeling terrible about it ever since."

What? "You've felt guilty for rescuing me?"

Matt pulled off his gloves and coat, hanging them on the rack beside the quilting table. "Of course not, but the way I rescued you meant some of your supplies got damaged. There was no reason for that—I had a chain and could have hauled you clear easy enough. Now, I'm willing to pay for what—"

"Oh no." Hope shook her head vigorously. "No bloody way. It was an accident, and you're not responsible for anything except pretty much saving my life. I could have frozen to death if you hadn't come along when you did."

He wasn't listening. Instead he was rolling up his sleeves, firm forearms coming into view, the dusting of hair over the muscles making her hyperaware of his every move.

She had it bad when even a glimpse of his arms was enough to get her wet. She crossed her own arms in self-defense and attempted to concentrate.

"What are you doing?" He paced the store, and she followed, dragging her gaze off his ass just in time as he spun around, wide smile beaming down.

"Just checking out the place. You've got some neat stuff in here. I mean, I already knew you had quilts, but there's a lot of different projects."

"Anytime you want to take up sewing..."

He leaned a hip on the cutting table, and the broad surface slid away from him. Matt stood rapidly as she grabbed for the edge and rebalanced it.

"Shit, sorry about that. I usually stand in the middle and brace it with my knee when I cut."

He held out a hand. "I can fix that for you."

Suspicion snuck over her. She turned and examined the bucket he'd had in his hands. The one he'd placed on the floor that she'd ignored while distracted by all the rest of him. It was filled with hammers and screwdrivers and other tools. "Matt, what are you doing here?"

He glanced around, feet shuffling in place like a naughty kid caught in the act. "Just thought I might offer you a hand. You know, brace the table, adjust shelves, anything that you need help with."

"And you would do this because...?"

"I want to?"

Yeah, right. "Sure. You got up this morning and decided 'I have nothing better to do today. I should volunteer my services to Hope.' Is that it?"

Matt shrugged. "Well, I had a coffee first, but then yeah, that was pretty much what happened."

Hope laughed. "Aren't you a shitty liar? Don't worry, you don't have to feel guilty about anything getting ruined when I went off the road. I got everything back and most of it survived the adventure. It's good, and frankly? Being saved from that ditch—you were right. It was just stuff and neither of our lives was worth risking. Please, put your guilt aside."

The door opened, the bell ringing sweetly through the shop. This time it was a customer, so Hope waved farewell at Matt and went to help the woman.

Only, he didn't leave, or not for good. At one point he headed out the door and she thought the strange visit was over, but before long he was back, coat once again on the hook, light tapping noises coming from the cutting area where he popped up and down like a broken jack-in-the-box. The entire time she pulled embroidery floss from the cupboard and helped her customer gather items for a project, he was there in the background. After the third time she'd forgotten what number thread she was going for, she steadfastly ignored him.

A few more people wandered in, and Hope got busy serving and chatting with the ladies, admiring projects and pictures of completed gifts they'd already mailed off to relatives for the holiday season.

It was over an hour later before she realized she was alone with him in the shop. It was obvious, no matter what she said, he was going to do whatever he pleased.

She wasn't sure if that pissed her off or if she liked his stubbornness.

After filling a mug with coffee, she brought it over and placed it in front of him. "If you're planning on staying much longer, you should know I will drape a display quilt over your back."

Matt stood, pausing to brush his palms against his thighs before picking up the coffee and taking a long swallow. He closed his eyes as he hummed in approval, and she allowed herself one brief fantasy of kissing her way across his firm jawline, tasting his lips.

She snapped her gaze back up to meet his, attempting her most innocent expression possible.

He was grinning. "Am I in your way?"

She shrugged. "Not really, but I still don't understand what you're up to. Go home, Matt. If you don't have chores to do, you certainly don't need to waste a day off in my shop."

He moved aside a basket full of patterns for Christmas ornaments and sat on the stool he'd cleared. "Yes, I've got some time off today, but I don't consider it a waste to spend it here."

Bloody fool. "What the hell is going on? Just tell me."

"I want to help you."

"I didn't ask for help."

"But you said we were going to be friends."

Hope opened her mouth to respond and nothing came out. *Friends.* The night she'd offered that word to him rushed back. Her brain flooded with too many erotic images. Him stripping

67

down, his cock tenting the front of his boxers. She might have had her eyes open a tiny crack as he stripped, and her penance was that now she had a good idea exactly what size equipment he was packing.

The sight of him, the feel of his hard body underneath hers in the tub—all of it rendered her speechless to respond.

Friends?

Good Lord. She was going to die right there in the shop.

He waited, sipping the coffee, one hand resting lightly on his thigh. The way the man filled out a pair of jeans ought to be illegal.

And while she had been the one to propose the friendship business, it had never been intended as anything more than a situation-saving comment. Friends with Matt? Bullshit on that, unless he meant the wave-to-each-other-across-the-street type of friend. That was the only safe kind considering how her body reacted to him.

Hope had to get out of this, and fast.

"Okay, friend, I don't need any repair work done right now."

"Fixed your table."

She reached for the edge instinctively and attempted to move it. Nothing shifted, not even when she used two hands.

His grin got wider.

"Okay, great. Thank you for that—I appreciate it, and I'll appreciate it even more the next time I have to cut some fabric and don't have to do an octopus imitation to keep everything vertical."

He put down his empty cup. "So, what else?"

"For you to fix?"

Matt nodded, his grey eyes taking in the shop. "You having heater problems? I can tweak the settings for you."

He was not giving up, but neither was she. "I turn down the

heat at night to save on my electric bill. It takes a while to warm up, that's all. The shop is a big space, and with the picture windows in the front, this cold weather doesn't help."

"How about a timer? Show me the thermostat and I'll explain how they work—if you're trying to save money but want the shop to be comfy first thing in the morning for customers, that's one way to deal with it."

She grabbed his empty cup and returned it to the small kitchen counter before taking him to the control panel. While he explained, she fussed with a couple displays, trying to balance this Matt with all the other ones crowding her brain. The staring-with-lust-filled-eyes version had been her favourite, even if his mistake last summer still made her crazy.

Years ago he'd been the older guy coming around the house, taking care of Helen, and by extension, little sis as well. To all of a sudden have that guy back was weird.

In a disheartening although sobering kind of way.

Fine. The friend-of-the-family type was safer. She could put her fantasizing back on the shelf next to her vibrator and leave Matt Coleman firmly in the just-a-guy category in real life. It's what she'd asked for, right?

"So you want me to install one?"

She scrambled to remember what they were talking about. Thermostats. "If you tell me what to buy, I can bring it in."

"I have time now—I'll go grab one."

Hope nodded slowly. "Fine, let me get you the cash you need."

He waved it off. "Don't worry, I'll—"

Anger bubbled up. She wasn't even sure where it came from. "I will not take your charity, Matt Coleman."

He caught her by the arm as she pushed past him toward the front of the store. "You a mind reader now?"

"If you want to help me out that's one thing, but spending money—"

"I was going to buy the thermostat then give you the receipt, since I have no idea how much it will cost."

Her annoyance fizzled away like a deflating balloon. Hope shuffled to a stop and stared at the ground. She forced a smile, the edges feeling twisted. "Well, seems I know how to jump to conclusions almost as well as I drive."

He made his way through to where his coat hung and shrugged it on. "Easy enough mistake."

"I'm sorry."

"No problem." He stopped at the door then turned to face her. "We really are two whacked-out fools, aren't we?"

There were too many ways to interpret that comment, especially accompanied by his serious expression. She sighed. "Can we blame it on holiday stress? That's what everyone seems to do these days."

He stared her down. "Hope, you were right the other day. When you said Helen deserted us both."

Deserted all right. "She's not my favourite person in the world, but I try to not dwell on it."

Matt nodded slowly. He didn't say anything else, just slipped out the door into the cold December day.

Hope walked to the front display window and watched him cross the street to the hardware store. She had no idea what was going on in his head, but she was dangerously close to making a terrible mistake. A mistake like letting him know that she thought of him more often than a friend should.

And after all the pain Helen had caused, dragging him though another dramatic situation was the last thing she wanted.

She leaned her forehead against the cool glass, the heated

air from her lungs fogging the window and slowly blocking her vision. Time for a change of mindset, starting now.

After all these years of pretending, dancing on stage and putting on a show, she should be able to do this. When she'd danced she'd made it seem as if she'd wanted every single man she looked in the eye more passionately than her next breath. This was another sort of illusion. Categorize him as hands-off— or even better, just a casual acquaintance. Make sure everything she said and did shouted that loud and clear.

Plus, Rocky Mountain House was a small town, but not *that* small. After Matt had done a few repairs to shed his guilt over her ruined things, she should be able to avoid him. They'd been out of touch for years at one point. With a little effort on her part, she could make that a reality again.

Letting Matt move on with his life was more than important, it was vital. Because it would be a sign she'd actually moved on with her own. Getting past the hurt of Helen's desertion? Financially she got enough reminders of that every damn month, but even there she was determined to win her way back.

But being caught up in longing for a man she could never have was slowly killing her. She had to give up these silly unanswerable fantasies if she ever wanted to find a way to be truly happy.

And fortunately, distraction had already given her permission to call. Hope stepped to the phone and dialed before she could change her mind.

Chapter Six

The cold air vanished in a blast of heat as Matt entered the bar, his cousin and brother following right behind. Gabe directed him to the side while Travis shrugged his way up to the bar and ordered three beers.

"You picked a hell of a night to go out," Gabe complained. He eyeballed the dance floor before brightening as he slapped Matt between the shoulders. "But then, since I see more than one group of females without company, I'll be magnanimous and forgive you."

"It's December in Alberta. It's going to be cold. Get over it."

"Hey, I'm not the one looking at lambing season starting within the month."

"Don't remind me." Matt took off his gloves and stuffed them in his coat pocket.

His brother sauntered up. "The only thing good about lambing is that we've got enough barn space they don't have to drop them outdoors. It's filthy and exhausting work, but at least it's moderately warm."

Travis set down two long-necked bottles, hanging on to the third for himself, and turned to get a better view of the room.

"I'll drink to that." Matt snapped up one bottle and passed the last to Gabe.

"You boys are lucky you switched your schedule. Still haven't convinced my dad that calving in February is old school and timing them for April is a hell of a lot easier on the body and the feed costs."

From then on, Matt pretty much ignored the conversation between Travis and Gabe. Ranching discussions had already filled his day. He didn't want it to be what he talked about all damn night as well.

But it was good to get out of his trailer. Maybe find a little companionship for the night.

Someone to get his mind off Hope Meridan, because she was pretty much all he'd been thinking about since last week, sorry son of a gun that he was.

It wasn't just the feel of her under him, but the little things he'd started to obsess over. Like her ready smile. Her stubborn refusal to allow him to do anything for her without complaining first.

The music was loud enough there was no need to pretend he wanted to contribute to the conversation. He leaned back on his stool and peered around, checking to see who was out that he recognized.

His gaze skittered over the dance floor, and his meager supply of calm and relaxed whooshed away.

Hope had her arms draped around Clay Thompson's neck, and they were both smiling way too much for this to be a first casual *hello* dance. Hell, he couldn't see any daylight between them either, and the way Hope was wiggling, Clay had to be pressed nice and tight to her soft breasts and...

Fuck it. Matt picked up his bottle and chugged back a few long swallows. No reason why she couldn't be here. She was a grown-up. Clay was too.

But it was impossible to pull his gaze away. She had on skintight jeans, faded patches on the ass, all her ample curves right out there and visible. Clay had tucked his thumbs into her belt loops, fingers spread over her butt as they swayed together. Hope rested her head on his chest, the motion turning her face toward Matt. She'd closed her eyes, face relaxed and a hint of smile on her lips.

It was the most peaceful Matt had ever seen her, and something ached inside.

He wasn't wishing her anything less than happiness, but there was this strange sensation that rushed him. He stared at Clay's hands as the man moved them slowly over Hope's body, and the ache switched to something sharper and needier.

Matt sipped his beer and deliberately rotated his stool so they weren't in his line of vision. That brought him into direct sight of a Christmas party group of women, gazes darting over him and the boys. Travis was already making a move. He lifted his bottle in salute, then grinned at Matt and Gabe when a couple ladies headed their direction in response.

"You guys know how to dance? Because we need some exercise and our favourite song is about to come on." Their spokesperson shook her head back and smiled enticingly.

"What's your favourite song?" Travis teased. He stood and stepped behind them, hands resting lightly on their shoulders.

"Any that we're dancing with you?"

"Well, I'm all for making your night a little brighter." Travis took her by the hand and led her toward the floor.

Gabe rose and reached for the other lady. He paused and motioned with his head as he spoke to Matt. "You joining us on the floor?"

Matt glanced away, catching sight of Clay moving toward the bathrooms. Hope sat at a table with a glass in her hand. Damn it anyway. "Yeah."

But he didn't head to the partiers' table to find his own dance partner. His feet carried him the other direction, and he found himself staring at Hope, wondering what the hell he was doing. "Hey."

She glanced up, and her smile vanished as she slammed

her lips together. "Matt?"

Awkwardness edged along his spine, and he felt about ten years old. "How are you?"

Hope snuck a peek toward the bathrooms. "Good. What're you doing?"

I have no fucking idea was the first thing in his brain. Couldn't say that though. Like a damn fool, he slipped into the empty seat across from her. That at least put the table between them so he wouldn't do anything stupid like dragging her from her chair and into his arms. "Just getting in some relaxation before the winter lambs start arriving. How are you?"

She leaned back, her uncomfortable expression twisting with amusement, and he realized he'd repeated himself. "Just fine. Not much changed since two seconds ago. Or since I saw you last week. Life's not that interesting."

Something had changed. Last week she hadn't been in Clay's arms. "Didn't mean...yeah. Well. I guess I meant more... I mean."

If he could have faded into the background, he would have. This frantic fumbling was not like him, but it seemed when it came to Hope, he had no style. He was so busy trying not to stare at the way her soft blue shirt stretched over her full breasts he didn't quite know where to look.

"Hey. I wanted to tell you that timer on the thermostat? Wonderful invention." She must have felt sorry for him. There was no other reason for her to actually be nice and try to put him at ease. "I've managed to adjust the times so the furnace is running at high for fewer hours, but the shop is toasty when I open in the morning."

Matt grinned. "Yeah, it might take a long time to heat up a space that big, but the heat lingers, so you can turn it off a couple hours before you close and no one will notice."

Their conversation was inconsequential. Furnaces and quilt

shops, and he still fought his attraction. Talking about rising heat—the irony wasn't lost on him.

He was so distracted by her blue eyes he didn't see Clay return.

"You're in my seat," Clay growled.

Matt stared up at a wall. He wasn't a small man himself, from working the land for years, but Clay was a bloody monster. "Resting my feet for a minute and saying hello."

He rose. Clay stared daggers at him. Neither of them said anything, but the tension was there.

"I'll be right back." Hope escaped her chair and raced away. She was halfway to the bathroom in no time, and guilt hit Matt. It was as if she was fleeing from them.

"What the hell foolishness you working, Coleman?" Clay pushed Matt aside.

"Nothing. Honest." *Just being a stupid shit.* Matt shrugged. "Thought I'd say hello and make sure she was okay. I pulled her from the car the other night."

"She's fine. Now that you've said hi, you can go find somewhere else to take a break."

Matt nodded and backed off. There was no reason for him to be defensive. No right to be worried about Hope and what she was doing with Clay.

The section of the bar where he'd sat with his kin was deserted. Gabe and Travis were both on the floor happily dancing with the ladies. Matt ordered a second drink and steadfastly ignored everything but taking measured sips from his bottle.

Especially paying no heed to the part that wished he were the one tucking Hope up against him and holding on tight.

Chapter Seven

For a Tuesday morning, the shop was crazy busy. Hope hurried to enter another sale before turning to help find some last-minute items for a gift. Sweet relief accompanied the rush—she was going to survive her first Christmas season and make the required profit to fill in the gaps from the first lean months.

She smoothed her hair as she passed the tiny mirror on the wall between the register and the sales floor. Her cheeks were bright red from moving around rapidly, but it was the fact her smile was real that made up for a lot of her previous stress.

Maybe this solo-ownership thing was going to work. First anniversary wasn't until May, but if she was careful she'd make it through okay, in spite of having Helen ditch her.

"Are you out of bright cherry-red piping?" Two customers waited beside the cutting table and Hope raced over to help them.

"There's more in the back. Is that all you need? Because if you have other items to grab, I'll be able to finish the orders for you in a minute."

The ladies waved happily. "Don't rush. We've got babysitters at home since the kids are out of school all week. The only thing left on our list is to stop for a cup of coffee."

Hope pointed to the back sitting area where she'd arranged comfortable chairs around a tiny Christmas tree. "Help yourself. I put out some deluxe mixes this week for a special treat. You can have a coffee, chat—I'll do up your orders when you're ready."

She watched with delight as three customers took her up on the offer and moved to the back, talking and dropping extra knickknacks in their baskets as they went.

Finding the extra piping in the back wasn't nearly as successful. She found the box she needed readily enough, but the shelving units were more decorative than sturdy. She cursed lightly as the entire load tipped forward and slipped to the floor, one surviving box clutched in her fingers.

The disaster sprawled everywhere, but she'd have to clean it up once the doors closed. Hope rushed back into the shop.

Time flew as she dealt with sales, satisfaction accompanying her creeping exhaustion. She passed over another shopping bag and smiled happily. "Thanks for coming. Merry Christmas."

Her cherry-piping sale pushed out the door, the front bells tinkling merrily, the same moment one of the hardware employees trolleyed in a tall box.

"Delivery for you, Hope. I've got three more in the truck. Where do you want them?"

The blast of cold through the door snapped off as he closed it behind him, but Hope examined his load with trepidation. "Why are you delivering my new shelves now? I thought no one could build them until the New Year? I asked for them to be stored until then."

He snapped to attention, a grin plastered to his face. "You were on the Secret Santa list. Someone is coming out today to set them up for you."

Mortification froze her feet in place. Only he looked so damn pleased about the whole thing she forced a smile. "Well. That's...nice. Umm, I don't remember signing up for the Secret Santa. In fact, I know I didn't."

"Your name was on the list, and someone volunteered to drop by. That's all I know. Love this time of year—people are so giving."

He pointed at his burden and Hope nodded. No matter how horrified she was, she couldn't leave him standing there. "Can you put them just outside the back storage room, please?"

All the while she served her customers and tidied the shop from the mad scramble of the morning, Hope tried to figure out who the hell would have put her name down for the Secret Santa.

It was a charity service. She didn't need help. In fact, she'd offered items herself, making a couple of quilts for the hospital and nursing home.

Being lumped as a charity case wasn't a happy thought. Even the pleasure of getting to organize the chaos of the back room onto sturdy metal shelving wasn't enough to eliminate the distaste in her mouth.

The phone rang, and she hurried to answer it, an additional flash of discomfort hitting as she recognized Clay's voice.

"How's my favourite fabric addict?"

She went with part of the truth. "Busy as the elves in the workshop. I can't talk for long."

"No worries. Just wanted to remind you I'll be dropping by later with lunch and a surprise."

Shit. She fumbled for words. "Right. Lunch."

He hummed in disapproval. "You'd forgotten, hadn't you?"

"Guilty." Although, if he brought food over as he'd promised after their last date, at least that would force her to eat. Otherwise she'd have skipped lunch completely today. "I can't guarantee a lot of time to visit."

"You should have hired extra help over the holidays."

Going solo was the only way to survive the cash drought. "I'll get by. See you in...how long?"

"Forty-five minutes, an hour at the most."

Hope dealt with customers and smiled and chatted, but half her mind was on Clay. He was a nice enough guy, patient and attractive...

And for some reason, he just didn't ring her bells.

Maybe there was too much on her plate right now, and the libido could only take so much stress, but all she wanted was to chat a little then fall into bed—alone. Most definitely alone.

Crazy, mixed-up, stupid female hormones.

With how swamped she was, dealing with the issue right now was out of the question. She'd just have to acknowledge her system was broken. After the holidays were over, things would kick back to normal and she'd be interested in something sexual again. That had to be the solution, because there was no other way she saw to fix it.

She smiled up at the next customer and all her thoughts about broken sex drives fluttered away like tinsel on the wind. Matt's firm jaw and cold-reddened cheeks were just visible above the raised collar of his thick winter coat—the coat he was removing and hanging on the rack. Like he planned to stay for a while. Tingles raced over her as if she'd hit an exposed wire on the Christmas light string.

"Can I get you something?"

He laughed. "Hi, Hope. How are things? Nice to see you too."

"Well, yeah, hi. What are you doing here?" Okay, that was borderline rude, but being shell-shocked didn't make for quick polite responses.

He held up a hand then dug into his back pocket. "My mom had a list of things she needed last minute, but she got roped into babysitting the nephews while Beth wraps gifts. Can you package these up for her?"

Matt passed over the list and she eyed it carefully. "It will take a few minutes."

"No rush."

He was rolling up his sleeves again, and she turned away to avoid staring. Damn, damn, *damn*. Why did her body do this? All the bubbling interest she kept hoping for with Clay burst out from wherever it had been hiding and rocked her with frustration.

Matt laid a hand on her arm. "Where are the shelves?"

Confusion swirled for a moment before she connected the dots. *Oh. Bloody. Hell.* "You're my Secret Santa?"

He waggled his brows. "Ho ho ho."

This wasn't happening. "There's a mistake. I didn't sign up for the program. You can go and help someone else."

Matt shook his head. "Sorry. You have shelves, I have tools and time. I'm going to build them. You have any specific instructions? Then I'll get out of your hair and get started."

The fact he ignored her protests added fuel to the fire. She managed not to stomp to his side, aware of the customers still wandering the small shop. Hope grabbed the front of his shirt and pulled him close enough she could whisper. "I don't. Need. Your help."

He frowned then shrugged in dismissal. "You were on the list—"

"I didn't sign up. It's a mistake."

Matt didn't hesitate. "But you do have shelves that need to be assembled?"

Blast. She didn't want to lie. "I do, but they can wait."

"As your friend, I'd be honoured to put them together for you."

The twinkle of mischief in his eyes told her he knew damn well whipping out the *friend* card would push her buttons.

81

Her anger still simmered, which was enough to help excuse the flush of sexual frustration that rolled over her every time he got within striking distance.

A customer waved in her direction, and Hope gave up. "Fine. Thank you. I want them three across the north wall and one beside the back door."

Matt tipped an imaginary hat and strode away, whistling a Christmas tune. She dragged her gaze off his butt and hurried to deal with her customer, even as she plotted revenge.

He worked as quietly as he could, the teeny screws giving him ample grief and plenty of time to reflect on exactly why he was doing this crazy task in the first place. It wasn't as if he didn't have chores to do at the ranch.

But when he'd overheard Clay talking at the hardware shop the day before, the seeds had been planted. When his mom had shoved the shopping list into his hand this morning and as good as pushed him into Hope's path, there was no way he could resist. His response to sneak into her shop ahead of the guy might be unreasonable, maybe even childish.

Fuck if he'd let some overgrown grease monkey make points with Hope by assembling her shelves. Maybe he hadn't known about the Secret Santa deal until a couple days ago. He knew enough to get the job done before Clay set foot on the premises.

He moved another pile of boxes to the side so he could manoeuvre the second shelf into place—she must have had some kind of a storm happen in the back recently. Either that or she was secretly messy, although he'd never have guessed that from the way her house and the outside shop were organized.

The front-door chime rang again and again. The sounds all reinforced this was a different kind of workplace than he was used to. There were no noises from the animals or rumbling engines. Instead there was laughter and conversation and the steady undertones of Christmas carols drifting through it all.

Then things got quiet for a while followed by a low rumble of a male voice entering the picture. Matt considered poking his head out of the storage area to see who'd come in, but he was near enough to being done with the final shelf he resisted.

When they moved closer, Hope's and Clay's individual voices came clear.

"You like vegetable soup? I got turkey sandwiches and coleslaw as well."

"Sounds good. You can put it on the table there and I'll get us plates. If someone comes in, I'll have to go and help them."

"That's fine, but that's why I waited until after one, because most everyone else is off their lunch break now. You might have a few minutes free."

"Aren't you supposed to be at the shop yourself?"

"Nahh. Dad and the guys, we all take turns for breaks. I arranged mine for the afternoon."

Matt took his time putting the final shelf into place. He'd been gone from his chores for a lot longer than anyone expected, and he still wasn't completely sure why.

It was weird, eavesdropping as the two of them talked about nothing in particular. Guilt hit over what he was doing, hiding out in the back room as the guy he'd intended to muck with sat out front sharing a meal with Hope.

"Want to know my surprise?" Clay teased.

"All depends. Does it require me to do anything other than relax?"

"Definitely not. That's the good bit—you know those shelves you ordered from Home Hardware?"

Matt grinned and glanced over the assembled units, the old

wooden ones lined up at the back door ready to be hauled away.

Hope answered hesitantly. "Yeah...?"

"I've come to put them up for you."

"Oh, really?"

Perfect timing. Hope was launching into her protests when Matt stepped into the room and their line of vision. "All done."

Clay's jaw swung open. He glanced quickly between Matt and Hope. "What are you doing here?"

"Matt set up my shelves." Her cheeks were flushed.

"What the hell he do that for? You ask him to?"

"He's..." she swallowed hard, "...my Secret Santa."

"But that's not possible. I signed up. My name was on the list."

Hope muttered. "Mine wasn't supposed to be."

Clay frowned. "What?"

Matt hid his smirk, the total confusion on Clay's face worth the effort it had taken to sneak away from his tasks for a couple hours.

Hope looked him over, her eyes narrowing with suspicion. Maybe he hadn't hidden anything as well as he thought.

She rose to her feet. "Guys, I have no idea what's going on. I didn't put my name on any list. I don't know why you're both here, but I don't have time for...whatever this is. Thank you for lunch, Clay. And thank you for putting up my shelves, Matt. But if you don't mind, I need to get back to work. I need the two of you to stop acting like children and let me get on with what I decide I want. This is my life, not yours. Butt out."

She glared at them in turn, almost daring them to respond. Matt wasn't stupid. He'd seen that expression on his mama and Jaxi before. It was the "pissed-off female, don't mess with me" look. The one the men in the family ignored at their own peril.

"Matt, the supplies your mom wanted are ready to go."

With perfect timing the front doorbell rang, and Hope turned her back on them both, heading to the front with a surprisingly cheerful call for her customer.

Matt's guilt dimmed as he caught the way Clay stared at Hope as she walked away. "Eyes off her ass. She's not a piece of meat for you to try on for size."

Clay swung back slowly to face him. "Coleman, you and I are going to have troubles if you don't get the hell out of her life."

"That's not your decision." Ultimatums didn't sit well with him. Matt might not know exactly what to make of this weird thing going on between him and Hope, but being pushed made him want to push back. "As she pointed out, Hope is a grown woman. It's not up to you who she's friends with."

Clay stepped in close, glancing toward the front of the store to be sure they weren't overheard. "It'll be up to me when she and I start hitting the sheets. Because I don't let my women fuck around with other guys."

Instant pain crippled Matt's intended response. He held his fists at his sides, containing the rage that wanted to explode out and take Clay to the floor in a scrambling heap of violence.

He shuffled off numbly to grab his tools from the back. By the time he came out, Clay was already gone, saving him from having to figure out what to do to the guy.

At the front counter, Hope didn't smile much as she rang in his mom's purchases. She wasn't rude, but what she gave him sure wasn't the same smart-assed take-charge attitude he'd come to expect. More as if she was resigned and upset, and her wretchedness broke through his protective wall, the one that snapped up involuntarily every time he was reminded about Helen.

She passed over the bag, and he caught her fingers with

his, forcing her to meet his gaze. "I'm sorry for making you feel uncomfortable. That wasn't my intention."

Hope paused. "I get that. And let me be real clear—I do appreciate having my shelves up, but I don't want to be used in some *my dick is bigger than yours* contest you've got going with Clay. I won't take it. You understand?"

He nodded, but as he wandered out into the bright sunshine and the cold that was enough to make him gasp, Matt wasn't really sure he understood at all.

Chapter Eight

The table remained crowded with bodies, although the highchairs had been pushed to the side. Blake and Jaxi's baby girls celebrating their first Christmas were being passed from arm to arm. The boys from Beth and Daniel's family bobbed and weaved through the post-chaos of Christmas dinner. Matt stared down the expanding line of his family, a strange mixture of warmth and lingering chill enveloping him, the cold having nothing to do with the freezing temperatures outside.

Jesse and Joel were home from college for a few weeks. Travis alternated between tormenting and confiding in them, just like old times, the three of them gathered together at the end of the table. Right now they were laughing under their breaths, glancing around guiltily every now and then, and he bet anything they were discussing their latest conquests.

He turned to his right and ignored the envy that rose at the realization his younger brothers were probably getting more action than he was.

"You guys heading into Calgary tomorrow?" he asked Daniel.

His brother shook his head. "Beth's parents went south for the holidays, so there's no reason for us to make the trip, not in the cold. Her sister said she'd come visit when the weather breaks, but right now traveling when we don't have to? Not a great idea."

"No kidding. Wind chill makes it nearly minus forty." Matt stared at the blowing snow in disgust. "You sure you don't want to come and check the newborns with me in an hour or so?"

Daniel laughed. "God, no. I openly confess my nine-to-five existence suits me far more than I ever imagined."

"Bastard."

"Uncle Matt." A tug on his sleeve made Matt slam his lips together with a guilty glance in his sister-in-law's direction. Beth shook her head but still smiled.

He turned to answer his youngest nephew. "Yes, Mr. Robbie. What can I do for you?"

"Come play a game."

"Well, sure, that sounds like a great idea." Little fingers dragged him upright, leading him away from the table and the grown-up conversations.

"Hey." He glanced back to see his oldest brother Blake grimacing. "You sneaking out of washing the dishes?"

"Of course not." Matt grabbed Robbie's hand and pointed. "I'm not sneaking, I'm being escorted."

He waved farewell to the laughter and went willingly with his nephews to the downstairs room to be introduced to their most recent board game, which he then lost in a spectacular fashion five times in a row.

Drifting. That's all he was doing. He'd recognized the truth more and more in the past week. Especially with the cold snap making it difficult to do anything but deal with chores as quickly as possible then hide out in his trailer with the newly installed wood-burning stove roaring as hot as possible.

With all the life and happiness around him, the contrast stood even bolder—he'd been a shadow for nearly a year now, and it was time to be done moping like a teenager over things he couldn't change.

Matt ruffled Robbie's hair and crawled to his feet.

"Well, boys, it's my turn to head out and give some Christmas cheer to the animals. Thanks for the games." He lowered his voice conspiratorially. "Thanks for saving me from dishes too."

He got a couple hugs and one fist bump from his oldest nephew who was far too cool for hugging. Wrapping up against the cold, going through all the chores with Blake's easy presence at his side—it was comfortable, routine, mindless. Yeah, drifting was pretty much the right word for his life.

It was time to shake himself up, even if he didn't know what that meant.

Blake headed toward the house, the lights along the eaves shining like crazy stars clinging too near the earth. Matt followed for a moment before changing his mind and heading toward his truck. He was halfway to town before he realized what he was doing.

Wondering why he'd headed her direction wasn't something he could explain either. Would Hope even be home?

He pulled into the parking area outside her shop, and his hopes fell when he spotted her empty parking stall. Still, there was a light shining on the second floor, so he dragged himself out, reaching into the extended cab space for the present he'd been hauling around all week.

Just in case he ran into her.

The doorbell at the top of the landing went off with a cheerful buzz, and he was delighted to hear noises approach. Hope's eyes appeared in the slim window to the side of the door, a frown creasing her forehead.

"Matt?"

He smiled and offered the package. "Merry Christmas."

She stared for a moment then shook herself. "Merry Christmas. Come in quick before we lose all the heat."

The heavy scent of peppermint in the air tickled his nose. It was warmer inside than the last time he'd been in her apartment, but not much. Mostly because he wasn't as cold to begin with.

"What brings you out on a holiday?" Hope shuffled from foot to foot. She glanced over her shoulder then excused herself, disappearing into the kitchen.

Matt didn't answer—didn't know how to answer. Instead, he put down his package. He was in the middle of taking off his layers when the realization hit he'd come straight from chores. "Hey, is it okay if I use your washroom?"

A burst of laughter rang from out of sight. "No problem, but if that's all you stopped by for, you need to learn to go before you leave the house."

He washed up, still wondering exactly why he was here. Kind of like he'd wondered the entire time he'd been working on the gift he'd brought her. It made no sense, but he wanted...

Nothing. He wanted nothing.

"Would you like a cup of tea or some apple cider?" Hope asked.

Matt slid into the living room, looking around, his curiosity rising. "Cider would be great. I left before they brought that out, and it's a Christmas tradition."

She bought him a mug and gestured to the lone chair that was free from swatches of fabric. "Have a seat. Don't mind the chaos."

"Did the shop explode?" He sat gingerly, wondering if the straight-backed chair could hold his weight.

"Just a few projects I thought I should get going."

Matt sipped his cider to avoid blurting out *On Christmas?* She knew what day it was as well as he did. "Can I help?"

Hope rocked back on her heels where she was kneeling beside the couch. "More help? Do you have a spinning wheel that whenever the hand stops on certain squares you go into the community and do random acts of helpfulness?"

"Good idea, but no. I was just…"

Just what? He stared down, at a loss for words. She rested on the floor with an expression of complete calm on her face. Her skintight leggings of bright red fabric and a patchwork-quilt sweater that hung nearly to her knees made her look vibrant and alive.

Hope sighed softly, placing her cup to the side and wiggling until she had her arms wrapped around her knees. She rested her chin on them and stared back. "Matt, why are you here? I mean, I'm not going to kick you out, but it's strange. You got anything more than 'I was in the neighborhood' to say?"

He opened his mouth then shut it quickly. How could he tell her anything when he still wasn't sure what had brought him in her direction, yet again. Matt raised his cup. "I honestly have no idea."

Something between mischief and sympathy flashed in her eyes. "Very descriptive. I understand completely. Make yourself at home."

She got on her knees and picked up squares of fabric one at a time, laying them on top of each other carefully.

"You're not going to call the men in white to throw me into the funny farm?"

She didn't stop working. "Nope, since I don't feel like occupying the padded cell next to you. It's not benevolence, Matt, it's self-preservation."

Matt watched her for a while longer. The sensation of loneliness blasted in harder than the icy-cold wind still sweeping the prairie fields to the east of them.

"Can I help you?" he asked again. "That looks interesting."

Hope checked him over carefully for a moment before her smile lit her face. "If you want. Pick a solid, drop on a square of batting, then layer on any patterned fabric you like. Keep repeating until you have twenty sets in the pile. We'll stack them on the table for now. Later I'll chain-stitch them together for the start of the top."

Matt put aside his cup and joined her on the floor. It was awkward at first, bumping her with his elbows as he reached for different colours. Music played quietly in the background, something with bagpipes, and he smiled, but didn't say anything.

The silence stretched out, but it was comfortable, not awkward. Matt stood to carry his fourth pile to the table when the buzzer on the stove went off. "You want me to take care of that?"

Her cheeks flushed pink. "There's nothing in the oven. It's a timer to remind me to stop what I'm doing and have some supper. I tend to forget otherwise."

Matt nodded. "Can I help make something?"

Hope shook her head. "Freezer meal, ready to nuke. You want one?"

"Actually? I'm still full from lunch. Jaxi and Beth were trying to outdo my mom in the kitchen." He stopped. It hit him. "My God, Hope. I'm sorry. It's Christmas. You could have come over..."

He wasn't sure how to finish that sentence. Suggesting she should have joined them was completely wrong, and yet completely right.

She saved him, patting his cheek almost playfully as she passed him en route to the fridge.

"You can stop being embarrassed by my lack of family, okay? Mom left years ago, Dad is gone. I have no idea where my sister is...but it's okay. I'm living here because I like Rocky. And the shop is doing well." She paused then wrinkled her nose. "Well enough, at least."

He nodded in sympathy. "First years are the hardest, I hear."

The microwave was warming her food before she turned back to face him. "So really, it's okay. Now, you want another drink? Or do you want to get back to the family? It's been nice to have your company, but I don't think you want to watch me eat."

Matt glanced at the table, covered with piles of organized material. "You eating in the living room?"

"Planned on it, and watching *The Sound of Music*. Tradition, you know."

The microwave pinged, but he caught her wrist before she could open it. "Hope, why did you let me help you with the quilt without arguing with me?"

She leaned back and crossed her arms in front of her as she looked him up and down. A slow smile snuck out and she laughed. "Because you were honestly interested. And I'm never going to say no if you really want to do something. I don't like charity, Matt, but I have no problem with a friend giving me a hand because they want to."

Something in her logic hit him hard enough his knees nearly buckled. His heart pounded as if he'd just run a gold-medal sprint, and the satisfaction filling him reminded him of the sheer excitement of Christmas morning when he was young.

Delight, unexpected but fresh and new in how it arrived.

Heading back to the house was impossible. Not because there was anything there he wanted to avoid, but because there was something here he didn't want to leave.

Even if he wasn't sure what it was, other than a...friend.

He cleared his throat. "Then, if I ask if I can stay and watch the movie with you, because I'd really like to just hang out with you for a while longer, what would you say?"

Hope didn't hesitate. She pointed to the fridge. "If that's what you'd like to do, and why you'd like to do it, then I'd say, 'Could you pour me a glass of iced tea and bring it with you when you come to the living room?' Because my hands are full."

Hope kept her eyes glued to the television, snuggled into the couch a little deeper and fought an epic battle. Hypocrisy didn't feel good, no matter who delivered it. She'd promised herself Matt was off the serving shelf. But the sensation stealing over her as she sat next to him and watched singing goatherds for what had to be the millionth time in her life—well, she liked Christopher Plummer plenty, but it wasn't the sight of him on the screen making her heart race.

And she was not going to muck this up. Hurting Matt? God, she'd cut off her own arm before letting that happen. He obviously wanted to spend time with her. Wasn't his fault he couldn't possibly want it to be for the same reason that teased her on a daily basis.

Not to mention during the nights.

Matt stretched and yawned, his left arm slipping farther into the space she'd mentally tagged "hers". The safe-zone line had been crossed—that was her cue to bounce up and go for more drinks. Or popcorn, or...or something.

"Okay if I pause it?" Matt waved the remote control.

She grinned as she hit her feet. "No problem."

He smiled back suspiciously. "What's that look for?"

"I just want to point out you took all of fifteen minutes to assume ownership of that thing."

"I'm a guy, it's genetically built into us to cling to the controls."

Hope laughed as she grabbed their empty glasses. "I've heard that. I've also heard shock therapy can help deal with it."

Matt headed down the hall toward the washroom. She watched, enjoying seeing his ass flex before mentally slapping some sense into herself.

It wasn't going to work, but maybe if she kept telling the lies they'd become true.

She had both hands full when the phone rang a couple minutes later.

"You want me to get that?" Matt called.

"Please." It was probably her friend Donna making a post-eggnog holiday shout-out.

Hope finished topping up their glasses and turned, nearly tipping both full loads over his broad chest, he stood so close behind her. "Shit, warn a girl, will you?"

"It's for you." He held out the phone like it was a snake. "I gotta go."

What? She scrambled to put down the glasses. "Oh. Okay."

He was already gathering his coat and slipping on his shoes. His face was white, body stiff. My God, what was wrong? Whoever was on the line could wait a few minutes while she discovered what was going on. She spoke into the phone. "Hang on a second."

"Hey, no problem, sis."

Hope froze, her sister's voice echoing in her ear loud enough he must have heard. Hope slapped a hand over the mouthpiece. "Shit, Matt. I'm sorry."

He shook his head, digging in his pocket, looking for something. "Nothing to apologize for."

Hope snapped the phone to her mouth. "Helen? I'll call you back." She hung up and tossed it onto the counter, grabbed hold of his jacket and yanked him to a halt in the process of actually stepping through the exterior door. "Wait."

Matt's broad shoulders filled the doorframe, the thick

layers of his winter coat like armor facing her. "Hope, I just…"

"Damn it, don't you leave right now."

Matt spun. "You're swearing at me? Fuck that. If I want to leave, I'll leave. That's what you said, isn't it? That if it's something I really want to do, then I can do it. And right now I want to go. In fact I want to go and get a stiff drink, and since I'm too fucking responsible to get shit-faced except when I'm safely at home, I'm gone."

She grabbed his collar, one side in each hand. "Fine. Go drink yourself into a bloody stupor. But this goes two ways. There's something I want before you run."

Logic flew out the window. It was the last thing she should do and yet it had to be done. She yanked him forward.

He was an unmovable wall, but she was strong enough the frantic jerk brought her to the mountain of his body. She lifted her chin and slammed her mouth against his, kissing fiercely. His hands hovered in midair for a moment, visible in her peripheral vision before she closed her eyes and simply took what she wanted.

His hands didn't stay unoccupied for long. She was lifted off her feet. The bulk of his muscular body shoved her backward as his tongue thrust between her lips. Her back hit the wall the same moment he switched from accepting her kisses to consuming her. She couldn't groan, couldn't let out anything but a brief gasp when he ripped his lips from hers and bit her neck, the entire front of his body rammed against hers, pinning her in place.

Hope raised her legs and wrapped them around his hips, squeezing as tight as she could with her still relatively strong dancer's muscles. If she didn't get her point across one way, he was going to hear it loud and clear another.

Oh God, he thrust his hips forward, making contact with her core, and his name burst from her, exploding like a cry for help. She clutched his head, jerking his hair to drag his mouth back into range so she could kiss him again. Excitement simmered in her core, tingles of pleasure radiating out from where he rubbed insistently against her, the solid ridge in the front of his jeans a magnet she was determined to stay connected with.

And his kisses? She melted under his assault. Heated, wicked, violent even. Burning and stripping away some of the pain, some of her lingering frustrations.

He slowed as she did, one hand cradling her head, lifting her chin higher to allow him to cover her mouth more easily. His tongue swept smoothly over her lips, hot breath flashing over her cheek and neck as his left hand cupped her ass and pulsed her against his groin slower and slower.

He eased away until her feet reluctantly hit the floor. Hope savoured the last touches of his mouth against hers, the smooth slide of their tongues as she withdrew, sucking in air. The final squeeze of his hand on her ass, the fleeting brush of her fingers escaping from his hair. Matt backed up, leaving her leaning on the wall for support.

His eyes were open wide, hands dropping to his chest as if checking to see if he was still in one piece.

She didn't want to hurt him, but damn if she'd let him hurt her either. And there was no way on earth she was going to let her sister drag them both through the barbed-wire pain all over.

Hope lifted her chin.

"You've gotten blasted by a painful reminder—but running away? That's not you, Matt. You're bigger than that. If you want to leave now, yes, you leave. Not to escape, not because you want to get piss-drunk over past hurts. Go because while we've had a great afternoon, we *both* think it's time to say good night."

The haunted expression in his eyes faded, though a darkness still hovered near. Now his expression looked more like unresolved desire than the urge to kill someone. Matt stepped back without another word. He left, the door clicking firmly behind him.

Hope lifted her fingers to her mouth to trap the lingering heat from his kisses. All her good intentions had been tossed away in a moment, but she couldn't regret it.

Whatever she had done—they'd both have to live with the consequences. But for now? She was going to hide away for a while.

Chapter Nine

He didn't want to go home. The temptation to hit the bottle and wipe away the confusion by fading into oblivion was too high. The previous year when Helen had left he'd spent a couple solid weeks drinking himself into a stupor every night before his brothers had intervened and talked him out of that stupidity.

The cheerful chaos of his parents—definitely not what he needed right now either. Not with the simmering undertones of sexual need still buzzing through him.

What the hell had she kissed him for? Matt drove the mostly deserted main street of town, shifting through everything he'd seen and felt that day.

He headed down the road toward one of the residential subdivisions, just on the off-chance. Lights glowed through the windows of Daniel and Beth's house, and Matt hesitated only for a minute before turning into the driveway and parking in the back beside the garage.

He'd never been in this position before, so it was time to do what he knew was right. Go to family.

Daniel met him at the door before he even knocked. There was music playing quietly in the background, but other than that it was a far more hushed house than he usually was welcomed into.

"You duct tape the boys to their beds?"

Beth's bright smile poked around the corner. "We left them behind at Gramma and Grampa's."

Shit. Now he was interrupting his brother's private time

with his wife. "Sorry. I'll go—"

Daniel's hand landed on his shoulder and pulled him farther into the house. "No running away. Come on, we didn't get much chance to talk during dinner. Have a visit for a bit. The boys are gone for a couple nights."

This was about the most awkward thing, made worse when he spotted two drinks on the coffee table, firelight shining from the fireplace. "Daniel, it's fine. Just let me call you later."

Daniel blocked him. "Stay."

Beth paused in the door. "You want a drink? And if you want to talk with Daniel alone—I don't mind, really."

"Great, now I'm not only interrupting your privacy, I'm kicking you out of the room."

"She's not going to complain if she gets to soak in the tub for an hour without anyone banging on the door." Daniel's slow perusal of his wife shot another round of daggers into Matt. Either he needed to talk this through or get the hell out of the room and suffer alone.

By the time Matt had grabbed a drink and settled on the couch, Beth had vanished, accompanied by a content smile and a full wine glass.

"She really doesn't mind, you know." Daniel lifted the footrest of the recliner and eased himself back more comfortably. "Time of peace and quiet without the boys isn't that hard to come by with our folks chomping at the bit to pull grandparent duty, especially during the holidays."

Matt nodded, then suddenly found himself tongue-tied. He snorted. "So after all that, I'm not sure what I want to say."

Daniel stared at the fire for a minute. "You were quiet during dinner."

"Yeah."

"Lot on your plate these days?"

"Right, with these temperatures? You know there's more navel-gazing going on than anything else until lambing fully kicks in." Matt paused. "I went and saw Hope this afternoon."

Surprise flashed onto his brother's face. "Really? Why?"

"That's...hell if I know." Matt collapsed on the couch, staring at the ceiling. "Am I some kind of masochist? The one woman in town I should avoid at all costs and I end up on her doorstep."

"Now you've got me confused. You spent the afternoon with her, but you're not sure why? What did you do over there?"

Matt opened his mouth then laughed. "We made a quilt top, or at least set up the fixings of one."

"A quilt..." Daniel smiled at him, the type of smile that edged over into something that looked suspiciously like amusement. "Can I ask a specific question, since you don't seem to want to confess you came over for any reason other than to shoot the breeze? Why is Hope the one woman in town you should avoid?"

"Don't be stupid." Matt shook his head. "Hope Meridan? Helen's sister?"

"I know the connection. But the woman you spent the afternoon with was Hope, not Helen."

"She called, by the way."

"Helen called? You?"

"Hope's apartment. I answered the goddamn phone."

"Jesus, you don't do anything the easy way, do you?" Matt shook his head. The fire crackled with a loud explosive pop before Daniel spoke again. "Helen wasn't the woman for you."

"Nailed that in one."

"But Matt, you spent years thinking you two would be together. You worked at that relationship with crazy dedication."

"Crazy is right—considering she never really wanted what I wanted."

"No. She didn't." Daniel pulled himself upright. "But she's gone. And now there's this other woman you're feeling interested in, and I'm wondering why you aren't going after her with the same enthusiasm you put into everything else you do."

Bloody hell. "You're not listening. This is Hope who I'm…"

"You're what? Attracted to? Great. Then ask her out."

Fuck a duck. "That easy?"

"That easy." Daniel sighed. "One of the biggest blessings of our family—the whole crazy horde of us—is that there's always someone around, right? Someone to talk to, someone to tease. When we were growing up and needed to let off some steam, there was always someone to fight."

Matt chuckled. "Usually more than one."

"The downside? There was always someone around that we got compared to. Poor twins—by the time they hit high school the teachers didn't give them a chance to muck around. They were already tagged and branded Six Pack Colemans, and all the sins of Blake down to Travis were sitting right there waiting to be dumped on their heads."

"They still got away with murder."

Daniel grinned. "Yeah, they did, but you know why? Because they're damn charismatic. Butter wouldn't melt in their mouths. They charmed their way out of more bad situations than you or I ever could have."

"Charmed their way into more girls' pants than us too." Matt shook his head. "Fine. So the twins, in spite of being Six Pack boys did things their own way."

"And…" Daniel threw a cushion at him. "And…connect the damn dots and don't make me say it for you, numb nuts."

Matt sighed. "And Hope is not Helen."

"Right."

The room grew quiet again. "I thought you'd be more 'what the fuck are you thinking' with me coming in here and telling you that Hope's got my attention. I thought I'd be getting warnings left and right about how I should stay away from her and get my head out of my ass."

"Hell, no. For a couple reasons. One, I know you, Matt. The harder anyone pushes, the more you resist when you've got your mind made up. Part of the reason none of us said much to you the entire time you were seeing Helen."

Matt started. "You really didn't like her that much?"

"None of us despised her—just didn't see the same things you saw. It was as if your version and ours didn't line up. She wasn't an evil witch we wanted to protect you from, but she didn't seem to exactly fit either. She hated family gatherings with a passion—if anything made her stick out like a sore thumb, it was that."

"I knew she hated the small town, but I never noticed that—the family side of it."

"Course not. And since I wasn't sure what made you care about her so much, I could never come right out and tell you she was wrong for you. Not until it was too late."

Regret hit hard. "I spent a lot of years trying to be what she needed."

"Like Beth with her first husband." Daniel stared down the hall, tenderness on his face as he turned back to Matt. "Now, I'm not saying Helen is anything like the bastard. But both Beth and you made the same mistake in dealing with people who were supposed to be special to you."

Matt waited.

Daniel shrugged. "If they don't care about you the way you are, then changing for them isn't going to make them care more."

"You been reading psychology books? What about the whole being what the other person needs?"

His brother grinned. "You change together—that's what makes it a relationship. Doing it alone is a sorry excuse for masturbation."

Matt nearly spat out his mouthful of beer. A glimmer of curiosity rose as he waded through all the information being tossed his direction. "You said you had more than one reason to not warn me off Hope—what's the second?"

Daniel waggled his brows. "She's hot."

"What?"

Daniel glanced down the hall and lowered his voice. "Whatever else happens? Enjoy the sex, because you two look as if you should set off fireworks when you stop dancing around each other."

"Bloody hell, is the entire town watching us?"

Daniel grinned harder. "I'll try to keep the betting pool quiet, but you know the minute you do start seeing each other, the cousins will have already—"

"Fuck that." Matt collapsed back on the couch and covered his face with an arm. "Small towns. Bloody small towns."

"Hey, give me a minute to top up Beth's glass." His brother left the room. Matt crawled off the couch and onto the floor, staring into the fire.

Fine. Hope was not Helen. Hope made his body ache and his brain tangle into confusion, and while he could still name a million reasons why he shouldn't be considering this, there were so many more why he should.

He liked her. That wasn't a bad place to start.

But he wasn't glutton enough for punishment to start anything official right now. Not when it was nearly a year ago that Helen had broken his heart and changed their lives.

After the New Year—that was when he'd do something. Only he needed a reason to get out of Dodge for a while. Daniel strolled back into the living room and placed the wine bottle on the table, picking up his beer and resuming his previous position.

"You got any shipments headed for Banff?" Matt blurted out.

Daniel snorted. "Looking for a reason to disappear for a bit?"

"Yes."

The honest truth rang clear enough Daniel's smile faded, and he swore softly. "Yeah, I guess you would be. If you'd like to do a haul, I'd appreciate the help. You'd save me money—if you can get away from the ranch."

"Twins are home…" Matt nodded slowly. "You know, this works. I agree, it's time for me to move on, but just not this instant."

"Come by on the twenty-seventh. You can help me load the furniture, and if you do display set-up at the shops, I'll pay you for that as well."

"You don't need to—" His brother's expression made it clear it was time to stop protesting. "Fine. Pay me. I'm always in need of extra cash to spoil my nephews with."

"Or maybe to spend on that new girl in your future."

Matt rose to his feet and gathered his weather gear. "Don't say that as if it's a given thing, me and Hope. You know there's always the chance she's going to shoot down this idea. Just because…"

The memory of her kissing him senseless drove the words right out of his mouth. There was something combustive between them.

Daniel burst out laughing. "And I'm glad you stopped that

bull, because I'd be sorry to have to end such a fine visit by rubbing your face in the snow for being a stupid shit."

"Who's the stupid shit? Talking to me when you've got a naked woman sitting in your bathtub?"

Daniel thumped him on the back then pushed him out the door. "You're so right. Now leave."

The love of family carried Matt all the way to his truck and kept him warm as he adjusted the heaters and cranked everything to high. Now he only needed to do one more thing.

He put through the call while waiting at the first set of lights.

"Matt?" Anxiety tinged Hope's voice and he hurried to reassure her.

"Hey. I'm sorry for... Well, I'm not sorry for kissing you."

Her light chuckle reassured him more than a rapid absolution would have. "I seem to remember I kissed you, Matt Coleman."

"How about we say we kissed each other and make it square?"

She laughed louder. "Is this another built-in guy thing? Like the remote-control gene?"

"What you talking about?"

"Needing to receive credit for initiating the attack."

Maybe. "Yeah, well, I'll give you total credit for kicking my butt in your own unique way." He paused. "You're right. You *were* right—I would have left your apartment and spent the night moping and getting smashed."

"You sound sober. My therapy worked?"

Holy shit, yeah. "Worked a little too well, I think."

There was a creaking sound in the background, then the music kicked up—this time delicate flutes tickling his ear. "How can me kissing you work too well?" she asked.

"I want to do it again."

Dead silence.

"Hope?"

She sighed. "Honest? I want to do it again as well. But that's probably not the best idea."

"Because I went out with Helen?" He hadn't expected her to have the same concerns he did. Matt turned onto the secondary road that led toward his trailer.

"Went out? Matt, you asked her to marry you. Yeah. Sticking with being friends would be much easier."

"But friends don't kiss."

She huffed into the receiver. "Nope."

"And I want to kiss you, Hope. I want to touch you, this time without fighting to keep my hands off private places. I want to taste your soft skin and feel—"

"Jesus, Matt, you trying to drive me crazy?"

He was making himself crazy, his body reacting to the thought of what he was describing. "But I also want to help you finish that quilt, and maybe make a few more things for your shop."

The line went silent for the longest time. Matt worried she might have hung up on him. When she did speak, it was quiet. Even. "I don't know what to say."

"I guess, in a way I don't know either. I'm going out of town for a week, but when I get back, is it okay...I mean, would you mind if I gave you a call?"

"Wait..."

Matt clung to the wheel with two hands, wondering what was up. Praying he wasn't going to get ditched before he made a real move. Shit, thirty years old and still fumbling with the girls. He needed lessons from his younger brothers or something.

"You have to wait until I open my present before I'll answer you." Paper crinkled in the background.

It took a moment before he remembered placing the gift against the wall when he arrived unannounced that afternoon. "You didn't open it yet?"

"I was waiting, because... Well, when I give a gift I like to be there while the person opens it. But I don't think you should come back tonight, so I'm breaking my rule this once. Hang on. What the heck did you use to seal this thing?"

"There was no invisible tape left at my place, so I used packing tape."

She laughed, the sound light and happy like a million sparkling stars. "Duct tape forever."

"You bet."

Paper crackled in the background for a minute then her soft voice returned. "A quilt hanger. It's very pretty, Matt. Thank you."

He resisted offering to come over right away and put it up. "So, can I call you when I get back?"

"Matt..."

Waiting was killing him. He was back to being fifteen years old and wondering if the girl he liked would—and he didn't want to think about that. About the memories of waiting for her sister. Those he needed to scrub from his brain. Instead, he thought about Hope's rosy-red cheeks when he'd opened the door that day, the surprise in her eyes that had shifted to something more.

He wasn't going to beg, but as Daniel had pointed out, he didn't usually do things halfway. "I'd like to spend time with you. No pressure. Just get together and enjoy each other's company."

"I'm not sleeping with you."

Jesus. Instant hard-on. Probably the exact opposite of the reaction she'd been hoping for, but the images in his brain were all soft skin and luscious lips, skimpy seashells and sultry eyes—that nearly naked woman from last summer he remembered in far too great detail. "Okay..."

"I mean, oh fuck this."

There were crazy noises going on in the background, and he struggled to figure out what the hell she was doing, especially after that announcement. "You okay?"

"No. To be perfectly honest, I'm not."

The quiet calm he'd associated with her was noticeably absent from her voice.

She went on, picking up speed. "I spent the morning by myself feeling a touch blue before concocting the best *make myself busy* plan I could—pulling together a couple quilt tops for samples in the shop. Then this guy I've been trying hard to put out of my mind drops in out of nowhere, turning my relaxing afternoon into an exercise in sexual frustration.

"I'm a dozen kinds of worried about this idea, and yet I'm still thrilled. I'm sure that somewhere along the line I'm going to end up in tears, or you're going to figure this was the worst idea of your life but frankly? I can't even pay attention to the red flags waving frantically in my face because I *really* want to see you again."

"Good—"

"No talking. If I don't say this now, I'll chicken out. So, yes, I will see you, but I'm not going to sleep with you. Because I really want to."

"That makes—" He stopped himself. "Sorry, continue."

Hope groaned. "You must think I'm a crazy woman. Maybe I should start rescuing stray cats or something. But I'm serious. I could have crawled into bed with you last summer without blinking an eye, but now I think that would be a huge mistake for us both. So I will see you if you can promise we'll try to keep this out of the bedroom for a while."

When she stopped he waited, making sure he wasn't about to interrupt again. "May I talk now?"

Her loud burst of laughter made him smile. "I'm a bossier shit than you thought, aren't I?"

"I don't mind. Well, I do mind. I think it's totally insane that you want us to keep this platonic. But you asked, so even though my balls are screaming *nooo* at the top of their lungs, I'll agree to your terms. One month no sex? Two? Six?"

"Six? My Lord, if we last six days I'm going to be impressed."

Him too. "Your idea is a good one for a bunch of reasons, though."

"Ha, you say that now, but I bet we're both going to be bitching about it in no time."

Matt pulled up to his trailer and sat in the running vehicle. "Hope, my turn to be crude. I can find someone to fuck."

"*Jesus.*"

"Well, it's true. I don't want to go out with you just because I can see us having a blast between the sheets. I want to try that friend thing as well, and having sex off the top could get in the way. So...although I can't believe I'm saying this...fine. No sex."

"Not until we say—I know, like a double-jeopardy thing. I have to say yes, and you, and then we can't do it for twenty-four hours or something."

She had to be kidding. "Don't try to make rules, darling. If we decide it's time, there ain't going to be any double-signed papers or anything like that bullshit."

"I could wear a chastity belt."

"I can pick locks."

She snorted. "Ha, you can not."

"With my teeth."

Matt was still laughing when he made it into his trailer. The fire had gone out, and he shuffled through the cold room to light it one-handed as he clutched the phone. "I'll call you when I get back into town, you crazy woman."

"Don't leave it too long or you'll find I've given your quilt space to the cats."

Matt clicked off, a high-energy rumba on a saxophone echoing in his ears, and the most optimistic sensation in his heart—happier than he'd been in a long time.

Chapter Ten

Hope checked out the menu, but she was more interested in examining the restaurant. Matt had asked her to meet him at a new spot on the east side of town, an eclectic place that was somehow wildly appropriate as a location for them to begin this unusual relationship.

She sipped her water as she glanced around, the butterflies refusing to settle.

"Is this seat taken?"

He slid in opposite her, and she was glad she'd just swallowed or drool would be dribbling off her chin. That facial hair of his got her every time. "Hey. No, I managed to keep that one for you. Just don't sit in the chair by the wall or my invisible friend will beat you up."

Matt's smile flashed white. "I hope he's not planning on staying for long."

A snort escaped. "Nahh, he's got a date."

"Invisible friends." He laughed. "Did you ever hear about the time the twins decided there were dragons living in the hayloft?"

She shook her head, not bothering to pretend she wasn't checking him out. Matt kept talking, but all the while she was examining his beard, the way his eyes sparkled as his hands rose to help with the storytelling. Hmm, hands.

She knew how firm they were. His lips as well.

Hope pinched her thigh and sat a little straighter in an attempt to throw her mental process from full-throttle forward into physical admiration to what this was supposed to be about. Making friends.

And then the sex, her mind whispered, and she pressed her lips tight to stop from moaning.

Matt leaned back in his chair and crossed his arms. "I think we might need to start again."

She shook herself alert. "What? I'm sorry."

"You're objectifying me already. I know this is going to be tough, but I thought you could at least keep your hands off me for thirty minutes."

His teasing smirk helped push her thoughts the proper direction. "Busted. I'll wait with the *guh* comments then. You're mighty fine, Mr. Colem—"

He threw up his hand. "Whoa. There's nothing more mood-killing than thinking you're checkin' out my dad with lust, okay?"

"Oops."

That deep chuckle of his sent goose bumps all over her. "What we need to discuss has nothing to do with the drool-worthy state of your being—although let me just get it out there that you look awesome—and everything to do with dinner. See anything you like?"

"Yes." She stared him over.

Matt laughed and poked at the menu. "This list."

Drat. "I haven't decided yet."

He winked then picked up his own menu.

Hope relaxed as she checked the options, impressed with his tactics. If he'd ignored the simmering heat between them, it probably would have made things harder to deal with. Acknowledging their attraction, putting it right out in the open instead of being an elephant in the corner—well, the desire was still in the room but it was a lot easier to deal with saying it was there.

That it was fine to feel the tension, but for now they could move on to the next thing.

By the time their food arrived, she was laughing out loud at his stories. They stole food off each other's plates and thoroughly enjoyed themselves.

Hope eased back in her chair and raised the last of her Coke in a salute. "Here, here. To a wonderful first date. Suggesting this place was fantastic. Ready for my addition?"

He nodded. "Movie? Walk? Are we going to cut innocent chunks of fabric into teeny tiny pieces then sew them back together?"

She snorted. "Innocent chunks of fabric?"

"That's my nephew Lance's description of quilting. Kind of the same concept as making trees into furniture, but what you do is nowhere near as manly, you know."

"Good thing my manhood isn't offended by that definition."

Matt took a long, slow gaze down her body, enjoying every minute of it if she was any judge of his expression, before meeting her eyes again. "Your manhood has nothing to be offended about."

Simmering lust shot way back up to a boil. Why, oh why, had she suggested no sex was a good idea? A change of topic was desperately needed. She sat up and clapped her hands together. "We're going tobogganing."

"Oh God, really?"

Hope nodded. "At the ski hill."

He lifted a brow and smiled with a little more interest. "Really?"

"Ha, you lazy ass. You didn't want to do it when it required hard labour."

"Damn right. I got enough exercise today." He rose to his

feet and held out a hand, tucking her fingers into his strong grip. Outside he paused in confusion. "Where's your car?"

She pointed and waited for the fireworks to begin.

"Okay..."

It was almost anticlimactic, his total lack of response as he walked her to the truck she'd pointed out and waited for her to unlock the door.

"Shall I meet you at the hill?" he asked.

Hope nodded.

He helped her in then shut the door and waved. Only he pulled out his cell phone as he walked away. *Uh-oh.* Seems a moment of brotherly love was about to take place.

She turned over the reluctant engine and shoulder-checked before slipping into the traffic and heading back into town.

Matt wondered how close to danger level his blood pressure was. Still, he wasn't going to take his concerns out on Hope.

But his brother? He had no trouble stirring up some shit there.

He put through the call. Blake picked up. "Yo, bro."

"What the fuck were you thinking?"

There was silence for a minute. "This is Matt I'm talking to, right? Calm, cool and collected—"

"Did you sell Hope that hunk of junk that's been sitting in the back forty for the past ten years?"

"Nope."

Matt swore as he caught up with her, positive he was going to be pulling over to pick up chunks of metal from the road as the wreck fell to pieces before his very eyes. "Well then, hallelujah, there's been a miracle, because somehow she's driving said wreck down the street in front of me. And so I repeat, what the fuck were you thinking?"

"I was thinking that she didn't have a car, and it must be damn tough to be a single woman with no vehicle. And since the shop figured it would cost more to repair the crap she was driving than it was worth in insurance, when she came here last week and asked if I would sell her—"

"What!" Matt pulled the phone from his ear and clutched the steering wheel tight to stop from flinging anything anywhere, including his own vehicle in front of hers to act as a guard.

He counted to ten. Twice. Then he spoke. "Hey, you still there?"

"For all of five seconds if you continue to be a shithead."

Matt collected his hard-won calm and forced it into his voice. "Sorry, that was just a momentary lack of concentration. Let me get this straight. Hope came to you and asked for the hunk of junk that's been out rusting behind the far barn for years."

"She did."

"And you sold it to her?"

"I gave it to her. Well, fine, sold it for a dollar. Just to make it legal."

Oh God. "Shit, Blake. Still...I mean..."

His brother rumbled back, his own annoyance coming through. "Yeah, I know the truck's a piece of crap. But she had valid reasons and insisted it would work. She brought over a new battery, a couple of milk crates to secure shit in the back and we used binder twine to lash the front seat in place."

Matt's temper raced upward again. "Did you say binder twine? Goddamn, Blake! So, what's going to happen if she's in an accident?"

"She said it's only temporary, but she needs a way to get

around."

"I don't like it."

Blake snorted. "Tough shit. I don't think it's your choice, is it?"

"Would you let Jaxi ride in there with her?" The silence at the other end of the line was enough to make his point come through loud and clear. Matt knew he had Blake. "Right. That's what I thought. Good luck convincing me you had nothing but—"

"Does she know you know she has the beast?"

"Since I just took her out for dinner and I'm following her to the ski hill, umm, yeah."

"What'd she say to you?"

"Nothing."

Blake sighed. "Not going to tell you your business, but if the DMV approved her, and she got the thing insured, not much you can do."

Not without coming off like the over-controlling jerk of the century. "I hear you."

"I promised to keep an eye out for a good deal. Something smaller. You got to admit, that piece of crap is a bloody tank. If she does lose control, she'd win the fight with ninety percent of what's out there for her to hit."

"You're not making this any better, Blake."

"Sorry." A high-pitched cry reverberated in the background. "Gotta go. Princess Becca is commanding my presence. Have fun at the hill."

"Yeah, run and hide behind the babies. I'm still pissed at you."

Hope made it to the parking lot in one piece, and Matt pulled in beside her, staring at the dash as he went through and discarded different responses.

Blake was right—it was her choice.

She was going to get her neck broken.

If she did get hurt, he was going to kill his brother.

The truck should have been driven straight to the edge of the dump and pushed off years ago.

A light tap on the window pulled him back to discover Hope staring in. She wore an old-fashioned jester cap on her head, complete with bells on the ends of the long, dangling tassels. Neon green and pink, it was hilarious and ridiculous, and made him smile at her total lack of self-consciousness.

So unlike Helen, who would have never been caught dead in such an outfit.

Hope didn't smile back. Instead, there was a tiny furrow between her eyes as she waited. "You coming?"

He nodded then grabbed his gloves and a spare toque from the back. He paused casually next to the rust-bucket mobile under the guise of pulling on his gear. Actually, he used the time to sneak a glance at the licence.

Insured and registered. *Dammit.* "So. New wheels?"

Hope squirmed, her gaze darting away. "Temporary. It passed inspection, but it's just until the spring. I've got leads on a couple others."

"Good." Matt took her hand and headed toward the service desk. That was as much as he could ask for right now. "If you'd like, I don't mind looking around for you as well."

Hope slipped ahead of him and slapped down the money for their tickets before he could. She offered a smile. "I would love your help."

They were on the hill then, and Matt had no more time to strategize how he was going to convince her to leave the deathtrap at home. Like sneaking her taxi fare, or maybe he could just sit at the end of the block and every time she came out to go somewhere he could "accidentally" drive past and offer her a ride.

"Come on, dreamer." Hope poked him in the chest and Matt concentrated harder. There were people scattered all over the hill. Some were newcomers to town while others he recognized from years back—schoolmates and the like. A few of them gave him questioning looks, their gazes bouncing back and forth between him and Hope.

And so it began. The watchful eyes of the small town were on them. He wondered exactly how long it would take for the entire community of Rocky to know he and Hope were on a date.

They slid their inner tube under the rope tow and crawled on board. Matt found himself cradling her between his legs, and suddenly the cold temperature around them wasn't going to be nearly enough to keep his body from reacting to the surprisingly intimate position. He'd never thought of sledding as potentially erotic.

"Ready?" She turned toward him, and the limited lights of the hill shone through the darkness and highlighted the flush on her cheeks.

He reached up and grabbed the rope. The tube slipped upward smoothly. Hope wiggled sideways until her chest faced him, clutching him tighter. There might be icy-cold air slipping into his lungs, but with the grip she had on him and the way her long legs slid against his, he was plenty warm.

"When was the last time you went sledding?" she asked.

"Boxing Day. Family tradition."

"That's right. I knew that."

Matt stiffened involuntarily. Hope looked out at the lighted sections of the ski hill, and Matt bit back his frustration. Yeah, she knew that from him taking Helen out year after year with the family. Or at least asking Helen to come, when she did deem it possible.

There was no way to get around it. He and Hope knew way more about each other than the average couple at the start of their dating career.

The comfortable banter they'd enjoyed earlier in the evening vanished, and with every passing second he wished he could turn back the clock. Change his response. He could ignore the awkward moment, but that wasn't going to make the truth go away. "We will have to deal with this at some point."

Hope adjusted position again, which brought her hips into contact, her crotch nudging his hip. "Deal with what?"

The erection he was carrying? The one going from a semi to a full faster than he wanted, considering they were going to hurl themselves down the hill in a few minutes. "We can't pretend that Helen doesn't exist."

Hope snorted. "Well, hell, can't we?"

"You know what I mean."

They were at the top of the hill, and she rolled, pressing her hands against his chest and pushing her way over him. The move teased as her body weight rested fully on him for a second before she slid off. He let loose the rope and scrambled upright.

They reached for the tube at the same time. Hope deferred to him and grabbed his hand instead.

"Yeah, you're right. She does exist, but you know, if we're going to do this...*dating* thing, then you've got to not tense up every time someone mentions her name or you have to talk about something you've done with her." Hope squeezed his fingers. "I'm just saying that the longer we're around each other, the more likely it is that someone will say something. Or, you know, remind you of her. It's time to move on. Ether that or we stay at my place and hide out, or we forget about seeing each other altogether—"

"That's not what I want." Matt stopped them on the top

ridge of the slope, securing the inner tube with a foot as he brought their bodies close together, tucking a loose hair farther under her crazy toque. "I'm not hiding, and yeah, you're right. People will talk, but I'm a grown man, so I can just get the hell over myself. You have permission to smack me whenever I get stupid. I'm trying."

Hope grinned, her head tilted to the side as she looked him over. "Smack you? Hmm, sounds fun. You mean like this?"

She leapt forward, and he jerked to attention, catching her as she wrapped her arms around his neck. Only with one foot up on the inner tube, his balance was far enough off-center that the force of her momentum tipped them both and she landed on him, squarely on the inner tube.

Their combined weight set them barreling forward, and Hope buried her face in his neck as they bounced down the hill at an increasingly breakneck speed.

"Holy shit." He scrambled for the handholds on the tube, spreading his legs to counter-balance their bodies. Hope lifted her head and shrieked with enthusiasm. Snow flew up on either side of them, a fine icy spray that coated everything before instantly melting to run in rivulets down his face and under his collar.

He laughed, the sound escaping in staccato bursts as they rocketed over a series of small bumps. "We're all going to dieeee..."

It seemed forever before they spun in a slow circle, coming to a stop. They were both still laughing uncontrollably. Matt relaxed his hips, and they sank into the hollow in the middle of the tube, Hope collapsing with him. They were cradled together, but it was the bright smile on her face and the enthusiasm in her eyes that beckoned louder than the sexual chemistry between them.

Hope kissed his cheek then scrambled out of reach,

slapping snow off her shoulders and knees. "That was awesome!"

"Next time I get to use you as a landing pad."

She grinned. "You told me to smack you."

"I did." Matt grabbed the tube with one hand and reached for her with the other. "May I suggest we go for the *spinning demon* my brothers invented?"

"Sounds scary."

"Only if you've had too many eggnogs first."

They took the tow again and again, laughing and sliding until they were exhausted.

Not even the thought she was going to drive home in the devil's junk heap could darken his good mood.

Chapter Eleven

"Four more companies have signed up already, so you guys need to look at the calendar and make some decisions about when you want to start your preparations." Hope taped the last corner of the poster in the shop's front window, advertising that *Thompson and Sons* were official participants in the spring Quilt Raffle contest.

Clay wiped his hands on a cloth and spun the desk calendar around, pushing it to the front of the counter. "Take a peek. Any time that's empty we can book for the first session."

Hope leaned over and checked the weeknights hopefully. She wanted to keep her weekends as free as possible to spend time with Matt when the shop wasn't open. "I can't believe your dad got on board so fast with doing the challenge."

Clay laughed. "We forgot to take into consideration that him and Captain Fraser at the fire hall have had a long-term feud going for years. All Len and me had to do was mention the captain was taking part, and Dad folded like a bad card hand."

She tapped the upcoming Wednesday evening. "I'm free here. What do you think?"

Suddenly, there were two rock-like bands of muscle on either side of her, Clay's big body a heated cage at her back as he stepped behind her and leaned in. "I think we can do that."

He reached forward for the pencil, his entire front pressing against her and Hope froze with uncertainty. Was it deliberate? "Clay...?"

"Hmm?" He wrote lazily, circling and adding her name to the seven o'clock time slot.

He didn't change position and she sighed. *Damn.* No action for the longest time and now she had two guys interested in her? Life was totally unfair.

"Back off, Clay. I told you I was seeing someone else." She wiggled free, snatching up the rest of the posters like a shield. "I'm not going to date you both at the same time."

"Matt. Yeah, I remember you said that." He looked her over, taking his time and not holding back from showing his interest. "I think you should reconsider. I'm a much better choice than him."

He turned that killer smile on, and Hope had to respond with a grin of her own. "And oh-so-modest?"

"As always." Clay eased away and shrugged. "Seems I've been waiting for you to be available for long enough to show I'm serious. But if you think he's going to make you happy, it's your life."

"Damn right, it is."

He stopped her, his hand gentle on her upper arm. "But if you change your mind and decide he's too much like baggage, let me know. I'll be watching."

Great. She didn't want another guardian. Hope pulled away from his grasp. "I think you guys should both get over yourselves. I'm not a needy puppy or something."

He returned to his spot on the other side of the counter. Those tight muscles may have walked him away, taking his bulk farther into a safety zone, but his too-perceptive gaze stayed put, staring right through her. "You're needy. You just won't admit it."

Hope batted her lashes and flashed him the finger at the same time. She joined him in laughing as she pushed the front door open and headed back onto the street. How she had gotten stuck in the middle of a male ego-fest, she wasn't sure. That sort of battle was fought over other women, not her. Sure she'd dated, but never had more than one guy hanging around at a time.

The temperature was well below freezing, but she enjoyed the short walk back to her shop. Even though it was Monday and the store was closed, she had a few things planned to keep her busy. From all the stats she'd learned during her college classes and her days of working part-time, she expected a lull in sales for most of the month. January was perfect for other moneymaking tasks.

She was in the middle of cutting out a jacket to sell on consignment when the phone rang.

"You're not hanging out at the shop on your day off, are you?" Jaxi Coleman scolded her over the line and Hope snickered.

"No. Of course not. I've been waiting anxiously for you to call. Because just like the past couple times you phoned, I have absolutely nothing on my agenda until you tell me what I'm going to do for the next four hours of my life."

In the background, little girls giggled and talked baby talk, and Hope smiled in spite of knowing the Jaxi-steamroller was about to flatten her.

"Am I really that bossy?" Jaxi asked.

Hope laughed. "You know you are, but that's fine. What's up?"

"I want adult company. The guys are all working and it's too cold to haul the babes outside, and I've already baked enough cookies my hips won't fit through the door if I eat them by myself."

"So you need me to come and finish them? Won't make a spot of difference on me, you know."

"Oh, *pshaw*. You're gorgeous. Don't go begging for compliments or I'll be all over you, even though I'm exhausted from keeping up with Blake."

125

Hope paused, images of trying to keep up with Matt racing through her brain faster than she could process and enjoy.

"Hope? You still there, honey?"

She shook herself. "Sorry, distracted."

Jaxi snorted. "Once you get undistracted, can you come and play? Stay for supper, help me wipe baby bottoms. Bring over whatever you're working on and I can help you."

"Like you need more hobbies."

"Seriously, I'm thinking about doing some more sewing. These cold days it would be a nice task to keep me busy."

Hope hauled her things together, tossing in a prepackaged baby quilt kit she had done up as a sample. If Jaxi was serious about wanting to try something—and knowing Jaxi and her endless energy, she probably was—it would be a great chance to discover if her kit would help newbies to quilting.

The drive to the ranch was no warmer than in the days of using Herbie, but the massive truck's tires gripped the road better, and she certainly sat high enough to have plenty of warning as she approached intersections.

She pulled into the yard at Jaxi and Blake's, the second of the original Coleman homesteads. The older buildings of the ranch were well maintained, barns on the nearby section tidy and everything in their place. Hope appreciated the work the family put in even as she ached a little.

There was so much pride and love visible among the Colemans—with her own messed-up family and the lack of trust, it hurt to acknowledge what she'd never had.

Now, stepping more fully into their midst? Where she'd longed to be when her own family had exploded into chaos? She'd have given anything back then for the Coleman clan's protection when the screaming and throwing and accusations had begun.

A horrible thought hit, and Hope actually stopped in the parking space and clutched the wheel hard. Was she with Matt to be with the Colemans? To experience the whole warmth of family because she'd missed it in her past?

Then his smile flashed to mind, the sexy lift of his eyes as he met her gaze, and she relaxed. There might be a part inside that wanted things associated with the man, but she was pretty sure the man himself was the first and most attractive draw.

Jaxi held the door open for her, a baby balanced on her hip. "I wondered if you'd gone to sleep out there."

Hope put her bags on the table and got rid of her warm clothing. "Just thinking."

"Good thoughts? And do you want a coffee?"

"I would kiss you for a coffee."

Jaxi pursed her lips and blew before heading to the counter to deal one-handed with their drinks. Hope rubbed her palms together to make sure her hands weren't too cold then reached into the playpen for the little girl staring up at her with wide eyes.

"You going to get fussy if I try to hold you?"

Jaxi laughed. "Becca will let you love on her all you want. It's this one who's being mama's girl. Ain't 'cha, Rae?"

Hope sat at the table and arranged the toddler in her lap. Rebecca played happily with the lace Hope had added to the collar of her V-necked T-shirt.

Jaxi passed over a cup then organized herself across the table. "Now, spill. What made you sit out in the car in the cold like that?"

Hope stared across the room at the pretty blonde. They'd been friends off and on over the years, more off for the past couple simply because of distance with Hope being away for school. Even though she was three years younger, Jaxi had been around the community since the start. She knew all the history of all the locals, including Hope's. "Remember my folks? Every time they started to fight, I cut out and hid. Helen had Matt to hang out with to get away from the shouting, but I didn't have anywhere to go."

"Wow, you are going back in time. What's making you think about the bad old days? You hear from Helen again or something?"

"Not since Christmas Day, but..." *Bah.* She didn't want to do this, and yet if anyone would understand, it should be Jaxi. "What if I'm with Matt for the wrong reasons?"

Her friend's grin flashed brightly and chased away some of the gloom threatening the shining goodness of the day. "Oh, you. Let's see—he turns you on big-time, he takes caring for people to the extreme, he's got an awesome sister-in-law—those all sound like great reasons to admire the guy."

Hope stuck out her tongue briefly at Jaxi's list before shooting back. "He used to see my sister, he takes care of everyone, and you're already my friend. Not good enough."

"Not good enough? What is this? I missed there was a checklist of things you had to have approved before you could get involved with a guy."

Hope sipped her coffee then slid the cup farther onto the table out of the reach of little fingers. "I like your family, Jaxi. I'll admit it. The Colemans, with their great big *take everyone under their wing* attitude makes something inside me ache at times. What if I'm just wanting that family thing, and going through Matt to get it?"

Jaxi's teasing smile faded, but her eyes lit up. "Okay, I do understand this one, more than you think because I had to figure it out as well. You know I wanted Blake for years before I got him to..."

"Cave?" Hope got a huge grin in response to that one.

"Yeah, eventually all his protests collapsed like a rotten barn. Hope, my folks are nothing close to the disaster yours were, but still not the type of people that I longed to be with. Did I marry Blake to become a part of a family that's huge and crazy and totally into being there for each other? Yes."

Hope choked for a second. She totally hadn't expected that answer. "Yes?"

Jaxi widened her eyes innocently. "Of course I did, but that's because it's the family around him that turned him into the man I needed. Everything he had growing up, all the fighting and playing with his brothers, and the hard work and the good times—that's what made him who he is."

"So me craving Matt's company isn't some weird obsession about wanting what Helen used to have?"

Her friend shrugged. "That I can't tell you. You got jealousy issues regarding your sister? You have to deal with them. But I think wanting to be with Matt isn't something you need to scrutinize this much. He's a great guy. He likes you. You like him. Isn't that enough?"

Hope looked around, feeling the warmth in the kitchen, taking in the wiggling girls and the contented smile on her friend's face. "Then I'll stop analyzing and we can enjoy some of those cookies. And some sewing, if you were serious."

Jaxi rose and came over to hug her for a second, toddlers' arms tangling the embrace like some crazy octopus of humanity, and Hope had to smile because it was completely what she'd come to expect in this house. Unconditional love, with sticky fingers and sloppy kisses thrown in as a bonus.

"You're coming in for supper, right?" Blake poked Matt for a moment and drew his attention from the motor repair he was finishing on the seeder.

"I said I would. You okay with me showering at your place or want me to head home first?"

Blake called over his shoulder as he walked away, ropes in either hand. "Just come in. Get cleaned up in the basement. You know you have stuff in the spare room still."

"I should get my things out of there soon. You're going to need the room for your family eventually."

"No rush. I imagine the girls will be sharing a room for a while. So until the next kid arrives, you're good."

Matt jerked upright. "You guys having another one already?"

"Who knows? The twins are already nine months, and just the other day Jaxi pointed out it takes nine months to grow one. She wants to space them out around two years, so if she gets pregnant during the next six months—"

The burst of laughter escaped involuntarily. "You're as bad as Dad calculating when the heifers need to be bred."

Blake turned and flashed a grin, calling down the length of the barn as he paced backward. "I want to be in the room when you call Jaxi a heifer. Go on, do it. I dare you."

"Right. And you promise to come and visit me in the hospital while I'm in traction?"

They finished their jobs and headed toward the house. Even after a full day working, Matt felt relaxed from spending time in Blake's easy company. His contentment grew as he spotted Hope's truck in the yard. Although, as happy as he was to see she was there, he still planned to get Blake sometime for that travesty.

They entered the house together, the scents of home wrapping around Matt and hitting him hard.

"Where's my girls?" Blake roared like a bear and squeals of delight echoed back. He ignored the little ones for a minute as they clamoured for his attention in the playpen. "I see one, two baby bears, but where's...ah, there's the mama bear."

He swept Jaxi into his arms and kissed her soundly. The noises from the babies got louder, but Blake ignored them for another minute before finally releasing a breathless Jaxi who now wore a rather pink-cheeked smile.

"Blake, you gonna do that every day for the rest of our lives?"

He nodded. "Yup. Which is why short stuff one and two can just learn that I greet you first. So, no more complaining, okay?"

Jaxi planted her hands on her hips and grinned at her husband. "Hell, I'm not complaining. Just making sure I know what's going on." While Blake stepped away to pick up his happy little girls, she turned her smile Matt's direction and winked. "Hey, you. Joining us for dinner?"

"Your cooking beats mine any day, and you know it." He looked around, but other than the telltale sewing machines on the kitchen table, there was no sign of Hope. He glanced back to find Jaxi's grin had gotten bigger. "What?"

"She's either setting the dining room table, since we've got a mess in here, or she's grabbing some potatoes from the cellar." Jaxi sniffed then wrinkled her nose. "And you might want to go get cleaned up before you try anything funny on her—Blake can get away with more because he's already signed, sealed and delivered."

"Am I that rank?"

She lifted one brow. "You need to ask?"

Damn. There went the idea of charging into the dining room and planting one on Hope before anything else.

"Fine. I'll be back in a bit."

Matt grabbed a clean set of clothes from the dresser in the spare room, then slipped downstairs and hit the shower. He'd enjoyed seeing Blake's method of greeting his wife after the day's labours. Of course, since his daddy still did pretty much the same thing to his ma every time they were apart for any length of time, he wasn't sure why it had surprised him.

And the fact he wanted to kiss Hope the same way? Hell, he wanted to do more than that. This waiting business was beginning to irk him more than he'd thought possible.

His body stirred as he pictured her sweet smile with that added twist of mischief. His cock hardened, remembering the brushes and contact between the two of them. Imagining what other things he'd like to experience along with the taste of her lips and the flushed heat of her skin.

Washing quickly wasn't going to work, not today. Not if he didn't want to be sitting at the table with wood, because even the thought of kissing the woman got him going.

Matt gave in and lathered up before wrapping a hand around his cock. Long hard stokes followed, the soap letting him thrust easier, his other hand cupping his balls briefly as he imagined Hope on her knees in front of him, her hands caressing and working him. As he tried to figure exactly how good her mouth would feel on his dick, warmer than his hand, slick with her saliva, her tongue pressing and lapping all the right parts of his length.

He leaned back on the shower stall and thrust slower, wanting like crazy for this to be real and not be him jerking off by himself again. Would she try to tease in the bedroom? He liked her saucy attitude, but in bed, he wanted her to be his. All the ways he wanted her, her pussy, her mouth—totally under his command. He groaned as he pictured her, naked and waiting, tousled and tied on his bed with pillows shoved under her hips. Another slow press forward into his fist followed as he pictured his cock entering her body, fucking her completely, no part unclaimed.

A tiny sound caught his attention. His hands still moving,

he glanced to his right. Hope stood in the now-open bathroom doorway, the slit between the curtain and the stall enough to reveal she was watching, her eyes huge, her lips wet from where she'd just licked them.

Whatever devil sat on his shoulder took control and he pushed the fabric back another couple inches, continuing to stroke his shaft with his other hand. He didn't falter, only locked his gaze on her face to see what exactly she would do now that she'd been caught sneaking a peek.

She jolted upright, but didn't flee. Their eyes met for a moment, then her gaze dropped, intent on his cock, staring as if mesmerized by his hands working his shaft.

God, he was going to last all of two seconds now. He squeezed harder, turning his stance slightly, giving her the best view he could. Tension built to the point of no return, and he slowed, his abdomen muscles tightening as his balls pulled up. Harder now, hard enough to ride the edge of pain. Semen blasted from the end of his cock, his head fell back against the stall, but somehow he kept his eyes open to enjoy every second of the expressions racing over her face. The way her cheeks grew redder, the way she squirmed, as if she was a part of the action. He slowed further, his breath escaping in short gasps, chest heaving as he fought for balance.

Jerking off with Hope as an audience was way better than by himself.

When she lifted her gaze to meet his, something violently wild and wonderfully intimate passed between them, and his cock jerked. Then she smiled and left the room.

Her ghostly presence lingered, urging him to hurry and dress. He had to sneak in a kiss before supper.

Chapter Twelve

"It all looked backward until the final minute." Marion Coleman peered closer at the sample swatch. "That is amazing."

"I'm glad you like it. Sometimes it's more complicated describing the technique than doing it." Hope handed the square back to Marion, then moved around the table to the next quilter.

There was warmth in the room that didn't just come from the fireplace. Hope smiled contentedly as she calculated the number of women who'd joined the new quilters club.

"Are you planning on holding the group classes here all the time?" one of them asked.

Marion spoke before Hope could respond. "I don't mind if you ladies are fine with it. The shop in town is lovely to visit, but there's only room for a few people to work at a time."

Hope nodded. "I've always got a workstation set up if you want to drop by the shop. But for these sampler classes? Mrs. Coleman has been kind enough to offer to host here. And if you know anyone who lives south of Rocky who doesn't want to drive this far, you can tell them I'll be out at the Macmillans' once a month as well."

She got them all working on the next step of their paper-piecing projects before having time to congratulate herself on having organized this brainwave. Every one of the women in the room had paid up front for a year's worth of sample materials and monthly lessons. This project alone was enough to get her through the lean months of the start of the year, and that was before any of them came in to spend money on extra material for more projects. After she got people hooked on a new technique, she always had a flurry of sales.

"*Psst.*"

Hope glanced over her shoulder to spot Matt's handsome face peeking from behind the kitchen door. A quick perusal confirmed all the quilters were busy working at their machines, happily chatting with their neighbors at the folding tables arranged around the room. She snuck past him into the muted lighting of the kitchen.

"Hey, you. I thought you were going to be busy all night in the barns."

"I got the lambs cleaned up and tucked in, and then, hallelujah, the last ewe finally dropped. Which means I'm free for a bit. Well, as free as it gets around here."

She leaned in as close as possible without making her actions too noticeable. A deep breath let her soak in the scent of his freshly washed body. The soapy fragrance clinging to him made her want to eat him alive.

It also reminded her of his very blatant display in the shower the other day.

Three weeks and counting. They'd made it this far without falling into bed, but it was getting tougher to remember why she'd insisted they wait in the first place. Not counting all the times he'd dropped in at the shop or she'd been around the ranch, they'd also gone to a movie and had a couple of game nights with his family. Each activity confirmed how much she enjoyed his company, but now that pleasure seemed to highlight their rising sexual frustration.

"Did you just sniff me?"

Hope looked up guiltily. "Maybe?"

Matt laughed softly. "Come here."

He wrapped a hand around the back of her neck and pulled

her in, not stopping until she was flush with the front of his body. He lowered his head slowly, giving her tons of time to retreat.

Like that was going to happen.

That first brush of his lips against hers made a shiver race over her entire body. The teasing rub of his whiskers against her lips made her hungry for more. She grabbed his belt loops, twining her fingers through them to resist sliding her fingers farther back to clutch his ass and grind them together.

Sweet kisses followed, accompanied by not-so-sweet mental images. Even as his tongue slipped between her lips, she was imagining his lips and tongue on other parts of her anatomy. The fine scratch of his facial hair dragging over sensitive skin.

"Hmm." He pulled back, dark eyes staring down. "So, what you playing at with my mom and the ladies tonight?"

She dragged her mind back into gear. "Paper piecing. The ultimate in chopping up defenseless scraps of material."

He grinned. "What time you working until? Because Jaxi offered for us to drop in over there and have a drink with them, if that's not going to make you too late."

"I'd...like that, I guess."

One brow rose. "Like? You guess?"

God. She bit her lip for a second then continued her policy of honesty as the best policy. "What I really want to do is go back to your trailer, but that would lead to more fooling around, and so yes, visiting with Jaxi and Blake is far safer, but I ain't going to lie and tell you it's my first choice."

Matt closed his eyes for a second, his throat moving as he swallowed hard. Where their bodies touched, his erection had expanded in girth, the hardness very clear as he pressed into her belly, as if refusing to hide. "You're killing me."

"Yup, and doing myself in as well."

"Why aren't we going to my trailer and getting ourselves over this crazy lust between us?"

"Because..." She had no idea anymore why.

He grabbed her hips and lifted her onto the countertop of the island, batted her legs apart and stepped between her thighs. Instant full-torso contact dragged a gasp from her as he returned to kissing her, his hands delicately cupping her cheeks as he worked his way across her lips methodically, thoroughly.

Hope widened her legs, clutched his shoulders and held on tight. Wrapping her legs around his hips increased the pressure on all the sensitive spots that were aching—*again*—for him to do more than simply kiss her.

He pulled away from her mouth and dropped a series of kisses along her jaw, moving up to play with the dangling lobe of her ear. His chin whiskers scratched, and she turned her head, letting him tease her further, scraping his teeth along her neck.

She had the top buttons of his shirt undone before she realized what she was doing.

He bit lightly and rocked his hips, and she shuddered. "Oh yeah."

His lips were warm against her skin, his voice deep and low as he whispered. "I'm thinking we need—"

The door swung open behind them, the glow from the living room hitting them like a spotlight.

"Oh dear." Gramma Martin, no relation but one of the local matriarchs whom Hope had known for all her life, jerked to a stop.

"Evening, Mrs. Martin. Sorry..." Matt stepped back slightly, holding Hope as she twisted her way to a less provocative position then off the countertop.

Gramma Martin waved off his excuses. "You never mind apologizing, only I need that young lady of yours for a minute. My twos and threes are getting mixed up on the pattern."

"Right, sorry for abandoning you. I was just..." There was nothing Hope could say. She was as tongue-tied as Matt.

The older lady smiled. "I understand."

Matt squeezed Hope's hand. "I'll talk to you in a bit. Sorry for disrupting your class."

Hope hurried back into the main room, cheeks flushed with embarrassment that she'd completely lost her head with Matt right next door to a room full of customers.

Everyone was still busy at their machines, although the chatter in the room was suspiciously lacking. Hope checked Gramma Martin's work and explained the problem.

"Wonderful. I knew I was getting myself turned around somehow."

"You're doing very well." Hope checked the next quilter and conversation slowly resumed. Still, from all the half-hidden smiles, she figured the fact she'd been lip-locked with Matt Coleman was no secret. She glanced at Marion, but Matt's mom only gave her a full-out smile and nod.

Nothing wrong there. Nothing but a lingering uneasiness— like someone was talking about her behind her back.

Hope mentally shrugged it off and concentrated on doing the best job possible in spite of the sexual distraction simmering through her veins.

Tonight? She was going to give Matt a rain check on doing anything after the class was over. But tomorrow?

All she knew for sure was that waiting any longer was beginning to seem like a real bad idea.

Matt shoved the gas nozzle into place and turned to lean on his truck as the tank filled. He wondered how pathetic it would look if he casually dropped in at the quilt shop. Again.

Poor Hope had to be either getting sick of his face or be nearly at the breaking point. He was willing to stop the no-sex rule any time now—he considered coordinating his arrival with her closing the shop down. That way he could work on convincing her that testing her bed's mattress springs was of vital importance to both their safety.

Or forget the mattress, her couch had awesome support. Or the floor. Or the fucking wall—he wasn't going to be picky. Three days ago, if they hadn't been interrupted, he would have had her in his parents' kitchen.

In spite of the icy wind blasting past, his cock reacted with interest. His need to get her into bed had grown beyond stupid. He'd been waking up hard, stroking himself off while still half-asleep. Spending time with her was fun, but they weren't children. The attraction between them was real.

And the whole waiting until she said it was time for them to move this into something physical? He had no idea why it had ever seemed like a good idea. In fact—

A horn blared from not four feet away and he jerked from his musings. Clay Thompson's monster truck swung past, the ass grinning as he hopped out, shoved a credit card in the gas pump and began filling his oversized four-by-four.

Matt turned his back. There was no need to give the bastard any attention.

"Hey, Coleman."

Ah, fuck. Matt glanced over his shoulder. "What?"

"You Six Pack boys are bigger wimps than I thought."

Jesus. "You think you got something worthwhile saying, then say it."

Clay raised his brows and whistled, checking out the gas register as this time he turned his back to deliberately ignore Matt.

Matt knew he should drop it. There was no reason to get into anything with Clay. Call it male pride. Or stubborn, foolish curiosity. He managed to wait all of twenty seconds before responding. "You swinging your jaw for a reason?"

"I didn't see your name on the list of teams working on the raffle that Hope is organizing." Clay shrugged. "Too bad the Colemans aren't as giving to the community as they've always made out to be."

Clay couldn't be serious. "A raffle? What the hell you talking about? I have no idea about any raffles. Hope never said a word to me."

The other man laughed out loud. "I guess that means you're not talking? As well as not fucking?"

Matt's anger flared. "Eat shit, Clay."

His opponent leaned on the gas pump, a derisive smirk across his face. "Not able to get it up? Maybe that was your problem with Helen. It takes more than a pretty face to keep a woman satisfied."

An instant roar of blood through Matt's brain made his vision go white, and he was around the pumps before his brain fully engaged. He grabbed hold of the front of Clay's jacket, cocking back an arm to throw a punch. The next thing he knew they were on the ground, the hard snow on the concrete below them not enough to cushion the impact. Clay responded with blows of his own, and Matt's head snapped back, pain ricocheting through his jaw and cheek.

Hands pulled at them, others from the lineup jerking them apart with loud shouts and concerned questions.

Matt panted as he and Clay squared off. "Stay away from Hope."

Clay raised a hand to his lips, wiping away blood. "She's a grown woman. Can make up her own mind. If she wants me, she knows she only has to call."

Matt spat at Clay's feet, shaking off the people holding him. He thrust away the gas nozzle, climbed into his truck and pulled out from the service station, careful not to spin the tires or do anything that would be enough to get the authorities alerted.

Then he turned and headed down Main Street, slipped into the parking space at the back of Hope's shop and steadied himself with a few calming breaths.

What the hell difference did it make that Clay handed him a line or two? The taunting was deliberate, like schoolkids prodding each other. There was nothing in it. He and Hope were only just starting to date—there was no way they could have talked about everything. And fighting over the mention of a raffle? What the fuck was he thinking?

Matt grabbed a few wet wipes from the glove box and cleaned up, grimacing in the mirror. He was going to have a swollen cheek at the least. He stared at himself, remorse and uncertainty in his eyes.

This wasn't about any bloody raffle. Clay seemed determined to grind against the rawest parts of his soul. Matt hated that it was true—he hadn't been able to hold Helen. No matter how hard he'd tried. Damn if he'd make the same mistakes with Hope. But...

The trouble was he didn't know what mistakes he'd made that had caused Helen to leave. He had no idea what mistakes he was making this time that would break him and Hope apart. And yet here he was, unable to stop himself from following after her like some lost little puppy.

She was at the sewing machine when he made it into the shop. Her happy greeting slipped into dismay as she rose and came over to gently touch his face. "Matt, what happened? Did one of the horses kick you?"

Not even close. He'd like to think Clay was more comparable to the asses they owned. "It's nothing. I just have a couple minutes. Wanted to say hi."

All his earlier plans for an extended seduction would have to wait. He didn't want that to be the first thing he did after getting into a fight with Clay.

"Well, hi, I guess. I'd say it's good to see you, but you look like shit. You going to be okay?"

He nodded. Then, casual-like, slipped out the question. "So...what's up with the raffle?"

She frowned for a second. "The raffle? Why? How did you hear about it?"

Matt stepped closer. "Is this something you've been working on? Something I can help with?"

"Well, I guess so. I didn't think you'd be interested." Hope shrugged. "Frankly, I didn't mention it since I knew the timing is bad. And it would mean you and your brothers—"

"Is Clay doing it?"

She narrowed her eyes. "Is this another one of your cock-fight things?"

If he'd been ten, Matt would have kicked at the ground and hidden his hands behind his back, the instant guilt that hit was that strong. But now at thirty, he'd learned to fake it a bit better.

"Not really."

She glared.

"Kind of?"

When she laughed, he figured he'd dodged a bullet.

Hope shook her head. "Fine. The Six Pack Colemans can be added to the list. I'll get you the details, and you can decide if

142

you want to officially go ahead with it or not."

She stroked his cheek again, and he caught her hand and adjusted it until he could kiss her palm. "Thank you."

Those expressive brows rose. "You can save the thanks for after you've explained to Travis and Blake exactly what you've gotten them into."

Chapter Thirteen

Matt opened the door to the trailer and backed up in a hurry as Hope forced her way past him. Tuesday night, nothing good on TV. It had been another freaking cold day with more bad weather in the forecast. He'd been considering heading to bed early.

"Umm, hello. Didn't know you were coming over."

She twirled, dropped a bag by the couch then tossed her gloves on the nearest chair. Her boots were kicked off as she grumbled out a complaint. "You know what? This town is fucked in the head."

"The town is? How can a whole town be—?"

"Fine, the people. Did you know there's a bloody betting pool based on when we have sex for the first time?" Hope planted both hands on her hips and shook her head in frustration. "Someone who was disappointed you and I weren't doing the mattress mambo yet accosted me in the grocery store today. Said we'd cost them over two hundred dollars."

She jerked off her coat and tossed it aside as well, and Matt's mouth went absolutely dry.

"Holy hell, what are you doing?" There was nothing under her thick winter coat but a blue bra. A very pretty blue, like the bright winter sky on those freezing cold days they'd had back in December.

And why he was thinking about the weather when Hope was partially naked, he wasn't sure. His brain didn't seem to be keeping with the program.

"There's too much speculation about us, and I don't see it ending. Which—*fine*. They got nothing better to gossip about than us, they can go right ahead. But I refuse to let anyone profit from when and where I have sex."

She pulled off her pants as she spoke, standing in front of him in a skimpy pair of panties with a duck on the front panel.

Matt sat heavily on his couch and prayed for strength. "So you're stripping in my place...why?"

Hope lowered her chin and gave him the best smoldering look he'd seen in a long time. "No one's got money on today. You want to piss off a lot of people?"

The sight of all her smooth flesh as she wove her way to stand only inches in front of him made him crazier than everything else had up to this point. "You want to have sex?"

"God, yes, don't you?"

"Right now?"

"Now. Because, while waiting has been oh-so-much fun, we're going to do it sometime, right? And I sure don't want them boasting down at Okay Autobody that we increased their coffee fund by doing it next Friday."

Matt laughed, the sound turning into a gasp as she crawled into his lap, straddling his thighs. She reached for his shirt buttons and he caught her hands in his. "Wait."

Hope paused.

God, the look in her eyes. Heat and fire and *fuck them all* mischief mixed together. "Forget the damn betting pool. And I'm totally saying yes, but first, why do you want to have sex with me?"

She leaned closer and rubbed her cheek against his, sighing with satisfaction as she pulled back. The second time she swung forward she pressed her lips to his, soft, fleeting. She'd planted her palms against his collarbone and slipped them down his torso as she spoke.

"I like the way you smile at me. Like you're constantly surprised that I'm there beside you and that me being there is a good thing. The way you smell—*hmmm*—totally turns me on. I snuck that spare T-shirt of yours upstairs the other day after you'd taken it off helping move the extra shelves into the quilt shop."

"I wondered where that had gone."

Hope slipped her palms around his lower back then sank her nails in deep as she pulled forward. "The way your voice buzzes against my skin when you whisper, like in the movie theater—it's this gravelly layer of sensation that trickles over me and makes me all achy inside."

Matt was less and less worried about the reason that had brought her storming through the door and more sure that what was about to happen had been too long in coming.

She covered his jean-enclosed cock with her hand, palm cupping his ready erection. "I want to have sex because you've been haunting my dreams for far too long, and I want to have something else of you to enjoy, more than your laugh or the way you try to save me from myself."

She squeezed, and his hips jerked. The top button of his jeans popped open under her fingers, and the first teeth of the zipper slid open, easing the pressure on his full, and getting fuller, dick.

Hope leaned in and breathed in his ear, the warmth of her skin melting against his T-shirt. She whispered, a throaty husky moan accompanying the words. "So, are those good enough reasons for you? Or do I need to mention the urge I have to be fucked hard enough I'm aching the next day? The fact I want you to tie me up and—"

He captured her mouth, silencing all the dirty things that he had no need for her to voice. Not right now, anyway. She'd made up the no-hitting-the-sheets rule in the first place. She'd just removed it.

Finally.

He held her tight, taking her mouth under his. One hand clasped the back of her neck, the other slipped up to flick the hooks on her bra, releasing the straps and freeing her breasts. He stripped away the material without stopping the kiss, his hands suddenly full with hot, rounded flesh. She gasped into his mouth, and he responded by squeezing harder as she writhed over him.

Screw this couch business. He stood, cradling her under the butt as he walked blindly into his bedroom.

Hope never stopped touching him. Their tongues danced together, sweeping past each other again and again. She groaned as he lowered her to his bed, placing himself on top.

"Yes." A huge sigh escaped as she wiggled slightly, limbs opening to let his hips nestle in tighter. "God, I've waited so long for this."

"Good thing you came to my place, then."

She smiled against his lips. "Good thing."

He was lost in what to do first. Rocking his hips against her when he was still wearing jeans wasn't going to be enough. And he begrudged the time it would take to strip them away.

So maybe a new tactic instead.

First, he kissed her again, making sure he'd had a good taste of what she was so willing to give. He pulled back and caught her lower lip between his thumb and forefinger, rubbing the softness.

"We got any requirements in that betting pool? Like did they specify any order for us doing it? 'Cause if we're going to fuck with their evil plots, let's tear it all down."

Hope laughed. "Nothing but a date. That was bad enough,

wasn't it?"

"Hmm, then I get to set the agenda. I'm going to take you alright. Fast, slow, somewhere in the middle."

Her eyes shone, heavy passion flushing her skin. He traced a finger down her body until he palmed a naked breast. He plucked her nipple once before lowering his head and tasting her.

Under his tongue the tip tightened, drawing up hard, and he rewarded her response by sucking. A needy moan followed, her hips rising as if trying to find him.

He rolled to the side and let one hand drop to play with the elastic of her panties while he kept teasing her nipple. When he used his teeth on her, Hope screamed and a shot echoed through him.

Maybe doing it all before their first time wasn't going to happen.

"Matt, what's your favourite position?"

He laughed as he stripped away the scrap of fabric from her hips. "All of them."

"Ha, typical guy response. Oh God, more of that. Yeah." She cradled his head and held him to her breast. "I like the biting. I like it hard. Doing it on all fours drives me crazy. I don't mind getting tied up—"

"Whoa, no need for the rundown." Matt leaned on one elbow so he could see her face clearly. "You nervous?"

She shook her head.

"Then why don't we just do whatever I want? That'll make it plenty fun."

She caught his tease but didn't react like he'd expected. Instead of goofing off or bossing him back, she nodded. "Do it."

He crawled down the bed, ignoring her breasts for a minute, drawn instead to where she eagerly opened her thighs.

Matt teased her. Kissed the inside of one leg, licking slowly along the crease of her leg and thigh.

She quivered and he smiled.

"Now touch yourself."

Hope turned her gaze his direction, and the blue there struck him—blue that wavered between the chill of ice and the hottest part of a flame. She obediently trailed her fingers down her torso, skimming her breasts and coming to rest between her open legs.

One hand opened her further to his view, with the other she circled her clit with two fingers, dipping into her body then returning to touch the erect nub poking out from its hood.

"Perfect. Keep going."

He leaned in, briefly lapping her fingertips, adding to the moisture. Then he tucked lower still and tickled the very tip of his tongue through her folds.

"I like that. You...*ohhh.*" She drew her thighs higher, lifting her knees in the air as she completely exposed herself.

"Not very shy, are you?"

"Why are you talking? Your tongue has so many more important things to do. *Ahh...*"

She screamed because he'd nipped the inside of her thigh. Then she moaned when he went back to licking. And when he grabbed hold of her fingers, dragging them out of his way so he could suck her clit into his mouth and thrust deep inside with his own touch, she called out his name and came.

He wanted to watch every second. Wanted to see her body react to his touch and pulse around his fingers. See if her skin would flush brighter, if she closed her eyes when she came. Or if she'd be able to look at him as the pulse of pleasure rocked her repeatedly.

There was only one way to find out. Practice. Lots and lots

of practice.

He'd never stripped off his clothes faster in his entire life. Jerked open the side drawer, scrambled to find a condom. It had been far too long, and when he came back, covered and ready, Hope was waiting with eager hands to guide him to her wet pussy.

"You sure about—" Her hand slapped over his mouth, and she lifted her hips, drawing the tip of his cock into her heat. He shook off her hand. "You're sure. I'm sure. Good."

Matt moved slowly, watching closely as he slipped inside. He rocked forward, small increments, her tight passage squeezing him as she shifted position.

"Holy...you're...oh *yeah*. That's so *so* good—" Hope puffed air upward and squeezed her eyes shut.

"You know how to make a guy feel proud."

"You know how to make a girl feel awesome. It's been a while." She wiggled, and he grabbed her hip, lifting her slightly and easing in farther. The moisture from her orgasm smoothed his way, but she was tight. It was better than anything he'd felt before.

He deliberately kept his eyes on her face. On the delicate arch of her brow and how her long red hair lay tousled over the pillow. This was Hope under him, and he had no doubts about mistaken identity. No flashbacks or comparisons, and that's exactly how he wanted it.

His groin hit her ass and he grunted out his happiness.

Hope grinned. Ear-to-ear wide with an accompanying light that made her face shine.

Matt couldn't remember ever having this much fun along with the physical pleasure of sex. "You're thinking something dirty or you want to make a smart-ass comment, right?"

"I'm with animal man. You going to growl for me later?

Howl? I could go for the beast escaping and having his wicked way with me."

She laughed out loud, and the motion made her stomach and core tighten, which felt incredible around his dick.

He was going to die happy. "Do that again."

Matt covered her, cupping her face and kissing her gently as he pulled his hips back and carefully pressed his cock in and out of her body. Every plunge smooth now, the motion wicked and hot. She tilted her hips, and he adjusted to grind over her clit.

"Oh. My. God. That. *That.*"

This time he was the one to laugh, holding her chin and licking her lips, tasting her mouth without changing his thrusts.

She let out a squeak when he pulled her nipple a second before squeezing it. Matt swallowed the sound and repeated the motion, pushing into her harder, following his tease by grabbing her thigh where she'd held it out to the side and dragging her open farther. The change in angle brought him directly in contact with her clit, and she tightened everywhere, shaking under him as she came.

There was only enough energy left in him for a couple more thrusts to enjoy the sensation of her clutching him internally, the tight motion triggering then dragging out his climax.

He shuddered then lowered his face to her neck, pressing a kiss to the pulse throbbing there. The scent of sex filled his room, soaking into his sheets, and he was very glad.

Oh yeah, there was no way that anyone was going to benefit from this other than them, Hope was right about that.

"You, Matt Coleman, are one dangerous creature."

He growled in her ear, soft and low, and she squeezed his ribs in a bear hug, rolling sideways. He went with her, ending with them lying side by side on the bed.

She was still smiling, still laughing. And he was torn between kissing her and thanking her for helping bring him back to life.

Chapter Fourteen

Hope rolled over nearly three inches before she got stuck, a heavy set of limbs pinning her in place. She paused then happily snuggled into Matt's side. He planted a hand on her belly and tugged her back, the hard length of his shaft nestled between her naked ass cheeks.

The air was chilled, but under the covers it was toasty warm and getting hotter by the second.

She lifted her head far enough to eyeball the clock radio. Five a.m. Tons of time before she'd have to crawl out and start the day. A minute wiggle confirmed the erection behind her was real, and she sighed contentedly.

Yeah, the waiting had gone on long enough.

"You squirm like that one more time, and you're gonna get more than a sleepy cuddle in response," Matt warned.

Oh really? Sounded fun.

She rocked her hips all of an inch before he moved, pressing her chest into the mattress, his entire body lined up over top of hers. After their third session last night they had both collapsed, but Matt didn't seem any less energetic for the lack of sleep. He canted his hips and speared his cock between her thighs, the hard length rubbing over the wet-and-getting-wetter opening of her sex.

"Hmm, my favourite way to wake up," he rumbled.

She gasped as the head of his shaft slipped through her folds and he pressed in, one full thrust filling her. "I like that too."

Matt reached down, fingers catching hold of her right hip as he worked in and out. The friction was delicious, and while the angle was wrong for her to be able to come, she wasn't going to complain. This—*taking*—was perfect in a whole other way.

She'd have died before confessing it, but the lack of control on her part turned her on almost as much as the previous night when he'd put his head between her legs and consumed her. Direct contact on her sensitive spots? Score.

But not being in control?

Hope shivered as he thrust harder, a groan of pleasure leaving his lips.

"You like this, don't you?"

She nodded, unable to speak.

Matt leaned forward, his weight holding her in place. He grabbed her right hand where it lay on the bed beside her. One twist later, both hands were trapped behind her back, his strong fingers holding her in place.

"Shit." His voice went from lust-filled and sleepy to totally alert. "No condom."

Hope blurted out the words quick before he could do something stupid like pull out. "I'm on the pill. I'm clean."

Matt waited a beat. "I am too. Got checked..."

Neither of them wanted to say they knew why he'd gotten checked, but the situation was real. Hope shoved aside the flash of anger that her sister's presence had intruded even for a minute. "Take me. Fuck me however you want."

She squirmed, fighting his hold, willing for him to come back to the place they'd been a moment before.

His cock never left her body. Matt pressed between her shoulders and adjusted his grip, and she groaned with pleasure as he resumed control. Thrust into her hard enough to make her grunt. Another slam. Matt moved over her, continuing his relentless pillaging. Hope wiggled harder. A delicious thrill raced through her when she couldn't budge, simply had to lie there and take the assault on her senses.

A deep chuckle stroked her eardrums. "Yeah, you like this a lot. So do I. In fact..."

He pulled free from her body and Hope moaned in protest. Only he didn't let her go, only forced his knees under her thighs and lifted her ass higher into the air. The position pressed her shoulders and face into the pillows, increased the uncertainty of her balance.

Changed the angle of his cock as he paused to line them up before thrusting home.

"Oh *God*."

He chuckled, his free hand massaging her bare ass, fingernails scratching lazy circles on her skin. Urgency rose in her sex, the precursor warnings to an orgasm tugging her nerves. Why had she thought she couldn't come like this?

He tugged her wrists and slammed in again, using her arms as a lever to smack their bodies tight. When he ran a finger down the crack of her ass, everything went sparkly and shiny, as if she'd been holding her breath for far too long. Maybe she had, maybe she'd forgotten how to breathe.

Matt pressed a fingertip against the hidden spot between her cheeks and everything went supernova. Her sex constricted, her ass clutched his fingertip, her breasts tingled. Every bit of her responded and took him along for the ride as the wetness increased, his seed pouring in.

He released her arms and collapsed on top of her, pinning her to the bed, his heated breath caressing her cheek.

"Sweet Hope, that was one of the best wake-up calls I've had in my entire life."

"Hmm." Much more of a response was impossible. A series of aftershocks hit, and she was awash with contentment even though the tightening pushed him from her body far sooner than she wanted.

Matt rolled to the side and rearranged their bodies until her head rested on him, his rapid heartbeat assuring her she wasn't the only one feeling the wow factor.

He ran his fingers through her hair, draping her long strands over his chest. "You're good for me, darling. I like that you let me have my wicked way with you."

"I enjoyed that too."

He tilted her chin until he could kiss her, a light brush of their lips together, almost chaste. Lusty and dark, his voice scratched up her spine when he spoke. "I'm going to take it all. Everything you're willing to give me. You know that, right? Every damn thing I've been dreaming about for the past six months. I'm tempted to start with the first thing, work my way through before I begin all over."

Definitely not chaste—not that look in his eyes that was a mixture of sexual heat and urgent need. "Well, we might not have time to do the entire list this morning."

"Nope, but I hope you ain't got anything else on your agenda for the next while because I'm planning on taking up a lot of your time."

"Are you now?" Hope blinked, leaning on her elbow to stare down at him. If she thought changing her position would make her have the upper hand, she was totally wrong. He grinned, as if glad she'd tried to challenge him.

A second later she was under him again, his hands holding her wrists above her head, his legs trapping her immobile.

"I am, and you'd better just get that expression off your face. I won't boss you around outside the bedroom, but in here? You're mine. That's what you want, that's what you're gonna get."

"Who says that's what I want?" Hope protested. It might be

true, but she didn't want him to know all her secrets.

A fire burned in his eyes. He ignored her question, instead lowering his head until his mouth hovered over her breast. She arched upward, trying to connect them, and he laughed again. Taunting her. A tiny lick to her nipple, just enough to wet it. Just enough that when he blew a second later, the tip tightened and sent a shot of pleasure back to her sex.

"Your body says. Listen to it." He scraped his whiskers over the sensitive surface and she shuddered, hard. "Yup, it's talking plenty loud, and you'll be happy to know I'm going to give you exactly what it's begging for."

He let her wrists free and covered her again, kissing her neck and tugging her earlobe with his teeth. Gentle caresses now, the rutting urgency faded to something sweeter. The position seemed less about holding her in place, more about enjoying lying together. She relaxed and let her hands roam over his shoulders, loving to finally be able to touch and admire him the way she'd wanted for so long.

"I have to get ready to head to town. And you've got chores, right?"

Matt groaned and rolled off, breathing heavily as he sprawled on his back. She would have sat up, but he caught her fingers in his and held her at his side, turning his head to smile at her as he spoke. "Yeah, we better get a move on. You can have the shower first, though, because I don't dare share with you, or we're both gonna be late. But tonight? I'm coming over to your place, and we'll make some of those dirty dreams I've been having of your bathtub come true."

In spite of just having climaxed, a zing of lust managed to rise. "Some?"

He grinned as he swung his legs off the side of the bed and rose, his perfect ass flexing as he stepped across the room and grabbed her a clean towel. "Some. Because there are too damn many to make it through them all at one shot."

Oh boy.

Matt pulled on clothes and forced himself out of the bedroom before Hope walked her naked self to the bathroom, because good intentions or not? Watching would be enough to set him off again, and he'd have her up against the nearest wall.

It obviously wasn't a one-time thing, the lust he felt for her.

He got breakfast started. Set the table and got the coffee going—all the things that were tough to find in another person's kitchen. When Hope called out asking for the bag she'd brought with her the night before, he chuckled the entire way in to the shower, slapping her towel-covered butt as he went past.

"Nice to know you came prepared."

She smiled. "If I'm going to do the walk of shame, I'm going to be dressed properly."

"If you organize ahead of time, it ain't a walk of shame."

They exchanged grins like conspirators before heading opposite directions.

She'd finished making the toast and the eggs, dishing them up by the time he'd rushed through his shower. Full cups of coffee, full plates of food—it was homey and yet nothing felt uncomfortable about the situation.

"You okay with me coming over at the end of your workday?" he asked before scooping up a forkful.

Hope looked up from her coffee, heat and happiness there for him to see. "More than okay. I'm done...oh, *shit.*"

"What?"

She coughed and stared out the window, cheeks turning bright red. "You're not going to like it."

He waited.

"I have to give sewing lessons tonight."

Shit was right. But not the end of the world. "When are you done? I'll come over later. If you don't mind my truck being outside your place, I'd love to stay the night with you."

"It's not that, and hell, yeah, you can stay, but the lessons—" She jerked off mid-sentence and literally squared her shoulders before continuing. "Now don't go all caveman on me. The lessons tonight are for the Thompson boys. We set this up a week ago. For them to start on their quilt for the raffle."

In spite of being prewarned, *caveman urges* as she called them rose, and he slapped them down, deliberately drinking some coffee instead of swearing his fool head off and calling Clay unmentionable things. A few seconds later, he was in control enough to lower his cup and nod slowly.

"Okay. What time will you be finished?"

Hope blinked. "Okay? That's it?"

"What, you thought I'd forbid you to go near the smartass wrench-monkey?"

She fought to keep from smiling, the edges of her lips twitching. "Yeah…"

Matt patted himself on the back mentally for keeping his cool and making points on this one. It just might be enough to smooth things over when she found out that he and Clay had tussled at the gas station last week. "Nah. Remember, I said I'm only a demon-obsessed male in the sack. You ain't going to be sewing these quilt squares then testing them out in the bedroom, are you?"

She snorted. "I think I'll probably be teaching them how to thread a machine tonight. Maybe straight stitching."

All of a sudden the room got a whole lot brighter. Matt was going to have to remember to kiss his mama an extra time or two. "Oh, the simple stuff. Yeah, might take those boys three or four lessons to get that figured out. Us Colemans—we can get right to the interesting stuff."

A puzzled expression crossed her face. "I thought you didn't know how to sew?"

"Are you kidding? My mom taught us every damn thing there was to know about housekeeping—cooking, laundry, sewing. And there's more stuff to fix around the ranch that requires stitching than you'd think, including saddles. Just hasn't been on the top of my list since I started working the ranch full time." He leaned forward and put a finger to his lips. "Travis even knows how to knit, but if you tell him I told you, he'll wring my neck."

"Travis? Knits? The boy wonder with women can turn a heel?"

Matt snorted. "Knit, pearl, all that shit. Ma worked on teaching all us boys one winter, but he was the only one who figured it out. The twins were too busy trying to kill each other with the knitting needles and us older crew were already tainted enough to think it was too girly a task to put the energy in. But sewing? We can all do the basics."

Hope grabbed his plate and stacked it with hers, rising to help him clear the table. "I was sure you said you could barely use a needle and thread—that night I went off the road."

Matt shook his head. "You expected me to confess I can sew in front of a room full of ladies? I ain't that brave."

He caught her at the counter, taking her in his arms and kissing her like he'd been dying to all meal. She hesitated for the first second then got right into it, tangling her fingers in his hair, stroking his beard.

They split apart for air long before he wanted to. He cupped the back of her neck, thumb rubbing her pulse point lightly. She swallowed hard, her pupils huge. "Don't you start something we don't have time to finish, Matt," she warned.

"Not planning on finishing it. Just priming the engine, so

you run good and hot all day. By the time you get back to your apartment, you're gonna have no reason to disobey when I tell you to strip naked."

She lowered her lashes, but her smile got wider. "You're a dirty man, Matt Coleman."

"And you like that very much."

Hope nodded.

Matt pulled on his winter gear, went outside to start her beast of a truck and let it warm up for a bit. She planted a final toothpaste-minty kiss on him before slipping a key into his glove and batting her lashes. "I'll be home for sure by nine thirty. Make yourself comfy. You know, maybe you need to be the one naked when I arrive."

He held her chin. "If I'm naked, it'll be so you can put your mouth on my cock quicker."

She blinked in shock at his crude words. A slip of pink tongue darted out, leaving her lips wet and shiny. *Oh yeah.*

She wasn't going to be the only one running hot and horny all day.

In fact, as he worked through his tasks, Matt wondered exactly who he'd tormented more with that comment, her or him, because for the next twelve hours all he could picture when he got distracted from a task were those shiny wet lips wrapped around his shaft.

He did up a couple extra jobs before calling it quits, just to force the time to pass faster. He showered quickly then headed over to her place for nine on the button.

There were lights shining through her windows, and he took the back stairs two at a time. The door swung open easily, welcome warmth hitting, the familiar scent of her relaxation candles teasing her senses.

Hot damn. He'd told her he had plans for the tub. Finding

161

her naked and wet in there? On one hand, his cock was already harder than it had any right to be. On the other, he was serious about remaining the one in charge in the bedroom. He'd still plan for fun in the water, but if she was in there, he'd be hauling her out damn quick for a little something else to get started.

He put his coat and boots away and decided against stripping to join her, because if he was naked and she was naked? All his plans about running the show were going to be over before he started.

But start he would. And now. He stepped forward and swung open the bathroom door, silent in his approach.

Only it wasn't a feisty redheaded Hope he discovered laid-out naked in the tub, but Helen. The woman who'd broken his heart and sworn she'd never come back to Rocky.

Chapter Fifteen

Matt jumped back like a snake had bitten him. "Holy fuck."

Helen twirled with a shriek, hands flying up to cover her breasts. Her cry died off in mid-holler, but Matt was already closing the door and retreating to the living room, a ball of fire blazing inside his belly.

The swear words came hard and fast, and he wasn't sure he could stop without adding a few violent kicks and punches, but there was nothing in Hope's apartment he had the right to destroy.

Helen. My God. The last time he'd seen her she'd had tears in her eyes as she begged him to join her. To try living in Calgary for a while and escape the rural prison they'd grown up in. Her words, not his, and the fact three days before her request she'd been screwing around on him had given him no reason to try to salvage the relationship.

Years of loving her, then his heart torn apart and left for dead.

And now after he'd finally taken a chance on trying a relationship, *now* Helen had to show up?

You gonna run every time someone mentions her name?

The echo of Hope's question was the only thing that kept his feet from marching out the door. Hell yeah, running away felt like an appropriate response.

Only there'd been no mention of expecting her sister to show up. This morning he and Hope had planned to get together for a far more intimate reason than an unhappy family reunion, and something warned him Hope would be just as surprised as he'd been. He couldn't leave and allow her to deal with this alone.

"Matt?"

His shoulders were rock tight, his upper body clutched into one giant knot. He deliberately breathed out and relaxed before turning toward the hallway. Helen had crawled out of the tub, but hadn't put on her clothes. Anger flared again. "For fuck's sake. Go get dressed."

She stood with one hand at the knot of the towel wrapped around her, the bare length of her legs still wet. "Shy? You've seen it before."

He kept his gaze on her face. "It ain't mine to look at now, and I'm not interested."

Then he turned his back again and checked his watch. Nine fifteen. Hope could be here any second. *Please, God, let her get there soon.* But that was selfishness on his part, because neither of them wanted this.

Noises rose behind him as Helen closed the door on the second room—the one he'd slept in that night after the accident. Matt considered phoning Hope, to warn her what she was walking into, but she could already be on the road and how much a warning would help he wasn't sure.

He sat, collapsed more like, onto the couch. There wasn't much time to sort through the layers of confusion that had just landed on him like an anvil. He closed his eyes and remembered Hope's laughing smile, the naughty flirting and the willing love she'd given him in the past twenty-four hours.

And like he'd turned a corner, that was all he needed. Helen was a part of his past. Hope was...his future? It was too soon to say for certain, but one thing was sure. If he let Helen drag him down, it was him letting her.

Did he want to give her any control over him? Fuck that—

she'd had a say in his life once before and tossed it away. Keeping control meant a whole lot more now that he knew what could result from giving it up.

Of course, making the decision in his brain that Helen was nothing but a pain in the ass to be politely ignored was easier when she wasn't in the room. The instant she trotted into the living room wearing nothing but a shiny red barely there nightie, his frustration level went right back up.

"So, Matt, better? I'm clothed. How you doing?"

He remained seated even though being rude was a juvenile response. He kept his eyes fixed above her neckline. "I'm good. Surprised to see you. Hope never said a word about you coming for a visit."

She shrugged. "Last-minute decision."

Matt mentally rolled through a list of things he could ask, but most of the usual questions he'd talk about with a stranger—he didn't really want to know her answers. Immature, maybe, but also the truth. He didn't care what she'd been doing, what she was up to, except as it affected him and Hope.

"How long you staying?"

Another shrug. "Not exactly sure. What're you doing here?"

Straight for the jugular it seemed—Helen's style had remained consistent. So he responded in kind. "I was expecting to see Hope, obviously."

"You two dating or something?"

He let a smile escape. "Yeah. She's pretty special."

Helen hummed and ignored him, turning into the kitchen and filling the kettle. He snorted. They had a ton to talk about, didn't they?

The front door opened and Matt shot to his feet. Hope's obvious pleasure at seeing him coloured her entire face. "Hey, you. Sorry I'm late, but you were right. The boys are going to need a little more work on the basics. Clay sewed himself to the practice piece."

Any other time her sharing that tidbit would have made him laugh out loud. Now he only shook his head. "You're right on time, but—"

Helen chose that moment to step forward, cup in one hand. She waved with the other. "Hey, sis. You were working late."

Hope froze. Literally not a muscle moved as she stared across at her sister. All the colour and anticipation Matt had seen on her face vanished. "Helen? What are you doing?"

Matt slipped forward and stood at Hope's side, taking her hand, rubbing her cold fingers. She glanced up, gifting him with a tenuous smile. They both turned to face Helen. Matt nearly laughed—like they needed numbers to stand against her.

Helen took them both in with a raised brow and a smirk. "Change of plans. I'll explain more later. But don't let me keep you from your date or whatever this is. I'm tired. Think I'll head to bed."

Nothing more than that, and she was gone, the door to the second bedroom closing with a solid click as she locked it.

Matt glanced down at Hope who was muttering steadily under her breath. When he leaned closer she cut off suddenly, then buried her face against his chest, arms wrapping around his neck.

Her scent, the one that made his knees shaky, enveloped him and soothed the tormenting itch. He carried her to the couch and arranged her on his lap. Hope kept herself tight to him and they didn't even try to talk. Instead he held her. Rubbed her back and caressed her shoulders until her breathing leveled out.

She finally relaxed her death grip and sat upright, adjusting her hands to press her palms against his chest. A wry smile twisted her lips. "How about I try that again. It's good to see you, Matt Coleman."

He met her as she leaned in to press her mouth against his. A soft caress followed by a gentle slick as her tongue darted between his lips. He took the kiss, the tender offering, letting her taste him and take what she needed. Didn't matter that someone else was down the hall—Matt pretended for a moment what he'd feel like if it were Travis or the twins in the next room, and pretty much decided he wouldn't give a shit.

So he ignored the fact the world had just blown up around them and kissed her.

His touch, the gentle caress of his fingers, centered her. Her brain raced a million miles an hour, but the shock of seeing Helen faded as Matt stroked away the confusion.

She leaned back and caught a glimpse of his face a split second before he adjusted his expression to a smile. "You're wishing for a lot more than a kiss, aren't you?"

His smile twisted into a dirty smirk. "Well, I had some plans that don't seem to be on the agenda anymore, but that's fine. How you doing? Seems you were inventing a few new swear words there a second ago."

"I can't believe she just waltzed into my place and—" Hope cut herself short. She was going to deal with her sister in a minute, but now there was something more important to address. "How are you?"

Matt adjusted his position on the couch and brought her hips in closer. "I'm horny and staying that way."

There was the evidence under her of his words, but she ignored the urge to grind down. "That's not what I meant, and you know it."

He shrugged. "Yeah, well, after I got over the shock that the naked woman in the tub wasn't my evening's entertainment I—"

"Fuck. She was in the tub?" Hope fought for control. Still, he hadn't run screaming from her place, which was more than she'd have been able to do if their roles were reversed. "Seriously. You okay?"

He leaned back, his hands possessive on her hips. There was a pause as he looked at her one section at a time, his gaze pausing over her breasts, lingering on her mouth. There was a happy heat in the depths when their eyes met.

"I'm fine. Honest." Then he chuckled. "Course, I invented a few cuss words myself when I first saw her, so you and I are well matched in that."

Hope nodded. "She's not staying."

Matt glanced down the hall.

Damn. "Well, I'm not going to kick her out tonight, but if she thinks she's staying for any length of time, she's got marbles for brains. But you'd better go home tonight. I'll call you when I get this mess straightened out."

It wasn't what either of them wanted, but it was the only way to deal with the situation before it became more of a muddle.

He nodded but didn't release her. Instead he tightened his grip on her neck, pulling her in for another drugging kiss. Her body heated under his touch, the firm control he maintained as his tongue stroked along hers. Gentle noises of pleasure escaped their lips. She gasped when he snuck his hand under her shirt, moving determinedly until he cupped her breast.

She should tell him to stop. Should push him away and go deal with her sister, but his touch was too addictive to deny. He had her pinned in place, his fingers forcing aside the cup of her bra to take possession of her nipple. He pinched in time with sucking her tongue, and she squirmed, unable to resist lining up her clit with the rock in his jeans.

He hauled her head back and sucked in a quick breath

before whispering, "Playing with fire, darling."

She deliberately rocked again, and he released her breast and neck to grasp her hips in a pincher-tight hold. Then he lifted her up his body, pressed a hand between her legs and forced the fabric of her leggings and panties into her folds.

He rubbed. Firm. Fast. The material slicked against her and rasped over her clit. Relentless. Nearly violent, and yet oh-so-much what she wanted right then.

Hope put her teeth to the muscle of his neck, keeping herself up with her thigh muscles to give him room. To allow him to bring her closer to an orgasm with each passing second.

"I'm going to fuck you here on the couch some time. Force my cock deep and make you come around me."

She whimpered, and he pressed harder, his fingertips taking hold of her sensitive clit and pinching.

"Yeah, and then I'll flip you over the back of the couch and start all over. Maybe even fuck your ass."

The dirty words continued, uttered low and deep, a whisper of sexual taunting meant to drive her crazy. Hope closed her eyes and tightened her muscles in time with his demanding touch.

She came with an impact that shook her from head to toe. He supported her in place, his solid body a brick under her. She, on the other hand, was a muscleless blob, panting for air, all the stress that had enveloped her upon seeing her sister flushed away for at least this moment.

The bathroom door clicked and Matt laughed quietly. "You need to have a chat with your sister regarding privacy and not staring after saying she's going to bed."

Oh. My. God.

"Was she watching us?" And was that orgasm some kind of *screw you* to her sister from Matt?

He relieved her fears when he tilted her chin and kissed her tenderly, pulling back only far enough to drop his forehead against hers and stare into her eyes. "I have no idea how long she was there for. All I was aware of was about two square feet around us, and how fucking sexy you look when your lashes flutter and your lips quiver as you get closer to coming."

"You're damn good at that sweet talk, Matt."

Hope breathed in deep, the faint aroma of her sated body rising around them. She would have been more embarrassed if he hadn't looked so content to just hold her and dance his gaze over her face.

"I'd better be going. But if you need anything, you let me know, okay?"

"I will." She squeezed him in the biggest bear hug she could before crawling off his lap.

Matt caught her hand before she could get out of reach. "I mean it. Anything. If you need *anything*, let me know. You're not alone, okay? And you've got Jaxi if you need a woman's touch. Don't try to deal with Helen on your own if it gets bad."

Her throat tightened. After standing on her own for more than a year, hell, fighting demons of doubt for a lot longer than that, his insistently spoken reassurance meant more than she could possibly tell him.

She saw him to the door and kissed him one last time, then there wasn't much left but to face the dragon in its lair. Although, giving Helen that much of a hold in the house was exactly what she didn't want.

Chapter Sixteen

Hope stepped to the bedroom door and knocked. "Helen? You still awake?"

She banged loud enough that there was no way her sister could claim to not have heard.

The door swung open, and the bright red scraps of fabric masquerading as a nightgown assaulted her eyes. "Your date over so soon? It wasn't anything I said, was it?"

Hope stepped in and looked around the room. There was an open suitcase on the dresser and another spread at the foot of the bed. "No—we decided to have an early night. What are you doing here?"

Helen sat on the edge of the bed. "I'm back. Figured I can work here just as easy as in Calgary for a while. Things were getting tough—it was too expensive to get by."

There was a sour taste in Hope's mouth and she straightened her spine. Poor little Helen. Things were getting tough? "Well, good luck finding work. I know there's an opening down at—"

"What? I'm working here. At the shop. Like we'd planned all along."

Hope shook her head in disbelief. "You can't be serious. And you're planning on living where? Not in this apartment. You know, the one you left me high and dry to make full payments on all by myself?"

Her sister wiggled back until she leaned up against the headboard. "I'm sorry about that. I needed to get out of town quick. I was dying. Suffocating."

Yeah, right. No sympathy coming from this quarter.

"So that made it all right to try and drag me under with you? It wasn't all roses and ponies after you left. I worked like crazy to not lose everything before the shop even opened."

Helen glared back. "I said I was sorry. What else do you want me to do? Open a vein?"

The urge to snap out a nasty response was so strong, Hope actually trembled as she contained it. This wasn't supposed to be a discussion. This was her announcing the way life was going to be. Nothing to debate. She leaned back on the wall beside the door and crossed her arms, getting into a safe, solid position to present the facts.

Because if she guessed right this conversation was about to get nasty.

"Helen, I'm sure all your reasons for leaving were very sound and logical to you, but they tore apart everything we'd worked for. I had to make big changes and sacrifices. The bank manager finally set up an agreement—hell, I'm not going into that because it doesn't involve you."

"My name is on those papers too." Helen wasn't so casual and relaxed anymore, perching taller on the bed.

"Ha. That's bullshit. Because even when we first started this venture you were always too busy to get the things done you had to. So if you remember correctly, it was my name alone on the original loans, it's been my ass on the line in terms of meeting the deadlines for rent, which in fact means it's my business. All of it. Stitching Post has one owner, and that's me."

Helen stared across the room, her face gone red as she shot to her feet. "You can't do that."

"Can't do what?" Hope stepped into the doorway. "Can't run my business the way I feel best?"

"You can't cut me out like that. It's not *only* your business."

"You try and tell a lawyer that and they'd laugh in your face. Especially since you've been gone for a full year. All payments, on time, in my name. Bank account, in my name. Insurance, orders—everything we were supposed to do together, done by one person. Me."

Helen stopped for all of ten seconds, like she was regrouping and recalibrating her demands. "You really won't let me work in the shop? You're kidding."

"Bullshit, I'm kidding. The place is just surviving, and I learned enough during school to know this isn't the time to make any rash financial mistakes. Which means not hiring on unneeded staff who have no idea how to deal with customers or how to sew enough to handle the average question."

Helen waved a hand. "I was going to do the banking and the orders and the...non-sewing stuff."

"Right, operative word, *was*. Get this clear in your head, Helen. Last January, I didn't kick you out. You left, and that changed everything. Don't go thinking I'll let you come in and destroy what I've fought for, because it's not going to happen."

"Well, there you go." Helen shook her head in disbelief. "You're just like Mom. So much for caring about family."

Hope had held it in pretty good until now, she really thought she had, but that stupid comment was enough to break through her fragile layers of control. She planted her hands on her hips. "You know what? You're lucky I do care enough about family that I'm not kicking you into the street right now, tonight. But I want you out of the apartment first thing in the morning. You will not hang around the shop, you will not try to get me to change my mind. If you find a place to live in Rocky and a job, then you can call me and we can see about having a coffee some time."

"A coffee? What the hell are you talking about?"

173

"A coffee in a coffee shop. Like somewhere I'd meet a stranger and start to get to know them. Because that's what you are—a stranger." Hope slowed her speech, squeezing her fists tight to stop them from shaking. "If you really are sorry for your actions, then I'm willing to forgive you. But I'm not willing to let you drag me around and use me."

Helen looked her up and down. "You're a fine one to talk about using people."

No more. Helen wanted to turn this into an all-night event? Hope was cutting that option right here.

She turned her back, tossing the words over her shoulder. "I'm not continuing this discussion. I'm going to bed."

"Well, fuck you too."

Yup. Sweet, sisterly love was alive and well.

Hope used the bathroom then retreated into her bedroom, locking the door. She didn't think Helen was crazy enough to do something stupid during the night, but the extra barrier between them was symbolic if nothing else.

She lay back and stared at the ceiling. How much of that conversation would she regret in the morning? She replayed it a few times, but actually couldn't think of anything she'd change.

No name-calling, on her part. Nothing but the facts, if a little emotionally presented, but damn it, that should be expected. Hope grabbed her cell phone and stared for a second before punching Matt's number.

"Hey. What's up? You okay?" His deep gravelly voice was reassuring. Solid.

"Just needed to hear a friendly voice before I turn out the light."

"That bad, eh?"

Hope sighed. "Not as bad as it could have been, but considering I had a totally different plan in mind for tonight—

yeah, it was bad enough."

Matt coughed lightly. "You had to go and remind me about our plans, didn't you?"

"As if you'd forgotten."

"Actually, I was sitting here worrying about you, darling, not thinking about how sexy you'd look laid out naked on my bed, but now that you've reminded me..."

He did this growly thing into the phone that would have knocked her knees out from under her if she'd been standing. "Thanks for worrying. It's still not finished, the thing with Helen, but I told her she had until the morning to get out."

Matt paused. "I meant it. If you need help, call. And if you're worried about me being upset having to deal with her, don't be. I'm over it. I'm over her. It's you I care about."

The tension of the evening was going to have her in tears if he kept that up. "Thanks. Really."

"Now, can I offer to bring supper over tomorrow night, or are you gonna be teaching the monkeys more sewing skills?"

The smile stretching her face felt good after all the forced emotionlessness of the past half hour. "You're never going to let me forget that comment are you? Please don't say anything to Clay."

"Wouldn't dream of it. Well, not true. I'll dream about taunting him but I wouldn't actually do that to you."

And he wouldn't. She knew it. "Supper sounds great. I'll be ready to kick back and relax."

"I can help with that relaxing bit."

She bet he could. "Night, Matt."

There was an ache inside from having to deal with Helen instead of spending the night romping with Matt, but maybe this was for the best. She'd known at some point Helen was bound to show up. Maybe getting her out of the way now instead of later would be a good thing.

By breakfast the next morning, though, it was clear that Helen wasn't going to take the high road. The fact she'd come to the table in her nightgown was the first sign Hope's request for her to leave immediately wasn't about to be honoured.

Then the begging started. "Just let me stay for a few more days. I can't afford a hotel right now."

Hope shook her head. "You've got friends in the area. You can crash with one of them. Tawny still lives in town."

"I can't just drop in on her unannounced. That would be rude."

My God. Can't muck up a friend's life, but you can do it to me? "You can't stay here."

"Why, because Matt is going to be over?"

Hope poured the last of the coffee into her cup before turning slowly to face her sister. "Partly. This is my place. I told you what I expected."

"When did you guys start seeing each other?"

Like she was about to share heart-to-heart stories with Helen. "Are you nearly done? I need to be getting down to the shop soon."

"Why are you acting all stuffy? I thought we were supposed to try to be friends."

Hope ignored her.

Helen shook her head. "So now you're not going to talk to me? That's mature. Fine, you can just listen."

The temptation to slap her hands over her ears was strong, but as Helen had pointed out, childish.

"I bet you're only seeing him as a thrill to prove you can

have what I had. Well, good luck keeping Matt interested in you. You're not the kind of woman he likes anyway."

"And what kind is that?" Even as she spoke Hope knew she should seal her lips shut. To not let the frustrations bubbling up escape, but the sweet pleasure she had shared with Matt was too fresh to let Helen taint it with bitter accusations. "Do you think he likes a woman who goes off and fucks complete strangers? Is that what he wants? I don't think so."

Helen's face went white. "You have no idea. You think you're so smart, but there's more to the story than you know. You've heard the rumours about the Coleman boys. There's a bit of truth in every one. He likes to share. Matt and me were with someone else, and he was the one who set it up."

"Matt's interested in me, not you. And whatever kinky sexual things you guys did have nothing to do with *our* relationship."

"You keep telling yourself that. All the way up until he asks you to do something with another guy. Then you can try to be all righteous on me."

Helen stormed from the room, and Hope eyed her retreat warily.

Fuck. She shouldn't have gone there. Shouldn't have stooped to getting involved in a dirty word war. Plus now, she was fighting against time because while she didn't want to leave Helen alone in the apartment, she couldn't let the shop sit unopened.

A solid knock landed on the outer door. Hope glanced at her watch and wondered who was up at eight thirty in the morning and crazy enough to come her direction.

A glance through the peek hole shocked the hell out of her. Hope swung open the door and gaped. "Jaxi?"

Her friend pushed into the apartment, the most fearsome expression on her face. "She still here?"

Sweet relief rushed her. "Matt called you."

"Damn right, he did." She turned and wrapped Hope in her arms. "Figured if you didn't need any backup, you'd need a hug."

Hope squeezed her before shuffling back and sharing quietly, "It was okay last night, but it got a little messy this morning. I told her she had to leave. She's not happy about that."

Jaxi nodded. "You need to open the shop, right?"

"In about thirty minutes, but yeah, I need to get things set up."

"Anything else I need to know? Other than she's supposed to get out?"

Hope shook her head.

Jaxi tilted her head toward the door. "Then go do what you need to get ready for the day. I'll stay until she's gone."

"I'm sorry for taking you from your work."

"You kidding? The babies are happy to get spoiled by Gramma for a couple hours, and there's no way I'd let you bear this alone. Matt would have come over himself, but I figured I'm a less likely target."

Hope's head was filled with fog. "Thanks. I'm just...I didn't want to drag anyone else into this confusion."

Jaxi pushed her toward the bathroom. "Don't worry about me. I can deal with Helen. Now, hurry, you've got less time to get ready than before."

Hope brushed her teeth and rushed through her final routine. All the while banging noises came from behind the guest room door, and she hoped her sister was being reasonable and packing.

She knocked then spoke before Helen could answer. "I'm off to work. Call me when you get settled."

There was no response, and she walked away, hoping that would be the last of the troubles. It was unlikely, but hey, her biggest coping strategy up to now had been to concentrate on the positive.

Yeah, the blue jay of happiness was sitting on her shoulder. A little battered and bruised, with a few loose feathers maybe, but still singing. Hope hugged Jaxi one last time and escaped downstairs into the warmth of the shop, where quilts for families and homemade signs with heartfelt statements like *Love Lives Here* surrounded her.

The irony made her smile and ache at the same time.

Matt hauled out his cell phone and answered on the second ring. "Everything okay?"

Jaxi snorted. "Hello to you too. Yes, Helen is out and the locks on the shop and the apartment have already been switched—Hope called the locksmiths the minute their shop opened."

"I talked to her a few minutes ago and she mentioned that. I'm asking if you had any troubles with Helen."

"*Ha.*" The volume of expression in the short word made Matt laugh in spite of his concerns. Jaxi cleared her throat. "No, Helen didn't really try, although the comments about 'you teenage Coleman bitch' would have been funnier if I could have planted my boot on her ass when she headed out the door."

"You didn't."

"Nope, I was amazingly reserved. Only showed my teeth for a second. The woman eventually figured out it was time to shut up. About five minutes later than she should have, but it's not as if I'm going to melt from a few cuss words being tossed my direction."

"Damn. I should have—"

Jaxi cut him off. "No, you were right to call me. Hope got the shop open in time, and it could have been far worse if you had been the one there. Hell, who knows? She might have even done something stupid like accuse you of attacking her or…something insane."

"How's Hope really doing? She called me, but she sounded so tense—I'm not sure what's going on with her."

Jaxi hummed. "I saw her before I left. She's upset, but okay. There were customers in the shop so we couldn't talk. But, Matt…"

He pulled in next to the barn. The day loomed long and monotonous ahead of him with everything that had to be done when what he really wanted was to head over to the shop to see for himself Hope was okay. "What kind of advice you hesitating over giving me now, Dr. Phil?"

"Do I really have that reputation?"

"From what I hear, you're cuter than him, but you know damn well you boss us all around, especially since you and Blake got married. So spill."

"Fine. It's possible this entire storm can smooth over in no time flat. I mean I wasn't happy about being insulted, but it's only words. They only have power if I let them. If Helen has moved back, so what? She knows now that Hope isn't going to cave instantly in to her demands. If Helen gets a place to stay, finds a job…she's just another person in town. Unless we give her the power to upset us. Right?"

Which was pretty much what Matt had concluded the previous night. "If all she does is live in town and act like anyone else who's sort of known to the family, then yeah. You're right. But if she tries anything to hurt Hope, then she's out of line."

"Agreed. But can we hope for the best? The woman isn't

stupid. I know she hurt you bad, and part of me hates her guts for that, but it's time to move on."

Matt stared out at the snow. The ice and cold that had wrapped around him for so long after Helen had left—he'd been free of it for just a little while.

Because of Hope's warmth.

"Not what I expected to hear from you, Jaxi. I thought for sure you'd be heating pitch to tar and feather Helen before running her out of town."

"The thought crossed my mind, believe me. Maybe I've gone soft after having the babies, but there are more important things to do than waste time on revenge. Happy things like kissing toes and cuddling and—"

Matt laughed out loud. "My images of those things and yours aren't the same, I'm thinking."

She blew a raspberry. "Dirty Coleman mind. So, anyway. I'm saying let's see what Helen does before declaring war. If she behaves, we can spend our time on the things that matter."

"Hope is one of those things."

"Right. I think she'll call you if she needs anything. Could be she's a bit embarrassed. Since you're going over tonight that should be soon enough to reassure her she's got people who care about her, even if she feels awkward. Hope's one of the most stubborn people I know when it comes to accepting help."

Matt groaned in frustration. "Yeah, I gotta get back to work if I'm going to get done on time. Thanks, Jaxi. For everything."

The sound of a kiss being blown hit his ear, then she hung up.

He headed into the barn and the dirty work of the day a whole lot more relaxed than he thought possible. But his plans for the night? He revamped what he'd had on the agenda. After the shock of her sister's arrival, Hope needed a different kind of care than to be ordered around like some sort of sex slave.

Although he was sure they would get back to that scenario another time.

Chapter Seventeen

Fortunately, there was enough business to keep her distracted all day long. After Jaxi had given the all clear on her sister's departure from the apartment, Helen hadn't shown her face in the shop even once.

The smooth resolution to the situation was almost anticlimactic. Hope had envisioned all kinds of shouting and tossing of breakable things. It was evil, but the idea of calling the police and getting Helen's ass hauled down to the cop shop had played out in her brain as far too attractive a scenario.

Hope pressed her palms over her eyes and exhaled her frustrations. All the relaxation therapy she'd learned over the past year was sorely needed right now, because that vindictive thought wasn't her style. The revengeful bitch-woman who wished her sister would just disappear and never be seen again—was someone else. *That* woman was the result of too much stress and too many hard moments caused by Helen's actions.

Still, Hope had to congratulate herself. She'd dealt with the pain and anger. Pushed through the rough times and moved on. Another couple deep breaths later she was ready to head upstairs. She needed a shower and some chocolate.

She turned off the shop lights and armed the security system, then paced up the inside stairs to her apartment. Hiding out sounded like a marvelous idea.

Only—she wanted to see Matt more than she wanted to be alone.

Upstairs, with the door bolted shut, she looked around the

apartment with new eyes. What had Helen seen, walking in after a year of being gone? Something she liked? Something she decided she wanted after all?

The phone rang and she checked the call display cautiously, happy to discover Matt's name and not her sister's.

"I'll be there in about forty-five minutes, and I've ordered supper to be delivered then as well. Sound okay?"

God, yes. "Wonderful. I need some downtime. Don't know how good company I'm going to be."

"Don't worry, I'm not expecting you to entertain me. Just let me come and give you a little caring."

It sounded far better than it should. She was supposed to be a strong, independent woman, but tonight? She'd take all the coddling he was willing to give.

Hope turned the shower as hot as she could stand it. Matt's comment regarding finding Helen in the tub flashed to mind. She grabbed cleanser and scrubbed the entire thing so that all that was possibly left was the smell of disinfectant slowly covered by the scent of her shampoo and the candles she'd lit everywhere.

It was a silly response, but she felt much better after finishing. Like she'd washed away a bit more of the heaviness that had descended upon setting eyes on her sister.

It only took a minute to tidy the bathroom. Far less time than standing in front of her dresser and deciding what to pull on for the evening.

Screw it. She picked her most comfortable pyjamas, which were flannel, faded and made her feel about twelve years old. Matt was going to get her as she was, in spite of what Helen liked to wear.

He hadn't mentioned what he'd ordered for dinner, so she pulled out a couple plates then poured herself a glass of juice, crawled onto the couch and tucked herself in with one of the quilts draped within easy reach.

No music. No television as white noise.

Just silence.

There was a faint rumble of sound from the street, but nothing too jarring. She took in the peace and attempted to spread it through every bit of herself.

Calmness.

Quiet.

The heat of the quilt slowly soaking in.

Her plan worked so well that by the time Matt knocked and she rose to let him in, she felt far looser and relaxed than she thought possible.

His gaze darted over her outfit as he held forward a case of beer. "You look comfy. Should have told me we were having a pyjama party."

"You're always welcome to wear whatever you want in my place. There was no way I was going to dress up tonight. Sorry."

"Trust me, I'm not complaining." He tilted his head toward the door. "The delivery car pulled in just behind me. Let me grab the food and we'll get cozy."

"You want a drink?"

He nodded then slipped outside. Hope wandered into the kitchen and found room in the fridge for his beer, opening one and setting it on the table. The scent of Chinese food wafted in with him, the door clicking tight at his back, and she hurried to grab the paper bags from him.

"Holy cow, who else is joining us?" There was enough to feed far more than two people, even hungry ones.

Matt squirmed but kept unpacking the silver-lidded containers onto the tabletop. "I didn't want to bother you and check what you wanted. But then I realized I had no idea what you liked or disliked, so I got a whole bunch of stuff. I figured anything you hate I can take home. Everything else? Dig in."

Hope caught him by the arm. "Thank you, but before we load our plates, you forgot one thing."

His confused expression made her smile. She'd been waiting all day for this. Actually, she'd been waiting all night as well. A light tug brought their bodies into contact and his eyes lit up.

The kiss was better than any appetizer she remembered. Matt held her an extra moment after their lips parted, his strong fingers caressing her neck. "You okay?"

The soft-spoken question carried a ton of meaning. If anyone understood the frustrations she'd experienced over the past day? He did.

She nodded. "I'm glad you're here tonight. And sending over Jaxi this morning? Brilliant. I should have thought of it."

"That's why being friends is a good thing. You don't have to think of everything on your own." He tweaked her nose then grabbed a plate and passed it to her. Matt glanced around. "You want to eat at the table?"

"You don't mind us being terribly antisocial and watching some television while we eat?"

He shook his head. "As long as I get to sit next to you, I'm good."

They got settled on the couch, plates loaded with food. Matt handed her the control and she laughed.

"The ultimate example of self-sacrifice."

"I will steal it back if you turn to one of those 'what not to wear' shows."

Hope found some *CSI* reruns and snuggled tight against him, their legs stretched side by side, feet on the coffee table, with quilts draped over their laps and around their shoulders. Matt got up and refilled his plate, and her juice glass, but for the next couple of hours all they did was eat and watch TV. When the food was gone, they just cuddled and vegetated.

Her head rested on his chest, her eyes almost closed. Their plates were pushed to the side, and Matt was as good as holding her up, his strong arm cradling her.

The sigh of contentment that slipped out wasn't anything but heartfelt.

"That sounds as if you're feeling better."

Hope groaned as she rearranged her limbs to sit more vertically. "Better, but stuffed. Man, you outdid yourself with the food."

He leaned over and pressed a kiss to her forehead. "I'll go pop the leftovers in the fridge. You stay and relax."

She was going to protest, but the determined expression on his face changed her mind. "There are plastic containers in the middle drawer if you need any."

He moved easily in the small space, loading cartons into the fridge and even wiping the table off before coming back to grab their dirty plates.

Hope pulled herself to her feet to work beside him. "There's room in the dishwasher."

The situation was comfortable. Easy. Another sensation rose as they bumped hips and shared the dishtowel. The third time he cornered her by the fridge she realized it was deliberate, the press of his hips against hers. The graze of their bodies together.

"You looking for a bigger kitchen, Matt?"

"Hmm, nope. This one is the perfect size."

She was in the middle of rinsing her glass when he moved behind her, muscular forearms framed in her peripheral vision as his arms surrounded her. Matt leaned forward and breathed deep from beside her neck, his whiskers tickling her bare skin, and she shivered.

His dark chuckle made it clear he knew why.

"You spending the night?" She barely got the words out. He'd pressed his lips to the sensitive spot he'd scraped and was sucking lightly, causing all kinds of interesting reactions inside her.

His tongue rasped over the same spot. A line of tiny bites followed all the way to her earlobe. She wasn't sure what he would do next, but one thing was certain, watching television had lost all its charm.

"I planned on staying. So if you want me, you need to put down the glass before you drop it."

Hope lowered the goblet with shaky fingers, the base rattling on the counter for a second before she steadied it. Did she want him? Here? Now?

Oh yes. Oh hell, yes.

She twisted in his arms, and his plan of going slow and being gentle vanished like the bubbles disappearing from the dishwater. Hope stared into his eyes, lashes fluttering for a moment before she lowered her chin and melted against him.

He caught her up, one arm scooped under her knees, cradling her against his chest as he took them straight back to her room. All the frustrations, all the aching tension between them—there would be time for a slow seduction later. Right now he felt the urge to distract them both, and the hotter and dirtier, the better.

Mat lowered her to the bed then closed the door.

Hope laughed. "You worried about someone dropping in?"

"Nope." He stared at the full-length mirror on the back of the door, mind racing through the possibilities it presented, before turning toward her. "Strip."

No hesitation. She reached for her top and peeled it upward. Her naked breasts appeared, the firm rounds bouncing at him as she arched her back and shuffled off her flannel bottoms.

Less than ten seconds. Long enough for his cock to go from hard to an iron spike. He stripped, his clothes discarded in a pile on top of the dark blue fabric of her pyjamas.

Nothing between them. Nothing but too damn much air.

"Kneel for me. Right in the center of the bed."

Hope tore her gaze off his body, the lust on her face switching to curiosity. Was she wondering what he'd do next? He wouldn't keep her guessing for very long. She obeyed his command, her knees spread wide as she found a balanced position. He stared, impressed that heat radiating off her could be felt where he stood two feet away.

"Turn around."

A whimper of need escaped her lips, the bed rocking as her knees dipped into the mattress. He waited until she faced the headboard, then spoke again, the words rasping out.

"Don't move."

Matt knelt behind her, nudging her knees farther apart. He pressed their bodies together and nipped her shoulder as he dragged his hands over her naked skin. One hand he slid up to cup her breast. One snuck downward until his fingertips skimmed her slit.

"Damn, you're wet."

"You do that to me." There was a purr of contentment in her voice, and he grinned like a fool.

"It ain't the only thing I plan on doing to you." He flicked her clit and she moaned.

Matt pressed one finger deep into her pussy and her hips rocked urgently against his hand.

Hope laid her head on his shoulder as he worked her, fingers rolling her nipple. Two fingers thrust in and out of her body, the heel of his hand pressed hard to her clit. She puffed air rapidly, crying out long and low when she came, body squeezing tight around him.

He released her and dropped to his back, pulling her hips down. He centered her pussy over his mouth and licked the moisture escaping. Hope tried to wiggle away, but he held her tight to his lips, using his tongue to explore all the folds of her pussy. She tried to escape again and this time he nipped the inside of her thigh.

Hope yipped in response, squirming hard.

"Stay in one place. I ain't done with you." He clutched her ass cheeks and dove back in. Assaulting her sensitive clit, lapping along all her most responsive spots until she shook, calling out his name.

Then she was flat on her back and he was over her. Matt grabbed her ankles and draped her legs over his shoulders, exposing her core completely. He stroked downward, starting at her belly, two fingers gliding past her sex and pausing over the pucker between her ass cheeks.

"You drive me crazy. You taste fucking marvelous, but now all I can think about is taking you hard. Your pussy, your ass. I'm going to fuck you there sometime, you know. Drive into you again and again until you're screaming."

Her response—was that a whimper? A plea? He recognized the sound as needy though, and definitely not a denial of his suggestions. But he didn't have the energy to wait and get her ready for that kind of possession right now. Today the longest he could stand to wait was to line up his cock and thrust home in one shot.

"Matt!" Hope clutched the bed sheets. Her eyes squeezed shut, her teeth dug into her bottom lip.

The feel of her pussy enveloping him drove out everything but the need to rut harder. One stroke after another, her wetness pouring over him, her cries pushing him hotter and harder than he thought possible.

Another thrust, even deeper.

"Oh God, Matt."

He was sweating, beads rolling down his face and spine. He leaned on his left hand and changed his angle. Their bodies smacked harder as he aimed to connect with her clit. She gasped and her eyes flew open.

"Oh *God.*"

He was so close to coming, so close. Staring into her face helped him hang on, watching her lips pull into a tiny pout as she moaned on every slam of their bodies together. Then she made this wonderful sound that somehow mirrored the rippling of her muscles clutching him tight. He froze and let himself enjoy her climax, her nearly violent shakes as she writhed under him.

He pulled out and took his cock into his hand and pumped, dragging out the orgasm that he'd held off. Strands of seed flew from the tip, spurted over her belly, her ass. Hope clung to her thighs, watching him with an expression of pure pleasure as he jerked off all over her.

The last pulse left his body, and he stared at her splayed before him. An enthusiastic blob clung to one nipple, the rest of his semen scattered like random brandings of streaks and dots painted on her skin.

Ownership marks. His brain was still kinda numb as he slicked a fingertip through the liquid, again from her bellybutton down. "That was damn nice."

"Nice?" Hope gasped for air. "Nice is for children's stories. That was spectacular."

He rubbed with a full palm, massaging his seed into her

skin. They were both sticky and messy and fuck it all, it turned him on more than he wanted to admit. "Hmm. Makes me an asshole, I guess, wanting to leave a bit of myself all over you."

She shivered but smiled.

"I want more. I want you to see how damn hot we are together."

"I think I figured it out, Matt. If we were any hotter right now my bed would be on fire." She sighed happily, relaxing her grip on her legs and letting them fall loosely to either side. Everything about her sprawl said contentment and sated satisfaction. The urge to grab hold and start all over, working up one side of her and down the other was strong enough to make him growl.

Then he paused as, out of nowhere, doubt hit like a sudden winter storm.

Chapter Eighteen

Matt wasn't confused about how much Hope turned him on. That was the easy part. It was the flood of other emotions that rushed him and froze his limbs.

Helen had abandoned him. After years of being together, after he'd satisfied her every request—he thought—she'd still left. Seeing her brought back all the previous mental ramblings he'd shuffled through, trying to see where he'd gone wrong.

Now his panic wasn't about Helen, but about Hope. About how he could keep from making the same mistake with her, because he couldn't bear to have her tear out his heart like her sister had. Couldn't bear to think that even now he could be doing something that would make her want to leave.

Worry that he would demand too much, or go past an invisible line Hope didn't want to cross, made him hesitate. Matt quickly revamped his plans. He'd been a brute when what she needed was caring.

He took her in his arms as he lay at her side, cuddling their naked bodies together. She was soft in all the right spots, and he rested his chin on her shoulder and pushed down all the raunchy things he wanted to do with her. To her. Maybe if he waited a couple minutes he could take her to the shower and wash her off gentle and slow instead of continuing to maul her like a wild beast.

Scaring her off was the last thing he wanted—they'd only been lovers for a couple days. She didn't need an animal in her bed, not with everything else happening.

Matt caressed her arm, her waist, teasing lightly with his

fingertips. He nuzzled the back of her neck and licked, unable to resist the tiny motion.

It stopped him from putting his teeth to her skin and fucking her into oblivion.

Hope lay motionless for a while, then rolled to face him. She cupped his cheek, her blue irises a thin slice against the wide black of her pupils. Then she frowned and wiggled back, pulling up her knees and wrapping her arms around her legs. She sighed and stared into the room.

Matt leaned in close. "What's up?"

A small hesitation, then she turned those beautiful eyes on him and damn near pouted. "Did I do something wrong?"

"Hell, no."

"Then...why'd you stop?"

Shit. "Stop what?"

She snorted. "Matt, you went from being a possessive beast to cradling me as if I was a china doll. Which, okay, I do enjoy cuddling, but it didn't seem like that's where you were headed a minute ago. I just got whiplash from the change in your touch. Did I send out some kind of mixed message? Because I was okay with what we were doing."

"I didn't think I should ravish you."

Hope stared for a moment. Then her hard punch to his shoulder—a serious, full-out blow—surprised the shit out of him.

"*Oww.* What the hell?"

"Don't be an asshole." She crossed her arms, but that only framed her breasts and he had to look up quickly to avoid getting distracted. Her eyes narrowed as she glared. "What happened to 'there are a million things I want to do to you'? What about 'I'm going to fuck your ass' and 'your body is telling me you want me in control'? You take some mind-altering drugs between yesterday morning and now that just kicked in?"

"Yesterday morning Helen hadn't dropped back into our lives." He regretted the words as soon as they escaped.

Hope froze. "I don't understand. What does that have to do with anything? You mean the way you enjoy sex doesn't apply anymore because my idiot of a sister returned?"

She would have leapt off the bed, but Matt caught her hand. "No, that's not it."

Hope jerked her arm, attempting to free herself. "What the hell is it then? Why all of a sudden are you acting differently?"

"Because..." Because he was afraid of losing her. "Just thought you'd like some tenderness."

All the fight went out of her and she shook her head. "Oh, Matt."

Hope crawled against him and laid her head on his shoulder, her arms going around him. He wasn't sure what to do, so he just held on tight.

They were sticky from sex and his crazy impulse to cover her with his semen. Their heart rates still rushed—he felt the pulse of hers against his chest, although now it was probably more from her angry outburst than the frantic sexual release they'd enjoyed. Her bedroom curtain was open and the glow from the street shone into the room, meshing with her dim bedside lamp into muted mood-lighting.

Quiet. Back to the low-key and subdued situation they'd enjoyed before hitting the sheets, but something remained tight inside him. Fear, hovering like a carrion bird, ready to swoop down and peck at him if he showed any signs of giving up.

Hope pressed her lips to his cheek and his apprehension lightened slightly. At least she wasn't kicking him out or punching him anymore. She worked her way to his lips, threading her fingers into his hair and drawing their mouths together. He tried to put his heart into the kissing—his

195

tenderness and his caring. Under his palms, her shoulders and back relaxed as he cradled her, drawing circles on her skin.

When she leaned away, it was to give him a tentative smile. "We've been pretty damn honest with each other, haven't we? Ever since you hauled me out of the ditch?"

"Like telling me you could handle my hard-on and it wasn't anything special? Or that we weren't going to fuck?"

That earned him a bit bigger of a smile. "Okay, maybe blunt is more the word I'm looking for."

"Blunt I can agree with."

Hope curled her hands over his shoulders and hung on tight. "Since we're here, and not having wild sex and it's kinda dark and all, can I tell you a really big, very blunt secret?"

Matt wondered where the hell she was going with this. "Do I need to grab the bottle of tequila for us to do shots to help with this truth session?"

She shook her head. "There is obviously no booze needed for me to be blunt, if our history has anything to show. Matt, I like you being in charge in the bedroom, and I'm not a delicate little flower."

His breath caught.

Hope lifted her chin, turning her gaze directly at him. "I have enough I'm responsible for with the shop and the volunteering I do around town, I don't want to call the shots in bed as well. But it's more than that. I just..."

Matt wasn't sure which way was up. He hadn't freaked her out with his roughness, but his stopping? "What?"

She blew out a long slow breath. "I want you to do whatever you like. It turns me on big-time. I trust you. I trust you to take care of me and make me feel real good. You've knocked it out of the park as far as me being satisfied every time we've fooled around. And the idea of... *God*, this is so tough to admit. Maybe

I'm broken, but I want you to just—*take*. Don't ask, don't try to temper your urges."

He covered her mouth with his, savouring her taste all over. That was enough of a confession. He didn't need further details, not anymore. He was still scared shitless that he would to do something wrong and tear them apart, and he'd be thinking long and hard about it a lot more in the future. But being handed the reins to their sexual adventures? Being told that was one area where he didn't have to worry about going wrong?

Sweet relief and violent need swelled simultaneously.

Her cheeks were flushed red-hot from forcing the confession, but short-term embarrassment was better than having Matt act like some damn yo-yo in bed out of *consideration* when that wasn't what she wanted at all.

Honesty. She'd committed to it before, and as he kissed the living daylights out of her, she had to smile. The best policy ever? It certainly seemed that way.

Matt managed to get to his feet without losing his grip, lifting her and carrying her into the bathroom.

It wasn't the biggest room in the apartment, but with the oversized tub she was happy. She knew from experience they both fit.

"Stand up." Matt lowered her slowly and gave her time to find her footing. She stepped back to make room for him, but instead of joining her, he fiddled with the curtains, sliding them to the side. He turned on the tap and adjusted temperatures, leaning over the edge of the tub.

"What're you doing?"

He stood and snatched the showerhead off the hook, twirling the hose to turn the head into the tub. "Whatever I want, right?"

"But I thought—"

He frowned and Hope snapped her lips together. Okay. Right.

She waited, wondering, as he flicked knobs and got the spray started. A gentle stream fed over her skin as he aimed the warm water. Liquid slid down in sheets as he changed the direction from her shoulders, over her breasts to her belly. The zigzagging motion reminded her of a brief, gentle prewash.

A laugh escaped.

He looked up from where he'd been staring in admiration. "What's that for?"

"I feel as if I'm standing in a car wash and waiting for the next cycle to begin."

Matt nodded, his pupils going dark as he examined her carefully. "There are a lot of things about to happen."

He hooked the hose around the faucet and jammed it in place to keep the water inside the tub. Then he grabbed her body wash and scrubbed her from top to bottom. Bubbles covered her everywhere. Tiny goose bumps rose in spite of the heat of the water and the heat of his touch. Every caress was a tease, a delight. He massaged her breasts with a full palm and fingers, circles and circles and more circles until her nipples throbbed against his slick hands. Then he moved farther south, cleaning all the signs of his seed from her. Yet even as his markings washed away, it was as if he painted her with a far more permanent brand. Something invisible, but undeniable.

When he slipped his fingers through her curls and along her labia she sighed happily.

Matt growled in approval. "You make the most wonderful noises. I can tell exactly how soft or hard to go by the sounds escaping your lips."

Hope considered sealing her mouth tight to see what he'd do, but where was the fun in that? Instead, she widened her stance, making it easier for him to touch her.

Matt didn't stop at her sex, or at least not for nearly long enough. He went all the way down, his thick fingers amazingly delicate on the back of her knees and between her toes.

She was all comfortable and content, especially when he grabbed the showerhead and rinsed her delicately, bubbles slipping down the drain with a quiet gurgle.

Then he rotated the showerhead off the widest setting to the tightest point, and her relaxation scurried down the drain as well.

"Now that you're cleaned up, I think you're ready for the next thing."

And the next thing appeared to be tormenting her. Hope gasped as he directed the pulsing stream directly at her right nipple. The pressure was hard enough to make her body tighten. A tingling began, leading from her sensitive breasts to deep inside where she grew achy and needy for him. She wanted him to put down the playthings and simply give her his cock.

Matt sat on the edge of the tub and switched the water to the other breast. Then he covered her right nipple with his mouth and sucked.

"I like that."

"Hmm." Matt mumbled around his mouthful, lashing his tongue over the responsive tip before using his teeth and dragging out a little scream.

She watched him—there was something so erotic about seeing his mouth on her that increased the wonderfulness of it. Observing his other hand approach, anticipating the second before he made contact with her waist.

What she didn't anticipate was him dropping the level of the showerhead until the hard stream pulsed in a direct line with her clit.

"Matt!"

"Spread your legs more," he ordered. Hope obeyed, then shivered as he put his mouth back on her breast and sucked hard. When his free hand snuck around her ass, she was ready to explode.

He fingered the crease between her cheeks, all soapy and slick. One finger circled her most sensitive spot. She was in overload. Her breasts, her clit...her entire body vibrated on the edge. So when he pushed that finger deep into her ass, it was no surprise that she came. Sex pulsing, constricting around a cock that wasn't there. Her ass clenching tight on his finger.

It was a miracle her legs didn't give out and let her collapse into the tub.

He finally crawled over the edge and joined her, putting the showerhead back into place and adjusting the spray to cover them both as he pulled her still-shaking body against his firm muscles.

Hope snuggled in tight. "I feel guilty. Or I would if I had the energy to feel anything right now."

"Really?" Matt helped wet her hair, stroking his fingers over her scalp and working the shampoo into a lather. "Why guilt?"

Hope leaned her hip against his groin in answer. His cock was back up to full strength. "I thought we'd do something about that for you."

He lifted her chin and unleashed his sexy smile on her. "Oh, you'll be doing something about it soon enough. But if you want me to call the shots, I ain't gonna always do what you expect."

That was for sure. "I like that idea."

His gaze dropped to her lips, his thumb rising to rub along her bottom lip. "I'm glad to hear it."

He pressed his thumb between her lips, and Hope sucked,

closing her mouth around the digit. She shivered as his eyes darkened, his body tightened.

It was hard to remember she'd started out early this morning dealing with her sister, and now? If the expression on Matt's face was any indication, she wasn't going to get much sleep for a while.

The day had definitely gotten better as it went along.

Chapter Nineteen

"Shove over," Jaxi ordered, nudging past her cousins and Beth to plop down at Hope's side. She leaned in close and lowered her volume, making it impossible for anyone else in the music-filled pool hall to overhear their discussion. "It took forever for the babies to settle. Now spill. What's the latest?"

Hope double-checked no one was listening. Tamara and Karen, the oldest two of the Whiskey Creek Colemans, were deep in conversation with Beth. All the Coleman males in attendance for the semiregular Friday night clan get-together, a scattering of the older cousins and their friends, were gathered around the pool tables at the back of Traders Pub. The urge to tease Jaxi was too strong to resist. Hope played with the tab on her can of Coke and shrugged innocently. "There's a great new valentine's fabric in the shop I bet you could use as curtains for the girls' room."

Jaxi pulled a face and poked Hope in the arm. "That's not what I'm talking about, and you know it."

A second's pause ensued as Hope considered what she wanted to talk about and what was easier to start ignoring. Just because Jaxi would keep things quiet didn't mean every dirty detail had to be shared.

And there was no way she was making public any parts of the conversation she'd had with Matt regarding their sex lives, even though a week later that was probably the first thing that still popped to mind, crowding out the frustrations of dealing with her sister.

Hmm, positive thinking was working.

She hid her smile and answered. "If you're wondering about Helen, I haven't talked to her since last Thursday. I heard through the grapevine she's sharing an apartment with an old friend."

"She hasn't called yet?"

"No. Although, she did stop in at the bank and ask a few questions. The manager contacted me to let me know that everything is still confidential—Helen's name wasn't on any of the access forms, and he simply turned her away."

Jaxi whistled low. "Bet that pissed her off."

Hope didn't give a damn. "I mean it, Jaxi. She's not getting her hands on anything I've worked so hard for."

"You don't owe her anything. Information or charity." Jaxi leaned against her side comfortingly.

"But if she does call and try to be polite..." Hope took a swig of her Coke. There was still a ton simmering under the surface in terms of fear and anger. "I hope I'm mature enough to forgive her. It's hard to overlook how much she's hurt me, but she is family. She's the only family I've got left."

"Deal with that later. Wait and see what happens, okay? I hate that you're tormenting yourself like this. Relax and try to forget her for a bit."

Hope nodded, her gaze darting into the room and focusing on Matt. He sent the pool balls spinning before standing and laughing with his brothers. He glanced in her direction, and the way he stared made her heart leap unevenly—the slightly lopsided smile with one side of his mouth quirked up in the corner. As if he had all sorts of interesting ideas running through his brain when he looked at her.

"Relaxing, I can work on." Hope gave Jaxi a quick squeeze before nudging her with a hip. "Let me out. I have some distracting to do."

Jaxi moved over to the next table where more Coleman

cousins sat shooting the breeze. Hope nonchalantly adjusted her T-shirt, tugging the neckline downward to strategically expose a bit more cleavage before pacing over to the pool tables.

Matt leaned over the pool table, his ass toward her as he bent forward. She was tempted to keep walking until she could slap both hands against his butt to enjoy his muscles flexing in the palms of her hands. Before she could make it all the way there, though, he'd taken his shot and turned, his grin widening as he caught a glimpse of her.

Hope let her hips swing a little extra as she approached.

"Oh, sweetheart. You keep moving like that and Matt's gonna have a fight on his hands keeping you to himself." Travis leaned a hip on the table, his gaze running over her body.

The brother standing closest to him, Blake, poked Travis in the shoulder. "Cool it, Casanova. I don't want anyone else in our family traumatized while at this pool hall."

Matt turned his sexy grin in Hope's direction. "Now, Blake. You really think any woman's crazy enough to pick Travis over me?"

"Rub it in, why don't you?" Travis grumbled.

There was something almost sad in his tone, and impulsively Hope went right up to his side and hugged him. He tightened for a second before squeezing back. His whispered *thanks* brushed past her ear, and she winked as he let her free.

A loud, exaggerated sigh rose from Matt. "Sure. Give him a hug before me. I'm gonna get a complex."

"Just making the crowd jealous, that's all." Travis twirled her to face Matt. "That's my admirers, I'm talking about, by the way. It's always good for them to see a pretty girl in my arms and know they ain't the only one wanting a piece of me."

"Then since you've usually got a woman hanging somewhere over you, you must have quite the jealous following." Daniel shook his head. "You and the twins. I'm waiting eagerly for you all to meet your match someday."

"Someday. But for now?" Travis waggled his brows and picked up his beer from the edge of the table, raising it in a toast in Hope's direction.

While she'd been watching the interplay between the boys, Matt had stepped to her side. He took her hand and pulled her against his body, speaking quietly.

"You made him happier than you know. Travis talks big, but sometimes I think he's a hell of a lot more lonely than he lets on." The smile on Matt's face reassured her. He tucked his knuckles under her chin and lifted her lips to his kiss. A slow, heated exchange followed that increased her pulse to a rocking tempo. A leg slipped between her thighs as he brought them closer, and she hummed happily.

"How's the game going?" she asked.

Matt shrugged, all his attention on her. "Who cares?"

He would have kissed her again, but she ducked away, slipping up the room toward the pool cues. "I care. I figure if you're losing, I can convince the guys to let me play instead of you."

Daniel laughed, holding forward his cue stick. "You want to take over for someone, you can play for me. I'd be happy to take a breather and see how Beth is doing."

"Hey. That means she's not on my team," Matt complained.

Travis scooted forward to take Hope's hand in his and lift it to his lips. "You and I will kick their asses."

He winked saucily before kissing her knuckles. Matt growled in the background and Hope laughed out loud. Travis was so obviously pulling Matt's strings, she returned the flirt's smile. "Ass kicking, beginning now."

The game was lighthearted and fun. Hope enjoyed the banter among the brothers, Blake and Travis and Matt all giving each other hell as they played. By the time they'd nearly finished three games, she wasn't sure if her stomach could take much more laughing. "You're supposed to be concentrating on the game. Give me a break."

Matt dropped the final ball for him and Blake, and won the deciding matchup. "Diversion works wonders. Now if you'd been ignoring us and snickering a little less, you might have won."

She stepped back against him and snuggled in as he draped an arm over her shoulders. "Winning isn't everything."

Travis tapped her on the nose. "What kind of dream world you living in? Winning is everything."

Matt batted his brother's hand away good-naturedly. Hope sighed with contentment. It was so nice to enjoy an evening out with people who didn't have an agenda.

Travis straightened up from his relaxed slouch and excused himself, heading for the front doors of the bar like his ass was on fire. She followed his gaze, but didn't see anything that should have made him move that quickly.

Then Matt distracted her by turning her back to the wall and leaning in close, lifting her chin and working his way over her lips as if he was determined to make her legs collapse. The heat of his torso pressed against her, and she relaxed back, luxuriating in his touch.

"Damn it." Blake's growl pulled her back to earth. "Bad enough I have to put up with Jaxi talking about you lovebirds all the time. Do you have to do that here?"

Matt didn't take his eyes off hers. "I think I need to do this just about everywhere. You got any objections, Hope?"

She shook her head. "Hell, no."

"Guess my brother is out of luck. Sorry, Blake. The show continues."

Hope laughed but slipped a hand between them to cover

his mouth. "Except, I need to go to the washroom."

Matt sighed and backed away. "I'll be at the table. You want another Coke?"

Hope nodded then scooted down the back hall to where the bathrooms were. This was wonderful. Just a relaxing evening out. No deadlines hanging over her head. Plus, the lack of interference from her sister seemed to imply Helen was coming to grips with reality.

Life was pretty damn wonderful.

And now that they'd dealt with that stupid hesitation of Matt's to being the kind of man he wanted to be in the bedroom—there was the potential for things to get even better. They'd shared a ton of good sex in the past few days—rocking-good sex where Matt made her more than glad she'd shared regarding her fantasy lover.

She exited the ladies room and paused. Out of the corner of her eye she'd caught movement. Pressed against the far wall beside the fire exit she spied a couple in pretty much the same position she and Matt had just enjoyed. A tall figure with a short crew cut leaned one hand on the wall, the other hand caught in his partner's hair. Hope peered through the darkness and hesitated. She had no intention of interrupting—especially not when the top kisser rocked his hips slowly. A shot of something wild and sensual flashed through her. *Hmm.* She snuck deeper into the shadows, the need to allow them piracy forgotten as she watched and listened.

Then the couple twisted slightly sideways and a jolt went clear through to her toes. The man with the jet-black hair had complete control over the person smeared up against the wall. And from the square jawline with the five o'clock shadow, the *kissee* was definitely masculine.

It was two men locked together and Hope's heart skipped a beat at the raw passion. The edgy, almost violent motion between them. A long, low masculine groan rang out as their hips ground together. The dim lighting didn't allow her to see their faces clearly, which was probably a good thing. Hope forced herself to retreat, peeling her gaze away. Watching could become a bad habit if she let it. She made her way back to the table, tingles of excitement still simmering in her system.

Good thing she was headed toward Matt, who she knew could do something definitive about her sexual tension.

Matt slipped away from the gathering to start his truck so it would warm up before they headed to Hope's. She had to open the shop early while he was off morning chores this weekend, and it made more sense to crash at the apartment.

He grinned to think that he got to consider such things. Where they would sleep, whose bed, which home. It was a neat stage to be at in their relationship—comfortable and exciting at the same time. He hit the john before turning toward the main room. A solid grasp on his arm jerked him to a stop, and he twisted to face his attacker.

Helen's bright blue eyes shone in the faint hall light.

Matt jerked his sleeve from her fingers. "What?"

She snorted. "So much for the legendary Coleman politeness. Nice to see you again too."

He stepped back a foot and looked her over quickly. Her outfit was far more revealing than it used to be when they dated, and the neckline seemed to be unevenly buttoned. "You want something?"

Because there wasn't much he wanted to talk to her about.

"Just thought we could visit for a minute or two. It's been a long time, and we didn't get to discuss much the other night. I figured I'd find you around here. Colemans' traditional Friday night meeting at Traders, and all that."

Now she admitted she knew about the family traditions? He waited. The way she dropped her shoulders—her entire body language—was far from the confident, almost demanding woman he'd been with over a year ago.

She lifted her head and stared into his eyes. "I've missed you."

A shot of pain stabbed him, not in his heart, but in his gut. If she'd come back a month after leaving—or even six months later and looked at him like this? Confessed that same thing? He would have given her a chance. Would have tried to find a way to forgive her for cheating on him.

But too much time had passed and it was no longer enough. He'd moved on, and all her confession did was make him sad.

"Sounds as if you had a lot of time to think." Matt leaned on the wall, his arms crossed in front of him. Putting up a barrier between them that was far smaller than the ones she'd shoved into place.

Her gaze fixed on his mouth. "About a lot of things. About how good you and I were together. Matt, this past year, not having you in my life? God, it was tough."

He didn't want to listen anymore. "It was tough for a while for me too, but things change. It gets better. Give it time, you'll figure it out."

"Matt, I want to get back together with you."

The burst of laughter couldn't be stopped. "You're fucking kidding me, right? Or are you drunk again like at New Year's?"

He was trapped in the back hallway of a bar with the woman he'd loved for most of his adult life before she'd taught him to hate. And only recently, he'd learned to forget.

She stepped against him, slipped her hands around his

waist and dropped her head on his chest. "Not drunk. I love you, Matt. I always did."

This was not happening. Matt grabbed her upper arms and peeled her off. She had to let go unless she wanted to actually cling as he forced her away. "Oh, no. Don't you dare. You're not actually doing this..."

Helen tilted her head to the side, tears shining in her eyes. "But it's true. It just took me a while to understand. I mean it. You always wanted me to say it. I can tell you now. I love you. I want to be with you."

My God, this was some kind of nightmare. Matt backed down the hall, trying to escape as she swung from smiling and seductive into a weeping mess. "Damn it. What the hell do you think you're doing? You're the one who ripped us apart last year. You left, Helen. Not me. And even if by some strange chance we had called it off together, did you really think you could just waltz back in and we'd be a couple again? You're crazy."

He turned on his heel and walked away. There was nothing more he had to say. Nothing she could say that he wanted to hear.

"Because you're with Hope? What did you do? Go looking for her as soon as I left town?"

Matt kept walking.

"She's not going to make you happy. Acting as if she's some princess of the country. She's just using you to get back at me..."

Helen raised her voice to a near shout. Matt paused at the entrance to the main room. From his vantage point, his entire family was visible. The girls gathered in a tight group, laughing and smiling as they eyed the guys at the tables. His brothers shooting the breeze and kicking back after a full day of labour. The kind of country living Helen had refused to see as valuable.

The love and family she'd turned her back on at every chance.

Matt twisted to face her. "You trying to convince me your sister is pulling a fast one?"

The calculating expression spread, Helen's eyes brightening. "She was so damn proud the first time you guys got together, she emailed me, gloating she'd finally gotten another thing I used to have. It wasn't enough that she got the business and the apartment. She went after everything I had in my life."

Weariness settled around Matt's shoulders like a blanket of snow. The complaints were familiar—Helen often had something negative to say about Hope. For years he'd listened with only half an ear whenever she'd moaned about her younger sister receiving special attention, thinking it was typical family grumbles. Like him and Daniel poking that the twins got off easy being the youngest in the family—nothing serious, nothing more than a temporary protest. Now? Blinders fell from his eyes. She really did want him to think evil of Hope.

Still, he'd give her the rope she so obviously wanted just to let her well and truly show her colours. "Why would she do that?"

Helen stepped toward him unsteadily, and he wondered again if she was drunk in spite of there being no scent of liquor. She lowered her voice conspiratorially. "Hope's jealous. You know that—she's always been jealous of me. Remember when we were young? She always managed to get the best of everything from my parents. Spoiled and greedy. She's the same now as then."

Matt watched as Helen placed a hand on his arm and rubbed her fingers over his biceps. "I remember you complaining."

She nodded. "See? She doesn't care about you."

The sour taste in Matt's mouth was enough to make him ill.

211

A profound sadness settled over him. There was no depth that Helen would not stoop to. One deception after another. And like he and Jaxi had spoken about—Helen had chosen her path.

She wanted a war? She'd get one.

Matt laid a hand over hers and stopped her from caressing his skin. The optimism in her eyes—did she really think he was that gullible? Some country hick willing to swallow any story? To go from saying she loved him to trying to ruin his relationship with Hope?

When he pulled her hand off and dropped it as if he'd held a dead mouse, her sparkling confidence clouded.

"If Hope has the best of anything, it's because she's worked for it. She deserves her happiness. The business, the apartment. After you left she put in the time and made it happen."

Helen's right eye twitched. "You fell for her lies. She used money that should have belonged to both of—"

"I don't know the financial details, and I don't care. I've heard enough and seen enough to know that when it comes down to who I trust, you have nothing to stand on. Hope says you don't own any of the Stitching Post? I believe her."

Helen lifted her chin, "And what about me being in love with you? How convenient that she's with you, at least for now."

Matt shook his head. "You don't love me. You never did."

"Neither does she."

"This conversation is over. I think it's best if you don't bother to try to talk to me again."

"She's not the pristine and pure thing you think she is." The words burst out like a gunshot.

Images of Hope wrapping herself around him and accepting his nearly violent lovemaking raced through his brain. Pure? Pure heaven. "None of your business."

"Remember what she did for a living while she was in school. She stripped, Matt. She did all kinds of things to the guys. Hell, I bet she was fucking a dozen of them a night all through college."

This had gone beyond stupid. "You know what, Helen? You're not getting it. What you and I had is over and gone. What Hope and I have is here and now. For all I care she could have fucked half the college and all the profs. But I doubt very much she did because that's not the kind of woman she is."

Helen laughed, a dark, dirty sound. "That's what you think. Who did you think I got the idea to ask you for the ménage from?"

The stab of pain returned, harder than before, but none of the agony was connected to Hope—all the blame landed firmly on the shoulders of the woman in front of him.

He was a stupid ass for having stayed to listen in the first place. But now that she'd tried to poison his life again, he was going to have his own say.

"Helen, you broke my damn heart, but you taught me a lesson I needed to learn. I can't make someone love me. For years you refused to say the words, and now I'm glad, because I don't think you ever did love me. And what I felt for you—well, it might have been a kind of love, almost a practice for the real thing. Whether I've got that now or not you'll have to watch from the outside because you're not welcome around me. Hope can decide if she wants you around her, but—"

"Hope doesn't want you around either."

A warm hand slipped over his arm as Hope nestled against his side. Helen stared at her sister with increasing dismay.

"You didn't learn very much in your time away." Hope stepped in front of Matt, as if to defend him, and he would have laughed if the whole situation weren't beyond unbelievable. "Please. You're making a fool of yourself. You've seen for yourself that the shop is out of your grasp. Matt isn't interested in you. Just give up and start again. There are plenty of things you can do instead. You can't have what I've worked so hard for."

Helen sneered and twisted on her heel, racing down the hall and slamming out the emergency exit door.

Hope sighed. "That was the most awkward thing ever."

Matt pulled her against him, cradling her carefully. Hope's hug grew stronger and she rubbed her face against his chest.

It was bizarre. He'd waited years for Helen to tell him that she loved him. Would have begged for the words at one point in his life.

All he could think of now was how fortunate he was that she'd never said it—and how much he wanted to hear that Hope cared about him in the same way that he was growing to care for her.

Chapter Twenty

"You can't be serious. It's going up to what?"

"Forecast calls for temperatures to rise to a balmy summer day. The Chinook's going to make that winter chill disappear and turn the snow into a slushy mess." Joel tossed Matt the wrench in his hands then stood and wiped his hands on a rag. "If you're interested, Dad gave us permission to play in the southeastern pasture. We're digging a new ditch there come the spring so he doesn't care if we tear it to hell. Want to join in?"

"Mud bogging? In the freaking snow?"

Joel snickered and Matt figured he must have looked borderline horrified. "You won't melt."

"It's going to be a pain in the ass when we get stuck."

"We won't get stuck."

Matt raised a brow, and Jesse laughed from where he was hauling stuff out of the truck's passenger seat. "He's right, Joel—we'll get stuck. But that's part of the fun."

Joel grinned back. "So, you in?"

Having the twins home during their February reading week was always an adventure. With Mother Nature cooperating this time and giving them a break in the weather, Matt should have known the boys would come up with something crazy to play at.

Fine. "I'll bring my block and tackle. I hope that we aren't the only idiots going."

"Hell, no." Jesse hung out the window like some ten-year-old on a caffeine high. "Everyone who's got cabin fever is going to be there around two, and we set up a barbecue after for those who want to stick around. Don't be late if you don't want to enjoy the truck equivalent of sloppy seconds."

"Jesse," Joel groaned.

Matt slapped Joel's shoulder.

Joel snapped his head up and pulled a face. "What you hitting me for? It was him that said it, not me."

Matt snorted. "Right, don't tell me you weren't thinking the same thing."

"I...well, fine, I was thinking it. But I have enough restraint to resist spitting out every damn thing that pops into my head."

Matt turned away and headed to his own truck, still snickering over his youngest brothers and their crazy ideas. Since the day was insanely warm, maybe a little downtime would be a good idea. While there was enough work to keep at it every minute, that wasn't good—all work and no play, that kind of thing.

Joel ground the old Ford into gear and spun out of the driveway, heading down the narrow gravel road toward the rough pasture. Matt laughed at Jesse in the passenger seat, who had his phone up to his ear and an evil grin on his face.

These two—barely controlled natural disasters.

They were right, though. The underground spring in the area had made the right side of that field too boggy to cultivate for the past few years. Turning it into a proper dugout might help deal with the excess moisture.

But in the meantime, seeing who could get their vehicles through the mess was a great way to spend the sunny Saturday afternoon. They were guaranteed to end up filthy and ready for more than a few drinks.

A little family bonding time was always a good thing.

The day flew past, the temperature rising high enough to make him peel down to a T-shirt outside the barns. Matt got stuck fixing a couple pens before he could get away, finally turning his truck toward the field. He dug out his phone and tried calling Hope, but there was no answer. He left a message on her machine and rounded the corner to see a virtual fleet of Coleman vehicles parked randomly over the field, a few running boards already covered with thick mud.

He pulled to the side and hopped out, figuring he'd check the situation before committing to the chaos. Cheers and roars of laughter rose over the ridge. He topped the crest, and his stomach fell.

"What the hell?"

His brother turned to wave. "Hey, finally. Great timing."

Matt pointed forward. "What the fuck is that?"

Jesse followed his finger. "You going blind? Hope and Joel are getting ready to cross."

Matt was tempted to drop his head into his hands and weep. "She's mud bogging in that bucket of rust?"

Jesse snorted. "Well, you got to admit, it's not likely she's going to damage much on the thing."

This was crazy. Matt stormed to the edge of the field that must have already seen a number of trips from the big trucks they drove. The day was warm enough the snow was melting, the ground was soft, and together with the weight of the vehicles, there were ridges and puddles appearing everywhere between one side of the field and the other.

He waved and the trucks stopped revving their engines. Joel stuck his head out and cheered. "*Whooo.* You gonna see her fall this time. No mercy from me."

Hope lifted one hand and deliberately dropped all but one strategic finger. Jesse laughed over Matt's shoulder. "You never told us Hope was a demon on wheels."

Matt's brain was in a fog. "What the hell you talking

about?"

Hope spotted him and waved. "Hey, Joel. Give me a second."

Joel gestured her forward and hopped up on the front of his truck to wait. Matt glanced around the field as he moved toward Hope. There were at least twenty people on the hillside all watching with interest.

"Hey! Good you finally got here." Hope stepped right up and snagged him in for a kiss. She was warm and slightly earthy, with mud all over her boots. Matt still wasn't sure what was going on, but he was willing to be distracted for a minute as he enjoyed the taste of her lips against his.

There was a bump into his shoulder. "Enough already. It's time for driving."

Matt leaned back and glared at Jesse. "Jealous?"

"Hell, yeah." Jesse looked Hope up and down far too intimately for Matt's liking. "If she can do everything as well as she can drive..."

The temptation to bury his younger brother in the mud grew rapidly. "Fuck off."

Hope laughed. "Don't worry, Jesse, I'll be glad to shame your ass after I finish dealing with Joel."

She grabbed Matt and tugged him toward her truck. "You want to ride shotgun?"

"You're actually driving this thing?" Matt walked with her, all sorts of disastrous scenarios playing through his brain.

"Of course. It's like the Sherman tank of the truck world. It's been fine."

"I didn't know you were going to be here."

Hope stopped beside the driver side door and looked him over. "Jesse called and issued an invite. The shop closed today at two, so I came out right after. I left you a message. But you want to think about why you're using that tone of voice?"

Fuck. "What tone?"

She crossed her arms. "The one that says you're pissed off I'm here, and you think I'm a little-bitty crazy thing and need to be protected, kind of all balled up into one ultra-bossy he-man package."

Matt dug deep, and fast, for an excuse. "Yeah, well. I don't want to see you get hurt."

Hope nodded. "I hear that. But it's fine. I do know what I'm doing."

Matt crushed her to him, kissing the hell out of her. She clung to his neck, her fingernails poking into the fabric of his light coat hard enough he felt them to the skin.

Then she pushed him away and crawled into the cab. She grinned down at him. "By the way, about riding shotgun? I just remembered you can't. There's no seat belt on that side."

Matt backed up reluctantly. "Have fun."

Being a spectator and hanging out on the hillside was way harder than any previous time he'd watched a pair take the field. Only she was right—he didn't get to boss her around out here. Matt accepted a bottle of beer from someone but ignored the lawn chairs. He needed to be on his feet.

Joel and Hope revved their engines again, rocking the trucks in place. Jesse waved them to start, and the trucks shot forward. Joel was ahead of Hope as they hit the first section of the field where the snow was down to brown soil and the faded yellow of dried grass. Hope drove farther to the right, avoiding a largish puddle. Her left rear tire hit the center of a pothole and dirty water sprayed everywhere. A loud cheer rose from the watchers, and Matt had to smile. Yeah. It wasn't going to be trouble.

Not until Joel jerked in too close, his truck shimmying sideways and totally cutting into Hope's path. She pulled up short and paused for a moment, then slammed it back into gear and took Joel on the opposite side. Crossing behind him and racing past, her truck jolted and swayed, mud flying as she spun and readied for the return trip.

She was well ahead of Joel by this time. He'd gotten stuck in a rut and was rocking his truck in a futile attempt to free it. Matt laughed and ignored his brother, instead enjoying how Hope barreled down the last third of the field, taking the most level path possible. The truck bounced and jerked, and people shouted.

Wild and crazy, simple and dirty. The sort of fun that made his parents roll their eyes good-naturedly. The fresh Chinook wind surrounded them like a promise, bringing a shot of spring into the middle of winter.

Hope turned at the end of the field and popped open her door to stand on the running board and raise her hands in victory. Matt whooped back and clapped as he sped down the hill, headed for her parking space.

Two new trucks came forward for their turn while Jesse drove around the perimeter to rescue Joel who was still stuck.

Hope's face shone with delight as she leapt into his arms. "Damn, that was fun."

Matt brought their lips together again. He was a bit addicted to the taste of her mouth. To the touch of her body against his. He leaned back but kept their bodies in contact. "You did great."

Hope snorted. "Yeah, the way I went off the road before Christmas, you probably thought I couldn't drive at all."

"Well, icy-road conditions are different than this. And Herbie was possessed."

She smacked a hand against his chest. "That's like the worst compliment I've ever heard."

"Fine, you're the queen of the mudhole."

They went back up the hillside. This time Matt grabbed one of the double lawn chairs his brothers had brought, curling Hope up in his lap and wrapping a blanket around their legs as they watched the rest of their friends and his cousins take turns tearing the field apart.

"I didn't know you enjoyed this sort of thing." Matt pulled off his gloves and slipped his hands under her shirt so his palms rested against her bare belly. Her warm flesh in his hands was the best part of the afternoon. She leaned back and closed her eyes, face toward the fading sun.

"I love it all. The picnics and the drive-in theater. Fishing and campouts. It's part of the reason I wanted to live in Rocky. I like it here, and I like the things people do for fun."

The fact he could tell it wasn't an act made her words that much more powerful.

They pulled the last truck from the mess shortly after the sun dipped below the horizon, a few final red and gold streaks crossing the sky to light their way back to the main Coleman house.

"I'll turn on the grill and get the food started." Joel gestured those joining them forward. "Anyone who needs to get cleaned up go ahead—guys use the bunkhouse shower room off the downstairs. Ladies, take the main floor bath and my folks'. They're out for the evening."

Jesse glanced at the young woman tucked under his arm. "Well, you're a damn spoilsport, Joel."

His twin sneered. "If I'm stuck cooking, there ain't nobody having fun in the showers."

Hope laughed as Matt reluctantly pushed her toward the upstairs bath. "I need to go—I ain't cleaned up since I finished chores."

She looked him over, long and hard, admiring everything from his jeans to his smile. "I volunteer to come and help scrub."

He smiled as he backed away. "You go on and keep thinking those thoughts. I'm pretty sure we can come to some kind of arrangement pretty damn soon."

By the time she'd washed off the mud and put on a clean pair of jeans, there was a delicious scent floating on the air. A plate piled high with ribs sat on the counter, a huge pot of baked beans on the stove. The crowd had dwindled to a dozen bodies, and after demolishing the food, that number dropped to just the unmarried Six Pack Coleman boys and three females—Hope included. Everyone else took their leave, happy smiles and sunshine-brightened faces following the laughter and content sounds of family.

Joel turned on music as Travis lit the fire in the downstairs family room, the long row of windows facing toward the ranch showcasing the lights of the outbuildings as they sparkled in the winter setting. "Temperature's fallen again. Those Chinooks never stay long, do they?"

"It was fun while it lasted. Did you enjoy yourself, Zoë?" Jesse leaned closer to his date and lazily drew a finger down the buttons of her blouse.

Zoë nodded. Jesse took her lips in a slow kiss, their tongues visibly touching as the young woman arched closer, lifting her hands around his neck. Jesse eased her to the floor and broke the kiss, whispering in her ear as he popped open her top buttons.

Matt shook his head and brought Hope with him to the loveseat. "Those boys—all eager to get to the end of the chase."

Across the firelight Jesse stretched out to the right of the laughing young woman. Hope stared as he leaned closer and pressed his lips to her neck. There was a stir of something heated in Hope's core as she watched them fooling around. Small touches, not too risqué, but enough she got hot watching. Beside her, Matt slipped his fingers into hers and pulled her closer. The guitar in the music strummed lightly, and Hope lifted her face toward Matt and eagerly accepted his kisses.

For a while there was nothing but a gentle crackle and the faint drift of wood smoke from the fire. Matt threaded his fingers into her hair, pulling tight and making her gasp with the touch of pain. He rubbed with the pads of his fingertips and eased the smarting, keeping their lips in contact.

Kissing wasn't enough. She should suggest heading to his trailer so they could fool around, but she was reluctant to leave the warmth of the house. Lazy relaxation mixed together with rising desire. Hope curled her body against Matt's and enjoyed all his long lean muscles pressed against her. Enjoyed the stroke of his lips over her cheek and the slow slide of his hand up her rib cage as he snuck a hand under her top and found her breast.

She should feel embarrassed to be groping like teenagers, all of them in the same room, but it felt too damn good to stop. Besides—no one was watching her and Matt. They were all into their own partners. Intimate kisses, nuzzling bodies. Motion caught her eye and she twisted toward the fire, a small gasp escaping.

Jesse was still with Zoë, but Joel stepped past and lay down on her other side. The woman rolled and eagerly kissed him as well, and a shiver raced over Hope's skin.

Matt followed the direction of her gaze then chuckled lightly. "Those boys are going to be in a heap of trouble some day."

There was nothing to say—besides, Hope's tongue was stuck to the roof of her mouth, her breath stolen as she watched the twins touching one woman between them. She couldn't tear her gaze away, not even when they removed Zoë's top. Joel drew a hand down her torso and followed the motion with his lips.

Hope swallowed hard. *Holy shit.*

Matt twisted himself around, sitting up and facing her. "You like watching, do you?"

Hope hesitated for a second, then nodded.

"Come here." Matt tugged her into his lap, arranging her legs on either side of his strong thighs. "I've seen it before. It's not my kink, but if you want to watch, you go ahead. In the meantime, I've got my own things to play with."

Hope stared over his shoulder for a moment, amazed that the boys were just going right ahead, right there. Licking and sucking Zoë's breasts, fingers slipping over her now naked hips.

They certainly weren't shy. Well, she wasn't usually either, in terms of dancing, but this—*this*—was a whole 'nother beast altogether.

Her own top was untucked and lifted away. A cool breeze hit her heated flesh, but it wasn't enough to make her want to stop. She gazed into Matt's face and smiled. He only had eyes for her—fingers dancing delicately along her bra and bare skin. He traced the edge of the cups before moving over the center where her nipple was taut and tingling.

"You object to me taking this off? I want my mouth on your tits…"

Hope paused, glancing the opposite direction where Travis was disappearing into his room, a hand curled around his partner's waist.

She looked back at the twins, and a sliver of her sister's tirade returned.

Just wait until he suggests you have a threesome.

She'd given him complete control to do what he wanted with her, but she hadn't meant *that.* Opening the door to unlimited sex with Matt wasn't the same thing as allowing more people to play with them.

And it wasn't as if there was another guy she had to worry about right at that moment. But he obviously wasn't stressed by his brothers' behavior.

Maybe it was stupid to start qualifying things, but...

Matt stopped his thorough exploration of her neckline with his tongue. "What's wrong? You've gone as stiff as a fencepost."

His whispered question was accompanied by a caring expression. Hands gentle on her body, along the back of her neck.

"I..." *Honesty. Damn it.* "I don't want to share you. Or be shared. You're not going to ask me to do what..." Hope tilted her head toward the twins.

Matt glanced at his brothers then swore under his breath. The next second, he was carrying her out of the main room into the bedroom to the right of the stairs.

He sat on the bed and held her close, tighter than she understood why. He finally leaned away and shook his head. "No, a thousand, a million times no. There is no fucking way I'd let anyone touch you. No bloody way I'd accept you giving yourself to another man. Not while we're together."

"I didn't think you... I mean, it's just... I thought, maybe..." She squeezed her eyes closed and hoped she hadn't mucked it all to hell and back. "Someone brought it up."

Matt dragged a hand over his mouth then shook his head in frustration. "Tell me. Helen?"

She was ashamed she'd given into the doubts. Let the horrible seeds her sister had planted grow so quickly. "I'm sorry."

Matt caught her by the back of the neck and pressed his lips to her forehead. He held her, stilled her. Controlled her and let her know he wasn't angry just by the way he touched her.

He dropped his forehead against hers. "She told me that you'd be asking. When she accosted me in the back hall? Said that it was your idea in the first place for her to ask me to arrange a threesome between us."

Hope sucked in air.

He didn't let go. Didn't let her run away from him. Her anger was there, burning at her sister in a brand-new way. "She's wrong. Totally and completely wrong."

"I know."

Matt tilted her head to reach her better, kissing her eyelids, brushing a row of gentle caresses across her face.

They were alone, and yet not. Through the open door she saw his brothers with Zoë, heard the noises of pleasure they made. Watching still turned her on, and now that he'd assured her sharing wasn't in his plans, she wanted nothing more than to allow him to take the reins.

He'd asked for one thing already. She could give him that.

Hope reached behind her and opened the hooks of her bra. The cups fell away and she was exposed, firelight trailing in the doorway to flicker over her. A faint memory of dancing in front of the gang flashed back—she'd had on the teeny seashell cups then, and basically her undies—it wasn't the first time she'd been nearly naked in public. She wasn't in public, but they weren't completely private either. The door might be open, but she doubted Jesse or Joel would bother looking their way.

But it was different than being alone in her apartment or Matt's trailer. What made it so much more meaningful this time was Matt, who stared as if he was a starving man and she was the first full meal he'd seen in days.

Inspiration hit—along with the desire to be a little more risqué. Behind them the twins were working on a very pleased woman, if the sounds rising from their direction were any

226

indication. They wouldn't care.

She stood and shimmied off Matt's lap. A furrow appeared between his brows for a moment, confusion over what she was doing. Hope cupped her breasts and started a slow undulation of her hips, rocking from side to side. Matt's eyes lit up, and he leaned back, his gaze darting over her. His stare hovered on her fingers when she lowered them to the snap on her jeans. Popped it open. Peeled the fabric down. Twisting and turning and baring her ass as she pivoted and preened.

She stepped forward clad only in her undies, and Matt grasped her hips, tugging her closer. He slipped to the floor, working his way along the line of her panties, licking with tiny butterfly-soft strokes. Then he grabbed the fabric in his teeth and tugged.

Hope laughed. "Let me help you."

Another twirl allowed her to strip bare. She was close enough he kept his hands on her, the warmth of his palms heating her up. When she was vertical, he took control and adjusted until his mouth and her sex were directly in line.

The first touch of his tongue through her curls made her gasp. The next moment the gentle exploration grew more intense, and he spread her with one hand and thrust his tongue in deep, eating her hungrily.

Over his shoulder Hope clearly saw the twins both making love to Zoë, her blonde hair flying as they moved on either side, one being ridden, one riding her ass. A curl of desire tightened inside, and Hope had to admit the sight was hot. But as she threaded her fingers through Matt's hair, confirmation that all she wanted was him hit strong and true.

She closed her eyes and ignored everything but the crazy-violent passion surging through her veins because of the man giving so willingly to her.

Another stroke of his tongue. Another. Matt pressed a

finger into her and did some twisty thing, and stars floated in front of her closed eyes. Hope widened her stance, pushing her hips forward. She thrust against his mouth rhythmically to try and find the final edge she needed. She cupped her breasts and pinched her nipples, loving the physical excitement that rippled around her. Matt sucked hard on her clit, abrading his teeth over it, and the first wave of pleasure approached.

"Oh yeah. Matt..."

He added another finger to the first, the thick digits pushing her over the top. Full, and breaking apart, Hope sighed happily as her climax surged through her.

He kept on for a moment, slowing a little, then brought her down to his lap. She was shocked to find he'd opened his jeans and her ass landed on his strong thigh muscles, her still-pulsing sex nestled against his erection.

"Hmm, what's this?"

Matt laughed. "If I have to tell you, you've not been paying attention. Now put me inside you, darling. I'm dying here."

Hope lifted her hips and slid forward, rocking over his shaft. The broad head slipped through her folds, hard and wonderful, and she pressed down slowly, the exquisite sensation of him filling her too good to rush.

"Hmm. There we go. Now lift up on your knees so I can reach those beauties."

Somehow Matt kept his hips pumping steadily, his cock sliding lazily in and out of her pussy as he gave one breast then the other his attention, licking and biting, driving her quickly toward another release. Over his shoulder, the twins were still playing with Zoë, but the sight had grown blurry, as if seen through a thick fog. Matt's lovemaking was powerful and addictive, and infinitely distracting. She didn't care what was happening back in the main room.

She understood the attraction of voyeurism a bit better, but when the main event was so incredible, she didn't need anything but him.

Matt picked up his pace, shifting her hands to his shoulders. "Hold on tight."

Then he grabbed her hips and she clung to him, riding him like a bucking bronco. Thick and hot, his cock pierced her again and again. Matt dropped a hand between her legs and caught hold of her clit, pressing the little nub.

Climax slammed into her as she screamed his name.

Matt groaned out his release, driving upward and pinning them together, groins grinding as he pulsed into her depths, his firm abdomen rubbing her clit and extending the aftershocks.

It was a good thing he held her upright, or she would have puddled to the ground. There was a cry from the main room, but the urge to peek simply wasn't there.

Matt caught her chin in his hand and kissed her, hard. His body and hers still connected, his tongue taking possession of her just like his body had claimed hers.

Chapter Twenty-One

Hope parked her truck and cursed at the horrible noises it made as the final rumble of the engine died away.

It seemed her temporary wheels were fast becoming just that. She probably shouldn't have used it to drag race through the mud a week ago, but it wasn't as if the truck was a classic or anything. She'd have to find something else to drive, and soon, but so far she hadn't had much luck.

She hopped out and headed around to the passenger side, chuckling to herself. If she was honest, she hadn't been looking too hard. Between the shop, the raffle and everything else she was doing—like spending tons of time with Matt—she'd neglected to look for new wheels. Only with the ominous sounds it had just made? She'd better move the search up the to-do list.

She pulled open the door and reached in for her grocery bags, hooking up all four at one time. That meant she had to use her hip to close the door. She gasped as she turned and looked up into Clay's smiling face.

"Let me give you a hand."

She couldn't justify pulling away, so Hope let him take a couple bags. "What're you doing here?"

Clay stepped ahead of her easily. "Waiting for you."

Really? "Why?"

He grinned. "Got a lead on a car for you. I've got the details in my back pocket. Let me show you."

Perfect timing. "Affordable? Reliable?"

"Not a tank?" Clay laughed. "Let's get these into your place then I'll show you."

Hope hurried up the stairs, excited at the prospect of getting to drive something that didn't take two blocks planning to turn around. She unlocked the door and dropped her groceries on the table, pointing for Clay to do the same. "Mondays as a day off is a wonderful thing, but I put way too much on my plate at times. So? Show me."

Clay pulled out a paper covered with notes. "Sorry, my handwriting isn't very good. I'll help."

He stepped beside her. All her concentration focused on the information on the page. Low enough mileage, the make looked good.

She pointed to the numbers. "What's that say?"

Clay bent over and examined his handwriting closer. "Seven thousand, but I think we could talk him down. It's old man Shedwick—he's buying a new car for his wife and didn't get offered enough as a trade. I'm pretty sure I can find out what they offered him. If you suggest a price between what he's asking and that, he'll take it."

Sheer willpower kept both feet on the floor she was so excited. "This is perfect. Thank you, so much. I can't tell you how much it means to me."

Clay stepped in front of her, his body trapping her against the fridge, and suddenly the position they were in felt far too confining. "It's the least I could do."

Hope planted a hand on his chest, intending to open up space between them, but he closed the gap faster than she could retreat. His mouth was on hers and she protested loudly. Or as loudly as she could without air. His bulk held her in place, his arms confining.

Hope simultaneously bit down and lifted her knee as hard as she could.

Clay folded in two, backing away as if she was a wild cat. One hand stretched out to form a blockade, the other between his legs cupping his balls. He gasped for air, his sputtering proof her knee had made direct contact. For a second she thought he might drop to the floor, but he caught himself, his free hand clutching one knee hard.

Hope scooted to the far side of the kitchen near the door, ready to run if necessary. Only Clay wasn't coming after her. He groaned a few more times before grimacing.

"What the hell is wrong with you?" he squeezed out, the words broken by his gasps.

She'd kicked him hard enough to make a real difference.

"What the hell is wrong with *you*?" she challenged back. "You bring me information on a car and then maul me? Did you expect I'd just fall into bed with you for that?"

"But you left a message. God damn, Hope, stop playing games."

"I never left any message. Not since the last time we did a quilting lesson for the raffle."

Clay shook his head. He planted a hand on the counter and shoved himself a bit more vertical, pausing to wipe a hand across his mouth. He examined his fingers as if expecting to find blood. "You called. Said you hoped I was still interested in spending some time with you. It was a damn tempting message too. Dirty, explicit."

What? "I'm seeing Matt. Why would I say such things?"

"Don't bitch at me. I'm not an idiot—ah, hell. This is fucked up. I didn't mean to..." Clay shook his head. "Someone's played me for a fool."

Helen.

"Oh, Clay. I can guess who. I'm sorry, but I'm not interested in anything but the car. Things are good with Matt

232

and me. I'm sorry you—"

What could she say?

He laughed bitterly. "Maybe I am kind of stupid. I fell for it. Should have known better."

Hope grabbed a washcloth and wet it for him. She handed it over with an apology. "Sorry about your mouth. And..."

He lifted a brow, the cloth pressed to his lip. "Sorry about my balls? In spite of being embarrassed, I'm glad to know you aren't shy about defending yourself."

She was totally mortified now, for a whole new set of reasons. And totally furious as well. "My sister has moved past the point of being annoying to the point of being dangerous. I could have really hurt you. Or this could have ended badly."

Clay nodded, slowly easing himself upright. Another groan escaped. "She's a bitch. Sorry—related to you and all, but it's the truth."

Hope paced back into the living room. "I don't know what to do about her. I thought I made it clear that my life was my own."

"Obviously not." Clay staggered forward a step. "I gotta sit down."

She didn't offer an arm or anything as he made his way to the couch—figured that would only make his humiliation worse. She did hit the fridge and grab him a drink, as well as soaking the cloth again and returning it.

He leaned his head back and closed his eyes. "Don't sit there looking at me. It's awkward enough to know someone a foot shorter than me brought me to my knees that easily."

Hope turned away, hiding her grin. It wasn't funny. It wasn't. "I am so—"

"Sorry? Don't be. I shouldn't have come on so strong. Just something about Matt rubs me the wrong way and when I thought I had the green light?" Clay's eyes popped open. "Shit. You think your sister is bent on making trouble between you and Matt?"

"Looks that way."

Oh no.

His hint registered the same moment Clay pointed to the phone. "If she goes for the obvious, you might want to give Matt a call."

His phone rang for the tenth time in the past hour. Matt cussed louder, but otherwise ignored the call like he had all the previous times. It wasn't a familiar family ring, which meant there was no emergency worth freeing his hands from the mud and muck he was elbow deep in. Should have turned the damn thing off completely.

By the time he had scrubbed himself clean, there were more messages waiting. He jumped into his truck and started through them en route to town to pick up supplies. He'd grab a quick burger, maybe stop in at Hope's for a minute if she was free for lunch.

When Helen's voice came over the line, he was tempted to delete the rest of the bloody messages all unheard. All her words weren't understandable—slurred a little at times, and again, he couldn't figure out if she was drunk or high on something.

She didn't make a lot of sense in the first couple messages, but by the third, her intent was clear enough.

"You might want to ignore me, but it's for your own good. There's something funny going on. I was headed to work and happened to notice there's a strange truck parked outside Hope's place. She's off work today, isn't she?"

It was enough. Matt clicked erase, then turned the phone off altogether. Helen continued to amaze him. As if he'd believe anything she had to tell him, especially about her sister.

Pulling into the Stitching Post parking lot and seeing Clay's truck there—the shot of anger that arrived was infuriating, but more at himself for continuing to have such a strong reaction to the ass. He didn't doubt Hope, but there had better be a damn good reason for Clay to come sniffing around where he knew he wasn't welcome.

Matt bounded up the steps at full speed, surprised to have the door swing open without using his key. Even more shocked to round the corner to find Clay sprawled on the couch, one hand rising toward Matt as if in surrender.

"Whatever you heard, it's not what you think."

The full-fledged pissed-off response that flashed anytime Clay was around was tempered by the guy's instant submissive stance. He didn't bluster like usual. Instead, he kinda folded himself up and guarded his torso.

Hope rose from where she'd been sitting, pretty much as far away from Clay as she could possibly get and still be in the same room. "Matt. Clay found me a car."

She sputtered to a halt.

Clay and Matt exchanged glances. *What the hell?*

She shook her head and growled. "Ahhh, dammit, now she's making my brain crazy. Matt, Clay is here because not only did he potentially find me a car to replace Goliath the monster truck, my sister has continued her Wicked Witch of the West imitation. Clay didn't do anything wrong."

Her insistence made no sense. "I didn't say he did."

Hope opened and shut her mouth a few time. "Right."

"Helen called and pretended to be Hope." Clay leaned forward and grimaced, shifting his hips uncomfortably. Matt stared for a second, trying to figure out exactly why that move looked so familiar.

"Helen called you?"

Clay nodded. "I usually have call display, but I just switched servers and haven't set up the new system. She left a voice mail—said I should come over and she'd make sure I felt a lot more welcome than the last time we'd gotten together."

The urge to chuck Clay's carcass out of the apartment was tempered by rising confusion. Even though this situation was fucked up, why hadn't Hope come and greeted him yet?

"I see. So, now you know she isn't interested." Matt turned to Hope. "You get the details about the car? So you can call and look into it?"

Hope nodded, still hesitating on the far side of the room.

Fucking hell.

Matt looked down at Clay. "Thanks for the tip. We'll deal with Helen. If you don't mind keeping this quiet for a bit? I'm not sure what we're going to do, but until we decide, we'd appreciate you not spilling the beans all around town."

Clay levered himself vertical, hips remaining lopsided as he took a couple staggering steps then caught his balance. "No problem. Like I told Hope, not the sort of thing I'd go boasting about. I'd prefer to win attention raising money for the charity. Speaking of which, you Colemans working on your entry for the raffle or did you give up?"

The damn quilt. Matt had hoped everyone would forget his impulsive signup for the auction. Travis and Blake had both given him so much grief when he'd mentioned it, he'd avoided the topic ever since. "No worries. You guys—?"

"Nearly done." Clay limped across the room and pulled his jacket on. "Hell, we might be the first ones finished, right, Hope?"

She nodded wordlessly.

"Hey, Hope? I really am sorry." Clay turned on his heel and left, tugging the door shut behind him.

Hope remained on the far side of the room. Matt checked her over carefully. She looked damned uncomfortable, and he still couldn't figure out why. "You okay?"

Words burst from her. "I canned him."

"What?"

"Clay. That's why he's limping." She dragged both hands through her hair, turning the long strands into a riotous mess. "My God, Matt, Helen seems to be doing everything she can to tear my life apart. There's this mess with Clay, plus she's bothering the bank and my landlord. She's been sending me emails through the shop's website contact button. I'm pretty sure it's her—stuff about suing me for poor quality products and stupid things that are just not possible."

Matt hadn't heard much after her first words. "You did what to Clay?"

She paused. "Kneed him in the nuts."

It was a good thing Clay was already gone. "And what was the bastard doing that got you close enough to his nuts to have to knee them?"

All the colour in her face drained away. "I'm sorry."

Matt tore across the room and caught her before she could escape down the hallway. "I'm not accusing you of anything. Why are you so damn spooked? The only person I'm fucking upset with is Clay because he should have known better than to give you a reason to bust his nuts. Even if Helen was yanking him around."

Hope burst into tears, burying her face against his neck.

Matt closed his eyes and breathed deeply through his nose, fighting for control, for balance to deal with this hellhole of a situation. It was nothing—a simple misunderstanding—and yet it was everything. It was a pain in the ass that shouldn't have happened in the first place.

"Hope. First, answer me. Are you okay physically?"

The response came out sniffly and muffled against his chest. "I'm fine. He didn't hurt me. I was scared, but instinct kicked in."

Another jolt of anger hit. Maybe he'd pay a visit to *Thompson and Sons* and make sure that Clay's balls were out of commission for a good long time.

She gasped for a second then pulled away, wiping her eyes. "Sorry for being so silly."

He wasn't done with her. "Your instincts to get out of a man's reach shouldn't have been triggered. Tell me what happened."

She went into her explanation, her hands moving rapidly, her chin lifting and her face becoming more expressive the longer she spoke. He led her to the couch and sat beside her, one hand on her leg as she faded off at the end.

"So what do we do? What do I do? My God, it's as if Helen's turned into some crazy woman, and not a good crazy cat lady like I joked about becoming. She swings hot then cold—it's as if she's not all there."

Matt leaned back and tucked Hope under his arm. She snuggled in closer, slowly sneaking her hand behind his body. Tentative, careful, as if she wasn't sure how he would react.

It drove him crazy himself to see her so timid. As if she expected him to reach out and hit her. Or that she thought he might up and walk away.

He was totally going to deal with that issue, but first, Helen.

"She's not the woman I remember being with for so long."

Matt stared into space, trying to recall her being this vindictive. Other than when she'd actually cheated on him and left, Helen had been careless at times, and selfish, but never truly cruel. "We can talk to the police, but Helen hasn't done anything illegal. Being a pest isn't a criminal offense."

Hope stiffened as he spoke. "But she's a nuisance. Isn't there a law about not bothering people? Can I get a restraining order or something?"

Matt shrugged. "Not sure. I'll take you down to the station and we can talk to my cousin Anna. Or you could phone her and ask for advice. Do you know where Helen's staying?"

Hope nodded. "I'd call her, but I'm afraid I wouldn't have much to say right now other than *fuck off and leave me alone*. Which would probably lead to me being shouted at, and things would go downhill from there."

He agreed. "Don't call right now. Give it time and consider the options."

She struggled out of his arms and surged to her feet. "Damn it. Why did she come back? Why could she not just stay in Calgary and get on with her life?"

It was a good question. "The main thing is to make sure she's not going to be able to get into your life anymore. We'll work together to find a way to do that. Are you with me?"

Hope turned from pacing the living room, her arms slipping in front of her as she hugged herself tight. She bit her bottom lip and refused to meet his eyes...and didn't answer his question. "I'm sorry about Clay—not about him being here, because you're right that's not my fault. But I feel like..."

Maybe she was going to bring it up. That weird sensation he'd gotten from her ever since he'd walked into the apartment—there had to be a reason. "Feel like what?"

"Like I've done something wrong. Like you're going to be upset because he was here."

Matt sighed. "This is because of that damn cock-fight Clay and I were having before you and I started dating, right?"

A tiny smile snuck past her frown. A fleeting sign of the woman he'd been spending his days with. The woman he'd been dreaming about at night.

"Maybe?"

Dammit. Mat rose to his feet and took her hands in his. He tried again. "I'm not upset with you. And I'm sure we can deal with your sister. Do you want my help?"

This time Hope nodded tentatively. "Can we put away my groceries before we do anything else? My ice cream is melting."

Everything about her remained hesitant. As if the vital, lively woman he was so attracted to was being smothered under a layer of something that Matt suspected was fear. But he'd been around his share of timid animals in the past. The ones who'd been hurt and learned to be suspicious of others. There was a lot some caring and loving could do.

Family held together. Friends worked through the tough times. Misunderstandings happened, but when people were honest with each other, they could work it out.

And that's what Hope was going to find out big-time, if he had any say in the matter.

Chapter Twenty-Two

Hope tucked the last of the vegetables into the crisper, wondering if he'd noticed it took an unearthly length of time to find places for what she'd bought.

There was a ton she needed to say, but she dreaded it so much that even a foolish prank like drawing out her chores seemed worthwhile. Just to keep him at her side for a few more minutes, their hands and bodies bumping, his familiar scent an addictive drug to her senses.

A couple days ago the realization had hit she'd somehow crossed the line. He was no longer a guy she was obsessed with. The one she could find instantly in a crowded room.

She had gone and fallen in love, and now her sister had to come and remind her all over why she'd avoided serious relationships. It wasn't anything Matt had done, not yet at least. But all her hard-won confidence from the past year was fading fast as Helen tore away her control.

This is why you can't have nice things. The smart-ass remark popped into her head, and she snorted in spite of her frustration. Yeah, right. If she clung to her sense of humour, it might help her get to the end of the day with her mind intact.

A quick turn brought her face to face with Matt, his grey eyes staring intently at her face. Like a Band-Aid, the quicker she did this, the better.

"Thanks for dropping in. I'll call the police department and..."

He was already shaking his head, moving in closer. "That sounds as if you're trying to get rid of me. What's the rush?"

The rush was she had to do this before her courage failed. Helen had pushed so hard, so often. At some point Matt was going to throw up his hands and wish he'd never gotten involved with either of them. Hope would prefer to cut the ties before her heart got more involved—as if that was possible.

She tried to make it seem casual. "I'm tired. All this melodrama has been too much. How about I'll call you in a few days?"

Walking toward the door was the hardest thing, but maybe if she actually opened it and pushed him out, he'd go.

He didn't budge.

If anything, he got a little more settled against the wall he was now pretending to hold up, his broad shoulders easing back. Arms crossed in front of him, the entire long length of him relaxed and muscular and good enough to eat.

Hope swung the door open.

Matt laughed. Outright laughed. "I don't think so, darling. Whatever it is that's biting your ass is gonna get worked out right now."

"There's nothing—"

"Hope." All the relaxation vanished as he straightened and moved in like a predator intent on its prey. "Go to your room, strip and lay on the bed."

Her mouth was open far enough if this was summer, she'd be catching flies.

Matt raised a brow. "You hear me?"

"You expect after this kind of day that I'm going to—"

"Listen to what I'm telling you to do without a single fucking complaint? Oh yeah. You said you wanted me to take, then, goddamn, I'm taking. I need to grab something from my truck, but by the time I get back I expect you to be naked on your bed. You got that?"

Hope swallowed hard as she clutched the door. The cool wintry March air floated in, knocking some sense into her.

It might be the last thing she got from him, so...why not? The *why* was easy—the goose bumps pebbling her flesh weren't caused by the chill brushing past her. It was all him.

His voice, his body—the way he stalked in and made every bit of her quiver.

The way he looked at her. Heated, dirty passion waiting to be forced on her, and she knew in the midst of all of the chaos that this afternoon would be something she'd never forget.

Pity it was bound to be their last time.

She didn't answer him. Just brought her hands up over her head as she stripped off her T-shirt. Eyes focused straight forward, she paced past him, brushing his chest, his fingers trailing over her bare shoulders as she moved to the back of the apartment.

She deliberately dropped one article after the other on the floor, like a breadcrumb trail leading toward safety. Only this was one of the most dangerous things she'd ever done.

Laying her heart on the line—and hoping she survived when he left.

The front door echoed loudly through the apartment far quicker than she thought possible. He must have run all the way down to the street level and back, and something about that made her feel very good inside. That he was as eager for her as she was for him.

Hope sat in the middle of her bed, arms curled around her shins. Hiding herself, holding herself inside. His footsteps sounded, louder and louder, and she lay down quickly, the cool of the quilt heating rapidly under her back.

She deliberately closed her eyes. Staring at the ceiling wasn't her first choice, and actually watching him round the corner and spot her? That was a braver thing than she was capable of.

She could tell he was there, though, standing motionless. Her ears ached for the smallest of clues of what he planned. What he thought of seeing her laid out like he'd requested.

Then he chuckled, and all her melodramatic buildup was wiped out by his sexy good humour. "You're grimacing as if I'm going to make you eat liver or recite the times table, or something."

"The square root of eight-one is nine. In a right triangle, the square of the hypotenuse is equal to the square of the—"

Another burst of laughter rang out, and she felt a tug on her leg. "You planning on keeping your eyes closed the entire afternoon?"

"You planning on skipping work all afternoon?"

"I called Blake—told him I had an emergency to deal with."

Her eyes popped open of their own accord.

"You what? This isn't an..." She'd scrambled up on her elbows to confront him, but the words vanished because *hot damn*. This wasn't at all what she'd expected. "You're naked."

Matt grinned as he looped a plastic tie-down around her ankle. "I noticed. You're naked as well, which makes it very convenient."

She eyed the restraining loop with a little trepidation, and a shiver of anticipation that was impossible to ignore. Or hide. "Convenient for what?"

"A little conversation. Now hush."

She kept looking him over, ignoring the urge to point out that conversation and being told to hush weren't exactly on the same side of the scorecard. He applied another plastic strap and closed it off with a couple fingers' looseness. She used the straps around the store to secure material bolts. The way he was attaching them, the plastic wouldn't tighten any further, but she wasn't getting them off without a pair of scissors or a knife.

Soon she was wearing bracelets as well as the anklets. Then he pulled out a couple small coils of rope, and the suspense was all worth it.

He didn't do any of the really kinky things she'd heard about. Didn't pull her legs apart and secure her to the bedposts or anything. Just tied her ankles and wrists together. All the while, he whistled softly and rubbed his body against her at every chance. Totally unselfconscious that his impressive cock bumped and rubbed as well.

"You going to tell me what's on the agenda now? Although I will admit your rope skills are impressive." Her voice had gone husky and she cleared her throat.

"This isn't playing with ropes. We'll do that sometime down the road, but now? I've got other things in mind."

Down the road? Hope's heart ached.

Then the bastard grabbed her locked together wrists and pressed them over her head, tying her to the headboard. He straddled her thighs, holding his weight off so she wasn't crushed.

Matt looked her over, a slow, thorough perusal, his smile growing as if he liked what he saw.

Her skin twitched, like a horse when a fly lands. Only she wasn't trying to shake him off, she wanted more of him. Not only on top of her but in her. Holding her, his contact squeezing out the weight of the day and all the concerns caused by Helen.

Somehow he made being trapped the most freeing thing she'd ever experienced.

"Tell me why you're acting like a skittish colt. No lies, just the truth."

Hope snorted. "You got me naked, tied me up, and now you

want to talk? Are you a girl in disguise?"

Matt rocked forward, sliding his heavy erection along the curve of her mound, rubbing against her clit. "Does that feel like I'm a girl?"

"Just saying…"

"Because I care enough to work whatever the hell is wrong out of you? Fine. I'll be an asshole." He leaned forward and took hold of her nipple with his mouth, sucking gently, then harder until she squirmed. Matt switched to the other side, his fingers pinching and teasing along with his mouth until she was bucking her hips against him, hoping for a tiny touch on her clit to get her over the edge.

Then…he stopped.

In response to her muttered complaints, Matt raised his hands from her breasts, instead dropping them to her hips and pinning her in place.

"You enjoy having sex with me?" Matt teased his thumbs along the tender skin by her hipbones.

No way. "Truth or Dare now?"

"Just truth."

She grumbled *asshole* then nodded.

"Say it."

"I like sex with you," Hope confessed, her tone cranky even in her own ears.

"Good." His eyes brightened, mischief and *oh my God* desire lighting them up to drool-worthy. "Because I love having sex with you. Next question. You like spending time with me outside the bedroom?"

Shit. "Yes, Matt, I like spending time with you. Just…"

He leaned forward, sliding his hands up her arms until he grasped her wrists. The rest of his body lowered one bit at a time until she was completely covered with a Matt blanket.

She shivered. Having him over her felt so good, she could barely stand to speak the words, already anticipating he would withdraw. "I promised to be honest. I'm scared I'm going to lose you. That all this shit with my sister is going to make you leave, and I really don't want you to go."

Matt turned his head until his lips stroked her cheek, warm air brushing her skin as he licked her earlobe. "Then stop trying to push me out the door. Because I'm not going anywhere."

He scooted backward, leaving her hands over her head. Hope clutched the bars of her headboard as he untied her ankles, immediately coming back between her thighs. Hands gentle on her belly, he stroked outward, drawing her knees apart, opening her sex to his sight.

Hope licked her lips. "You're not leaving?"

Matt glanced up and smiled. "Oh, hell, no."

A gasp escaped as he slipped his thumb into her core, bending to lick and nibble as if he were starving. His tongue pressed firmly as he lapped at her, as he used every trick in the book to drive her crazy. The orgasm that had retreated while they'd talked roared up with a vengeance and slammed into her only moments after he'd begun.

She was still shaking as he rose, aimed his cock at her folds and drove in all the way. Hope clutched the headboard, staring at him, memorizing him, feeling him all the way into her heart as he lifted her hips and fucked her hard.

She lifted her legs into the air and caught him, ankles crossed at his lower back as she tried to help. Opened herself to his possession, enjoying the heated pummeling as he took ownership over her. That's what it felt like—a seal, a brand. He claimed a place and she gave it.

"I'm gonna come, Hope. I'm going to fill you and make you mine." Matt reached between them and pressed on her clit in time with his thrusts. He slowed enough to suck at both nipples for a second, before pressing her upward. "You nearly there, darling?"

Hope squirmed. Nodded.

He stopped and she cursed. Loudly.

Matt nodded. "That's right, I'm a bastard. Because I'm going to take it all. Every damn bit of you."

He levered her thighs into the air, spreading her wider. A cold sensation brushed between her butt cheeks, and she gasped. One of his fingers, slick with lube, pierced her ass.

Oh God, oh God, oh God.

Did she want this?

Matt leaned up and stared into her face as he moved quickly and opened her on two fingers. The burn continued, edged with something else. "Yeah, you like that, don't you?"

"Yes. Oh *damn...*"

The shot of cold as he squeezed lube directly into her ass warned he wasn't giving her a lot of prep time. Which was fine. She wanted this. Wanted this reminder of being taken. Being used a little—for the right reasons.

His cock touched her. The broad head slick as it pressed against her resistance, popping through the muscle with a sharp flash of—not pain. Not from Matt. A sharp pleasure that made Hope groan.

He stared down at where they connected, shaking his head slightly. "Prettiest thing, seeing you take me into your body. Your pussy, your ass. All of you fits all of me so damn fine."

Another rock sank him deeper. He withdrew until just the head of his cock was inside her before pressing forward. He worked his way in slowly and yet quick enough. Less than a dozen moves and his groin was tight to her ass.

Matt breathed out ragged and harsh. "Dammit. I hope

you're ready for a wild ride, because there ain't no way I can go slow after seeing that."

He didn't need her permission, but she wanted to say it anyway. "Do it. Fuck my ass, Matt."

He squeezed his eyes tight for a second before grasping her hips and doing just that. Quicker and quicker he pulled out only to slam in hard enough the bed shook, her breasts bouncing. Her ass burned, but it was a good sensation. Edgy, violent pleasure. He pounded in, making her crazy, aching for release. A single brush of his fingers over her clit and she came, pussy clutching, ass squeezing. He shouted, but didn't come, just took her again and again until every last pulse had died away. Matt pulled all the way out, smiling as he looked down. She had to be wide open to him, his fingers light on her hole before he pressed in smoothly once more.

"I'm not done, but I want your hands on me."

Matt reached up, cock slipping from her ass as he folded her like origami paper and let loose the ropes binding her to the bed. He pulled her fingers into his hands, massaging until the blood returned.

Then he grinned as he put his cock against her now-closed hole and reopened her all over again.

Dirty? Wicked good.

"That feels so wonderful."

"I know." He used the back of his forearm to wipe sweat from his brow. "I like how your body accepts me. Takes me in. Gives me what I need."

She grabbed hold of his shoulders and let her fingers dance over his muscles. Face to face as he rode her ass, slowly now, thoroughly, until his eyes kind of rolled back and he shook, his groin tight against her, heat and passion and wonderful connection all mixed into one.

Chapter Twenty-Three

Matt brought her to the shower and cleaned her from head to toe. Removed the plastic tie-straps. Washed her hair and wrapped her up like she was precious before bringing her back to bed and cocooning himself around her.

He was going to use every possible means to show what she meant to him.

"Your brothers are going to kick your ass if you don't get back to the ranch soon."

Hope's tired but contented comment earned her another kiss. He couldn't seem to stop touching her. Kissing her.

Wanting her.

"I've done the same for them before. This is important. You're important." He rolled her over to discover what the tiny gasp escaping her had meant. "Oh damn, I made you cry. I'm sorry."

Hope shook her head. "It's not you. I just don't understand why all this is happening. Well, some things have sucked, but on the whole, I've been so lucky lately—it doesn't seem possible. I'm not the kind who gets an easy break. If things work out, it's because I've put in the effort. I just don't know where you fit into the picture."

"In terms of luck or work? Because, darling, if you're talking about you and me as a couple, from what I've seen, relationships are work. The good ones—both sides give a hell of a lot and there ain't much luck involved."

She lay still for a moment before nodding. "I guess. Just

haven't seen enough good relationships myself to know that. I mean, I've been trying, but..."

Talking about relationships.

"Tell me about when your mom left."

Her blue eyes widened as she went completely rigid beside him, kinda like he'd expected she would. Only the protests that her mother had nothing to do with this, or her slamming her mouth shut and refusing to answer didn't happen. Instead she looked directly into his eyes, their faces only inches apart as she started.

"It felt as if they'd been fighting for a long time. I guess it was only six months or so, but it came out of nowhere and suddenly nothing he did was good enough, and nothing she did was right—accusations and cutting words flew at the strangest time. We'd go from 'pass the yogurt' to 'you stupid asshole', and that could burst out from either side."

Matt stroked his thumbs against her wrists, making tiny circles, letting her speak. Willing her to share whatever was propping up that wall behind her eyes.

Hope sighed. "You really want to have this conversation while we're naked?"

Hell yeah. Matt lifted and rearranged until they were tangled even tighter together, his cock nestled between her legs. "Distracted?"

"Yes."

"Tough. Tell me."

She tilted her head and gave him a dirty look, but kept talking. "I would take off when I could, but I was only fifteen. Helen would disappear to spend time with you or her friends, but I could only organize so many sleepovers, could only hang out at the teen club for so long, and for some stupid reason my parents decided my whereabouts was closely tied to their fighting. Whoever had control of me had the winning hand."

251

Matt dropped his lips against her cheek. "I had no idea."

"You were busy with your family, and with Helen. And I'm sure she told you all sorts of things."

That was true. "I was surprised when she said the two of you were going to open the quilting shop together. I always thought..."

Hope's smile twisted. "That I was this spoiled creature who got away with murder?"

"Actually, no. I figured most of Helen's whining was just that, whining, but I sure didn't see the two of you working together well."

She shrugged. "It might have been okay, but yeah, I would have had to be the one who caved in any argument. It didn't help the stress between us that before Mom finally packed her bags, she gave me a bunch of stuff, and nothing to Helen. I think because I'd shared the items were important to me— Grandma's old quilt rack, things like that. All Helen talked about was getting out of Rocky someday. And then it was Mom who left. Dad missed her more than he wanted to admit, and he started hitting the bottle."

Another piece of the puzzle fell into place. "That's why you don't drink."

"Damn right."

Matt could have kicked himself. Why had they not had this conversation before? "Helen moved out, but you still lived with him?"

"Yeah, and then he died. I was the one who found him. Didn't know he was dead at first, just thought he was dead-drunk like usual."

He stroked a hand along her arm, all the way up to her neck. Caressing until he could cup her face. "He left you too, didn't he? Not only physically, but mentally and emotionally— he checked out long before he was gone."

"I think my family is cursed. We can't keep it together. And that's why even though you're lying there looking so damn understanding, I think eventually you're going to have enough of the crap and you'll wish you'd never tried to be with me."

Holy shit. "You really think I'm going to hightail out because your sister is making your life hell?"

"She made your life hell once before, and she seems damn good at causing trouble. Unless you're some kind of glutton for punishment, I'm not sure why you'd stick around me waiting for more pain to come your way."

"Doesn't sound like you think much of me, Hope Meridan."

She wiggled upright, indignation on her face. "It's not you—I mean, I just said I wouldn't blame you for leaving. You're not a crazy bastard, why would I expect you to put up with me and my insane sister?"

Because he didn't mind dealing with the craziness if it meant he got to be with her? Didn't want her to have to deal with it on her own?

Because he'd fallen in love?

He pulled her into his arms and held on tight. "Remember what I said about relationships being work?"

Hope sighed. "You sure you want to keep hanging around me?"

"You sure you can put up with me being a demanding asshole at times?"

She cupped his face in her hands. "I like you as a demanding asshole."

Really? He was about to find out if she meant it.

"I think there's a bigger trouble than you being worried I might leave. I think you're still curious if I'm thinking about your sister. Comparing you to her, that kind of thing."

Her face tightened. She swallowed.

253

"You know what? I'm glad she came back from Calgary, even though we have to figure out what the hell is wrong with her. I probably wouldn't have brought this up otherwise, if she hadn't shown up. If she hadn't been going out of her way to come between us. And this whole issue would have been hovering over us the entire time, like some damn ghost in the background."

Matt grabbed her wrists and rocked her to a sitting position right between his thighs. He caught her by the back of the neck and forced their mouths together, his tongue possessive against hers. His teeth harsh, kisses demanding.

She answered him back like a wild creature, crawling into his lap and pressing her breasts to his torso.

Matt thrust his fingers into her hair and tugged until their mouths parted.

"You need to know this, one hundred percent. It's you I see, not any ghost of the past. You are not your sister, not at all." She looked down until he repeated his tug to lift her face. Blue pools reflected back as he looked deep into her eyes. "You, Hope, are an amazing woman who kicks my ass, in and out of the bedroom."

She took a deep breath, her chin rising. "I've worked so damn hard trying to be brave and reliable. And staying honest, because that seemed to be what was missing in my family."

"You're honest. We had that conversation before, remember?"

"I thought you said I was blunt?"

Matt adjusted their position so the entire front of her body made contact with his, her legs straddling his hips. "That too. But you're not blunt to be mean. Or selfish. You're doing it because you care. And so honestly? I think Hope is a pretty damn fantastic woman. I think you deserve to be happy."

She grinned. "I kinda like this conversation. You go right

ahead—tell me more."

They laughed together, hands moving, exploring. Her kisses began to distract him. Matt didn't want to lose the point he had to make, so he pulled away and caught her by the chin, holding her in place. "You want to know what I see?"

She nodded rapidly.

He whirled them to face the door of her room, turning her in his lap, placing her legs wide on either side of his. The mirror he'd noticed days earlier lined up perfectly with them, their reflection right there, explicit. Undeniable. The position put her naked body on display, the wet folds of her pussy open, moisture shining in the light of the room. The reddish cast of her curls dark against her winter-pale skin.

"This is what I see. A woman who is bright, beautiful. Determined. More than just your body, even though, *hot damn*, I love everything about you." It wasn't what he'd originally planned, but it would work. Matt reached around and covered her mons with a hand. Possessive. Like he was stalking a claim. Liquid and heat pressed to his palm. "This is where I want to be. Inside *you*, Hope. My cock fucking into *your* body, making you feel real good."

He swirled his fingers over her, smearing cream over her labia, letting the reflection show glimpses of her body through his fingers. Flashes of intimate touches, fingers dipping in deeper, circling up over her clit. Hope arched her back and attempted to push harder into his grasp. The motion lifted her breasts, nipples thrust out and reflected back in the mirror.

Matt rested his chin on her shoulder and her gaze darted up in the mirror, their eyes met. He stared into her face as his hand moved, teasing her, bringing her pleasure higher.

"Not just our bodies, but working together. Playing together."

He saw it—that moment right before she was about to roll

into orgasm, and he slowed. Controlling her release, dragging out the sensation for her. Making her wait.

"*Dammit*, Matt. You do that one more time today and I'm going to get mad."

He laughed quietly. "Stand up."

His hands on her waist were all that kept her from stumbling as her legs wobbled. Matt adjusted his position, sliding forward on the bed then lifting her over his cock. He ignored her protests. "Put me inside you."

One hand guided his cock to her opening, and he lowered her with a groan of satisfaction. Warmth, wetness—the tight glove of her body enveloping him felt so right. He caught the thick band of her neck muscle in his teeth and bit down lightly.

Their reflection was there in the mirror. As he used his hands on her ass to lift and lower her over his cock, the image added a new layer of intimacy. It wasn't just physical sensation involved anymore—although his cock pierced her again and again, her tits swaying as her body rose and fell.

Hope's eyes widened, her gaze locked on where they joined. Matt couldn't blame her. It was incredible to see and feel, and suddenly there wasn't much left in his brain other than desperate need. The angle was awkward, his balance on the verge of teetering over, but there was no way he was going to stop.

Another thrust. Another. Hope whimpered, her head falling back, and he felt her constrict around him, tightening.

"Make yourself come," he ordered.

Hope lowered her hand, her fingertips gliding over the side of his dick as she brought moisture up to her clit. The muscles in her forearm tightened as she rubbed and that was all she needed. All they needed. The squeeze of her body became an undeniable command, and Matt gave in. His climax hit like a landslide, the shot of electricity racing through his spine and spurting from his cock into her. Brain going numb, body shaking.

"*Matt...*"

Hope shook over him, hard jolts that would have torn him from her body if his grip on her hips had been less than rock solid.

Panting for breath, dragging in air and still attempting to keep his balance, Matt made a last-ditch effort and pushed them both backwards to rest more fully on the bed.

The motion seated his still-erect cock harder into Hope's body and she groaned happily, another series of aftershocks rippling through her.

If he could have collapsed backward he would have, but he wasn't sure Hope would stay vertical if he let her go. So he nuzzled along her neck instead. Cuddled her in his lap, intimately connected.

When he peeled his eyes open, the first thing he saw was their reflection in the mirror—two bodies, merged into one. Her sated smile, her long hair more disarranged than usual.

"God, you're beautiful." It was the only thing to say.

Her eyes shone even brighter. Matt was floored by more emotion than he expected. It truly wasn't just a blinding physical interest he felt, or friendship. He had fallen head over heels in love, and the idea no longer scared him to death. Because this was Hope—and honestly? She was something truly good in his life.

Chapter Twenty-Four

The organized chaos around the table was just as loud, just as deafening as it had been at Christmas. But there was an extra something meaningful added to the mix as Matt eased his chair back and considered popping open the top button on his jeans.

"You look a little too content for a man who's about to disappear into the hell of calving for the next month." Joel prodded him in the arm as he did his own slide back into a more comfortable position.

"Got too much to be content about right now to worry about the coming apocalypse." Matt dodged his younger brother's continuing attack, finally adding a fist to the scramble until Joel backed off. "I'm glad Easter is early this year. When it falls in the middle of calving and seeding, I almost begrudge the time off to eat."

Blake laughed. "Good thing you said almost, because I don't ever remember you turning down the opportunity for food."

A bell rang and their conversation stopped instantly as years of training from their ma kicked in. Inside, Matt chuckled, although he'd never let her see it. No matter how old they got, she had them under control.

With all attention turned her way, Marion waved a hand like the matriarch she was. "Don't worry, we have more food coming later, but I thought I'd remind you boys to get a move on with the dishes. And this time? Take the little ones with you. I think they're all big enough to help."

The oldest of her grandsons, Lance, grimaced, but the littlest cheered and Matt laughed as he joined the rest of the men headed for the kitchen.

Everywhere he looked he saw family. Blake and Daniel had Robbie up on a stool, rinsing dishes before passing them to his brothers to fit into the dishwasher. His dad and Travis were transferring leftovers, sneaking final tidbits off the nearly empty platters. The twins were already into the hand washing in the second sink, a loud conversation-slash-argument about something inconsequential flapping between them.

It felt good to belong, to be a part of the whole. But the real reason he was a happy man was the woman sitting out in the living room with the other ladies of the clan. The woman who'd come to mean more to him than he thought possible.

Joel was right. They were sailing into the busiest season on the ranch, and he still had a few commitments to meet. A bit of advance planning was in order and what better time than now, when he had a captive audience. Matt pushed himself into the middle of the room where they could all see him and cleared his throat.

"Guys, you can rag on me all you want later, but I need your help."

Hope held Rebecca from falling as she teetered on unsteady toddler legs. "Things are good."

Jaxi and Beth exchanged *looks*.

Hope frowned. "What's that for?"

Beth shook her head. "I know I'm newer to the area but even I've figured this one out. Things aren't *good* when you're involved with a Coleman. They're either pissing you off or making you crazily content. So spill. You and Matt?"

"Pissed or crazy? Definitely crazy."

Jaxi laughed. "And...that's all I could get out of her as well. Hope, you're the most closed-mouth person I know when it comes to some stuff."

"You tell me. You really want me to describe our sex lives?"

The little one on the floor, Rachel, clapped her hands and laughed as she shook a rattle enthusiastically. Jaxi snorted. "Oh no, baby girl. You're gonna stay sweet and innocent for a long, long time. No cheering for Auntie Hope to spill details about the luscious sex games her and Uncle Matt are playing."

Something twisted inside at being called auntie. Hope turned her attention fully on Rebecca to hide the mix of pain and pleasure the word brought.

Jaxi squeezed her arm quickly, as if she understood. "Now since you won't talk about the juicy stuff, what's the word on Helen? How's she behaving these days?"

"Better since Matt's cousin had a word with her."

"You talking about Anna Coleman? You did call the police, then? I'd heard bits and pieces, but Daniel and I didn't get the full story." Beth put her tea down on the side table and pulled Rebecca into her arms. The little girl tucked her head against Beth's chest and sighed heavily, wiggling in and closing her eyes. "Jaxi, I swear you've got these girls bewitched. She's going to sleep with no fussing?"

Jaxi grimaced. "No, not bewitched. They save all the wild antics for when they've got Blake and me alone. In public? They're the sweetest things, just so I can't complain about them being cranky without people thinking I'm out of my mind."

Beth laughed then turned the question back to Hope. "Did you have to bring charges against Helen?"

Hope shook her head. "Matt had Anna come talk to me— she suggested a friendly conversation was the best first step. Something witnessed by an official-type person, but not in an official capacity, if you understand what I mean. I didn't want to have to get Helen arrested—and Anna agreed, she didn't think Helen had done anything but cause mischief. So Anna and I set up a meeting with her."

"Did she explain herself?"

That was the most confusing part. "She didn't seem to know what we were talking about at first. I thought she was lying, but Anna suggested to me later that Helen might have been drunk and simply not remembered what she'd done. Matt said she'd sounded funny when she'd called him."

Jaxi shook her head. "I still think there was too much forward planning for it to all be some drunken binge. Calling both Clay and Matt, knowing it was your day off? Doesn't make sense if she was so drunk she was out of it."

It did seem organized, but Hope was ready to put that behind her.

After all, the results had turned out rather spectacular. She tried not to think too hard about the afternoon she and Matt had spent in bed after the misunderstanding.

Yeah, things had moved forward the right way that day, and she was so thankful.

Beth adjusted the sleeping baby in her arms. "And the situation is better now?"

Hope sighed. "I've heard nothing from Helen lately, which...well, it's not what I want in the long run, but it's great for temporary. I don't have time to deal with her and whatever it was she was trying to accomplish."

"Maybe someday she'll come around." Jaxi shrugged. "I understand that part. The wanting things to turn out the way you want, but really, the ball is in her court. Helen's got to make the first move, and one that's positive and not an attack."

Hope could acknowledge that in her head, but her heart was still hesitating. "I'll just give it time, I guess."

Beth nodded. "Sometimes that's all you can do—wait and see. But in the meantime, enjoy the *good* things you've got."

Hope grinned.

Marion chose that moment to return, and the conversation turned to other topics. Hope listened with contentment, her pleasure increasing when the guys rambled back into the room. Matt made a beeline for her side and wrapped himself around her. Taking her into his arms, his family.

His heart? If she was lucky—

No, if they worked at it right.

Chapter Twenty-Five

The noises of the Spring Fair rose and fell around her as Hope hurried through the freestanding booths toward the main hall. There were too many things on her to-do list and not enough hours in the day right now. Which was wonderful, because it meant the shop was in full swing and doing well, and terrible because she hadn't seen Matt in nearly three weeks.

They'd talked on the phone, briefly. When his phone didn't die, or he didn't get called away for the arrival of another calf, or he wasn't crashing from exhaustion. The ranch was small enough they dealt with calving season with just the Coleman boys, but big enough they were run ragged keeping up. And when the April calving was completed, they'd be busy in the fields.

She'd been tempted to go over and crawl into his bed. To be there when he did stumble in, but figured that wouldn't be fair when he was burnt out. Last thing he needed was her keeping him from his well-deserved sleep.

Even though she ached to be back in his arms.

Ahead was the wall where the quilts up for auction were displayed, large banners at their sides announcing the sponsors' names.

The Thompsons had completed a simple four-patch, and she had to say she was impressed. The dark colours the guys had picked went together well, as did the bright reds and whites of the fire hall's contribution. In all, there were eight offerings, ranging from a baby quilt to a slightly lopsided queen-sized. She'd hung them the previous night with the fire chief's assistance, pleased to be able to give back to the place she'd chosen as her home community.

The only quilt missing when they'd set things up had been the Colemans'. Matt had called earlier in the week and promised it would be delivered by that morning. Hope had to wiggle through the crowds waiting and pointing upward, shuffling slowly along the line as they dropped their raffle tickets into the bags for the fundraiser. A whisper went ahead of her and the faces turning toward her were smile-filled—as if they all knew a secret she didn't.

"She's here..."

A path opened, and Hope wondered what was going on. "Don't let me get in your way. I don't need to do anything else for the raffle."

Gramma Martin stood to the side and ushered her ahead. "Oh, there's one more thing you need to take care of this morning."

Shoot. Had one of the quilts fallen off? She hurried forward, gaze darting over the wall, but she couldn't see anything wrong with the display. There was an extra quilt tacked up on the right edge—the space she'd left for the Colemans' contribution. She looked eagerly to see what they'd managed to come up with.

They'd made a wall hanging. Smaller in size, maybe two feet along each side, a little rough in the finishing, but still a quilt by any definition of the word. A border filled with flying geese surrounded four different squares. A log-cabin patch on the bottom left, a lopsided star in the upper right, the brand for the SP Coleman ranch burnt straight onto a piece of fabric, and a...

Hope moved closer to examine the final square. Half triangles of icy blue contrasted against a buttery yellow. The occasional solid square strategically placed—it wasn't the prettiest pattern she knew of, but she was swallowing hard as she reached to touch it.

Single wedding ring.

Did Matt know the symbolism of what he'd picked?

A long piece of thin twine was tacked directly in the middle of the patch, and something shiny flashed where it was nestled against the knot. Oh my God, maybe he did know.

There was a ring tied to the quilt and she was standing in front of a crowd of people and if what she thought was happening, Matt had just proposed to her and yet he was nowhere to be seen.

Her cheeks flamed hotter by the second, but she managed to get the bow undone, even with shaking fingers. The shimmer of pale gold slid down the coarse twine to land in her palm.

There were tiny diamonds on the top ridge, the gold band worn but beautiful. Behind her back, Hope heard whispers of conversation, but no one came right out and said anything. Asked anything.

And all she seemed to be able to do was stare. He'd made a quilt and used it to propose?

"He was supposed to be here."

Hope twirled to find Mrs. Coleman smiling at her. "He...I..."

Yeah, speaking was going real fine this morning.

"The boy's been burning the candle at both ends trying to get this done and deal with the calves. You want me to take over for you? Man the raffle table?"

Hope nodded, her fingers playing with the ring, clutching it like a lifeline.

Mrs. Colman smiled. "You go on."

In the middle of turning away, Hope paused. She moved to the wall and removed the Coleman quilt. She couldn't possibly let it be auctioned off. She folded it carefully, pressing it against her chest before trying to find her voice.

"Whatever the top amount is given for the other raffled quilts, I'll match it for this one." She looked up at Matt's mother. "Do you think that would be okay?"

Marion Coleman grinned. "Nope, it won't work, because Mike and I already said we'd double it."

Hope bit her lip, fought the tears. "Really?"

"Matt talked my husband into making a quilt square. You think it's gonna be up on anyone's wall but family?"

Hope gasped out a laugh. There was more to the story than she'd imagined.

Marion waved a hand. "Now, go on. Go find Matt."

Quilt tucked under her arm, ring squeezed tight in her fingers, probably the goofiest grin ever on her face. She somehow made it back to the parking lot and headed toward the Colemans', wondering where to start looking.

Her first guess was right. She pulled in next to his truck outside his trailer and jumped down. A spring breeze floated past, songbirds escorting her on the trip to the front door and inside.

The quiet was all the hint she needed to find him, stomach down on his bed, face turned to the side and completely relaxed as he slept like a rock.

She didn't wake him. Just stood there and soaked in the sight. He'd stripped down to boxers and dirty socks, his feet hanging off the bed as if attempting to keep the sheets clean.

The muscles in his back moved as he shifted position, rolling halfway to his back. Long, delicious arms, his wide muscular thighs, six-pack on his abdomen visible even as he lay in repose.

Waking him up seemed cruel. She'd wait until he came around on his own. It wasn't as if she didn't have enough to entertain herself, looking him over.

"You going to stay way over there, or come and give me some sugar?"

Hope threw decorum out the window and pounced, body slamming against him as she offered her lips.

He wasn't as asleep as she'd thought. Not from the way he took her body under his, heavy erection pressed to her thigh, tongue and teeth working her mouth, her neck.

"I've missed you." He breathed the words against her chest before going in for a second round.

"Missed you too. I didn't want to bother you."

Matt lifted off where he'd been using her as a chew toy, nibbling along her bra. "You bother me by not being here, got it?"

Hope nodded. Then she didn't know what to say. There was a ring in her pocket and a quilt on the side table, both things that seemed to ask a pretty big question, but she wasn't sure how to turn the conversation that direction.

Matt snapped upright. "Shit. What time is it?"

She checked her watch. "Nearly noon."

"Fuck. I mean, what day is it? I've been buried up to my eyebrows in calves and—" He glanced at the bedside table and rumbled to a stop. "Oh. It's Saturday, isn't it?"

Hope couldn't stop herself. She laughed, soft at first then louder. His expression of total dismay turned the situation into something she was going to remember for a long, long time.

Maybe even forever.

Matt pulled the quilt over and opened it up, smoothing it over his pillows. He fingered the empty twine then looked at her expectantly.

"Oh no, Matt Coleman. You ain't getting out of this one."

He mock-pouted. "Sewed my fingers to the bone—figured

my message would be clearer if I spoke your dialect."

She still couldn't believe it, that he'd found the time to do up a quilt. Rough as it was. "You going to make me beg?"

His grin flashed bright—that one that said sex and mischief and too much Coleman to argue with. "I like making you beg."

She sat up straighter, intending to crawl over him and make him squirm, but he beat her to the punch, pulling her hand forward as if looking for something.

"Where is it?"

"Where's what?" Hope tugged her hand free. "Ah, I need to do my nails—"

He rolled off the bed and scooted her hips forward until she perched on the edge of the mattress. "May I have it please?"

It took a moment to dig in her pocket. She had to lie back to get at the ring.

Matt growled in approval. "Hmm, maybe you should just stay in that position for a while."

A sharp nip along the inside of her thigh made her gasp. She sat, the ring trapped between thumb and forefinger. "Later. First, I think you left this lying around in public. You should take better care of special things."

He was up on one knee, pulling the ring from her grasp, holding her hand captive. "I intend on taking very good care of something special. If you'll have me."

Hope let him slip the ring on her. "You just try to get away."

They grinned at each other. She opened her arms and he scooped her up, twirling her around before depositing them both back on the bed, all tangled together.

There was a whole lot of kissing and caressing going on, but Hope wanted a few answers before she gave in and enjoyed herself. "Whose ring was it?"

Matt rolled her on top of him, his hands slowing but not

stopping. "My gramma's. My mom gave it to me a while back. Said if I wasn't a stupid mule I might be able to figure out the perfect woman who could appreciate not only me, but being a part of the Coleman family."

"Your mom said that?"

He nodded. "She likes you. They all like you. Hell, my dad even chipped in and made one of the quilt squares. Of course, he called me a few names first considering the bad timing. And the fact that Mom refused to help him, but he did good. All of them did."

His family, drawing her into their midst. "Who else?"

Matt laughed. "Blake made the log cabin. He said Jaxi was twitching so hard watching him use her machine he finally gave up and hand-sewed straight seams and then cut until it looked right. Travis—that boy surprised us all and did the star. Not sure what the idea is behind it, but it's kinda appropriate."

"You calling your brother shiny?"

"No, unique."

She just listened, took it all in.

"The twins did the triangles around the edges—I guess they're called geese?"

Hope nodded.

"Then they dumped the lot on me and told me to put it together. So I've been working it in-between pulling calves. And you'd better take care of it, because it's the last time in my life I'm ever sewing."

"Appropriate, because it's the last time you're ever proposing as well." She couldn't believe it. Her oversized cowboy had been juggling chores and making something that would have never been on his list if she weren't important, real important, to him. "Matt, I love it. So much. And the ring—it's perfect."

He caught her hands in his and kissed her fingers. "And me?"

She shrugged. "Well, you'll do."

Matt roared with laughter and took control, rolling her under him, stripping her bare. Drawing their bodies together in the same way their hearts were knit together. All too soon, and not nearly soon enough, he slid into her core and she moaned her acceptance.

"I love you, Hope." He hovered over her, filling her, giving her a place to be with family and a place to be herself.

"Love you too. Really." She breathed out her contentment as he made love to her, taking her higher. Bringing her with him as they both slipped over.

Hope curled up against him when they were done. Matt's breathing calmed, his fingers slowing where he was caressing her neck. He fell asleep again, and this time she didn't wake him. Just lay in his arms, plotting how to make a quilt of her own with snowstorms and bathtubs and mirrors in it.

No one but the two of them would understand, but she never wanted to forget what kind of work it took to make love happen.

To make love stay.

About the Author

Vivian Arend has hiked, biked, skied and paddled her way around most of North America and parts of Europe. Throughout all the wandering in the wilderness, stories have been planted and they are bursting out in vivid colour. Paranormal, twisted fairytales, red-hot contemporaries—the genres are all over.

Between times of living with no running water, she home schools her teenaged children and tries to keep up with her husband—the instigator of most of the wilderness adventures.

She loves to hear from readers: vivarend@gmail.com. You can also drop by www.vivianarend.com for more information on what is coming next.

It's all about the story...

Romance

HORROR

www.samhainpublishing.com